IN THE 1930'S, THE
OLD AMERICAN PULPS
GAVE THEIR READERS
SAM SPADE, DOC SAVAGE,
THE SHADOW, CAPTAIN FUTURE
AND THE LONE RANGER.

NOW, IN THE 1970'S, THIS
NEW AMERICAN PULP BRINGS
TOGETHER TEN OF THE
MOST POPULAR WRITERS AND
ARTISTS IN THE FIELD OF
POPULAR FICTION. THEIR GOAL:
TO PRODUCE FIVE OF THE MOST
EXCITING, MOST INCREDIBLE,
MOST OUTRAGEOUS CHARACTERS
YOU HAVE EVER SEEN - - - - - - - - -

WEIRD HEROES VOL. I

UNITING THESE GENRES OF POPULAR FICTION — ADVENTURE, SCIENCE FICTION, FANTASY, DETECTIVE FICTION, AND GRAPHIC STORYTELLING — UNDER ONE COVER

A NEW AMERICAN PULP!

FEATURING

GREATHEART SILVER
BY PHILIP JOSE FARMER • ILLUSTRATED BY TOM SUTTON

QUEST OF THE GYPSY
BY RON GOULART • ILLUSTRATED BY ALEX NINO

ADAM STALKER
BY ARCHIE GOODWIN • ILLUSTRATED BY SHERIDAN

ROSE IN THE SUNSHINE STATE
BY JOANN KOBIN • ILLUSTRATED BY JEFF JONES

GUTS, THE COSMIC GREASER
BY BYRON PREISS • ILLUSTRATED BY STERANKO

Pyramid edition published October 1975

ISBN 0-515-03746-X

Library of Congress Catalog Card Number 75-27066

Printed in the United States of America

Pyramid Books are published by Pyramid Communications, Inc. Its trademarks, consisting of the word "Pyramid" and the portrayal of a pyramid, are registered in the United States Patent Office.

Pyramid Communications, Inc., 919 Third Avenue,
New York, N.Y. 10022

WEIRD HEROES, A New American Pulp is a trademark of
Byron Preiss Visual Publications, Inc.
The logotypes for each character in this book are trademarks of
Byron Preiss Visual Publications, Inc.

TYPOGRAPHIC DESIGN AND PRODUCTION
BY ANTHONY BASILE

Edited And Developed By
BYRON PREISS

PYRAMID BOOKS  NEW YORK

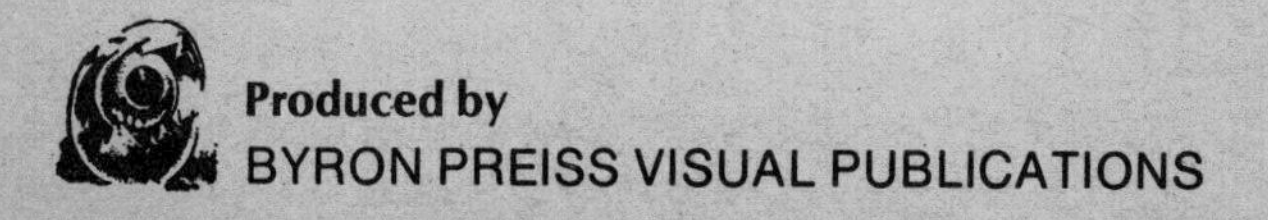

CONTENTS

Quest of the Gypsy

Stalker:
The Darkstar File

Guts

Rose In the
Sunshine State

Minstrel of
Lankhmar

Greatheart Silver
in Showdown at
Shootout

by Ron Goulart
Illustrated by Alex Nino 17

by Archie Goodwin
Illustrated by David Sheridan 39

by Byron Preiss
Illustrated by Steranko 93

by Joann Kobin
Illustrated by Jeff Jones 135

A discussion
with Fritz Leiber 175

by Philip Jose Farmer
Illustrated by Tom Sutton 191

Design Consultant/Logotypes—Steranko

Acknowledgments

To the creators of all the fantasy that has made my life so much fun, my appreciation.

To Ray Bradbury, Isaac Asimov, Fredrick Pohl, Joe Kubert, Nicholas Von Hoffman, Christopher Cerf, Bill Effros, Dick Giordano, Mark Hanerfeld, Barry Malzberg, David Gerrold, George Plimpton, Mike Friedrich, Chuck Neighbors, Bob Weinberg, Rich Buckler, Steve Axelrod, Mark Howell, Lem Rouk, Jim McIntyre, Mary Traina, the administrative staff at K.K.P.P. and P, P.C., and Julius Schwartz, my appreciation.

To Norman Goldfind, who said yes, my appreciation.

To Archie, Ted, Phil, Harlan, Steve, Joann, Charlie, Ron, and Elliot, who wrote, my appreciation.

To Fritz Leiber, who took the time, my appreciation.

To Neal, Esteban, Stephen, Dave, Alex, Jeff, Ralph, Paul and Tom, for their craftsmanship, my appreciation.

To Mrs. Jessie King, who didn't throw out the comic books, my appreciation.

To Manuel Auad, Orvi Jundis, Allen Milgrom, and Johnny Wolfe, for their friendship and consideration, my appreciation.

To T.R., for wonderful times with you away from the book.

To Jim Steranko, for his time, talent, and friendship, my appreciation.

To my creator, who blessed me with the ability to create, Thanks.

Introduction

Weird Heroes is a collective effort to do something new: to approach three popular heroic fantasy forms—science fiction, the pulps and the comics—from different and exciting directions.

Each story in this book is experimental. There are revitalizations of classic fantasy themes such as time travel and jungle adventure. There is innovative use of some of the most dynamic graphic story talent in the world, from Philippino illustrator Alex Nino to American cartoonist Ralph Reese. There is a strong and conscious effort to encourage storytelling which does not rely on violence as a primary source of drama.

Weird Heroes is a collective effort to give back to heroic fiction its thrilling sense of adventure and entertainment—the heartbeat of the old pulps. The pulps used heroes to bring fiction to a grand level of excitement—a level which incorporated the reader into the experience. *Weird Heroes* refreshes that concept of fiction as an adventure in itself, without relating to the new wave of violence and pornography in the production of exciting stories.

Weird Heroes is a collection of memorable firsts. It represents the first major publication of prose stories by both science fiction and graphic story writers. Within volumes 1 and 2 you will find the first published appearances of famous pulp biographer Philip José Farmer's epic pulp character, "Greatheart Silver." You'll be witness to the first major book publication of an interview with award-winning science fiction and fantasy writer, Fritz Leiber. You'll experience the insanity of *Superman* author Elliot S. Maggin's *"Gonzo Storytelling"* and discover the new hero by a literary descendant to Dashiell Hammett on *Secret Agent X-9*, Archie Goodwin.

Weird Heroes contains the first American book illustration work by award-winning Spanish artist Esteban Maroto. Jim Steranko and Neal Adams, two titans of the modern graphic story field, appear for the first time under the same cover in Volume 2. Tom Sutton, an unsung hero of the comics with a comedic style that blends Kurtzman, Elder, and Eisner, also makes his book debut with five plates for "Showdown at Shootout."

Perhaps this book would be more appropriately titled *New Heroes*, but in their own ways the characters herein are all very *different* sorts of new heroes and heroines. **Different or, if you prefer,** *weird.*

The people responsible for these weird characters are no strangers to the world of heroes. The writers and artists involved with the book can take all or most of the credit for the chronicles of *Wonder Woman, Batman, Superman, Amos Burke, Flash Gordon, Nick Fury, the old Captain Marvel, Harlequin, the new Captain Marvel, the Avengers, The Avenger, The Beast, The Justice League of America, the new Manhunter, Doc Savage,* and *Phineas Pogg.*

Why, then, our new heroes? Do we really need "heroes" at all?

Need is a strange word. Certainly we could do without Superman, Doc Savage or even astronaut Frank Borman; but these men were more than individuals doing some outstanding activity in the name of some cause. They were *symbols*—and that's what all America's lasting heroes are: *symbols*. Superman was and is a basic statement about humanity's ability to do the apparently impossible. Frank Borman was and is a symbol of humanity's ability to explore, discover, *expand*. Some heroes, such as Jack Kirby's and Joe Simon's *Captain America*, were symbols of their time. *Captain America*'s roots in 1941-vintage patriotism have since become the core of a new series of introspective adventures in which "Cap's" WW II ideals are interfaced with the skepticism and challenges of a post-Watergate democracy.

In a time when our supposedly "real" heroes—elected officials, peacekeeping world bodies, chiefs of state, and public administrators—are too frequently being revealed as fraudulent, incompetent, or unscrupulous, the public affection for many of our fantasy heroes and heroines has remained intact. It has endured because those characters represent basic hopes and dreams which people continue to share. They represent peace, justice, tenacity, and freedom.

For this, they are "needed". It is a healthy and important indicator that these heroes persist. It is less than healthy to see the parade of many of the new heroes: the Destructor, the Baroness, the Penetrator, the Eliminator. Death. Violence. Symbols that "justice" can be bought with the muzzle of a gun.

So we return to our new heroes. They are an outcry. A statement of **"No!—that's not the only way things can be done."** **Weird Heroes** is one alternative to other new heroes. Our characters are symbolic of different ideals, or at least of different ways to reach the same ideals. Ted White's avocation of the sciences of the mind as a viable way to solve personal and social problems in "Doc Phoenix." Archie Goodwin's call for social responsibility and the recognition of the need for affirmative action in "Adam Stalker." Joann Kobin's delineation of the realization that old age does not always mean inactivity in "Rose."

A central message of some of the old pulps and many of the new paperback adventurers is: **Violence can solve your problems**. A central message of this new American pulp is **Respect life and enjoy it**.

If there is a common ground between this new American pulp and the old pulps, it is a feeling of enthusiasm. A feeling of fresh creative effort and a hope that what we are doing is exciting.

If you have gone to a newsstand in search of the whereabouts of wonder, I hope you'll find some of it here.

Ten Heroes, ten dreams, ten hopes.

Have a good time.

Byron Preiss
New York 1975

For my Mother and Father, for their immeasurable love and support

Introduction to Volume 1

On the cold, sunny day that I delivered the manuscript for *Weird Heroes* to Pyramid Books' monolithic headquarters on New York's East Side, I had pains in my fingers and aches in my arms.

The book was heavy.

Pyramid agreed. Not only was the book heavy; it was too heavy. In the publishing world this can mean one of two things: either the *book* becomes the *books* or the book gets edited down to a slimmer form. Fortunately for Byron Preiss Visual Publications, Inc., Pyramid Publications, Inc. decided upon the former.

So here you are holding half of *Weird Heroes*.

Not quite. We have spent many hours deliberating about a way to split up the work so that each book would be a satisfying self-contained entity. We went as far as to commission an extra story from Philip José Farmer for Volume 2 so that Volume 1 could contain the five stories we felt were most appropriate for it.

I think we've been successful. While the two volumes combined more fully represent the scope of this effort, Volume 1 is an exciting dose of what we hope is innovative heroic fiction. Within the pages of this book you will see over twenty pages of the most incredible fantasy art by some of the most popular paperback and graphic story artists in the world. You will find three novella-length adventures and two remarkable short stories, the first of which is a self-contained prelude to an epic tale of paradox and discovery. You will find the combined efforts of Philip José Farmer, Jim Steranko, Joann Kobin, Dave Sheridan, Jeff Jones, Archie Goodwin, Tom Sutton, Alex Nino, Ron Goulart, and, oh yes, five weird heroes.

What Is an Old American Pulp?

Since we call these stories *new American pulp,* it is our obligation to define original American pulp.

The American pulps had their heyday in the first half of the twentieth century. They were first developed by publisher Frank Munsey, who saw them as an economical alternative to dime novels.

Dime novels, cheaply printed tabloids containing adventure stories and fiction for children, gained popularity during the nineteenth century. Railroad construction helped their prosperity by enabling copies to be shipped across the country.

When Frank Munsey switched his dime novel publication, *Argosy,* to a cheap, fat, and rough pulpwood paper in a smaller size—somewhere between *Time* Magazine and a 25c comic book—it enabled him to get the less expensive, second-class postage rate which had been denied the standard dime novel.

This economic change had a significant secondary effect. The public liked the new form. Munsey's "pulps" became popular and by the 1920s there was an entire industry producing pulpwood paper magazines. Companies such as Dell, Street and Smith, and Fawcett went into the pulp publishing business. In 1911, Edgar Rice Burroughs created John Carter of Mars. In October 1912, Burrough's "Tarzan" debuted in *All-Story* Magazine. The jungle and exotic adventure genres were firmly established.

Before the twenties were over, specialized pulps for the Western, detective, athletic and romantic fiction genres were established. *Amazing*, the science fiction pulp started by William Clayton and edited by Hugo Gernsback, was born in this period. It is still being published today as *Amazing Science Fiction* magazine.

The genre pulps continued to be popular into the nineteen thirties. Simultaneously, there was increasing reader support for series heroes. The *detective-adventurer* hero, popularized by America's Nick Carter and England's Sherlock Holmes, had proved to be an effective figure to the public and publishers were eager to perpetuate him.

In an effort to find something new, pulp writers began to mix the basics of the detective story with exotic settings, incredible adventure, super abilities, strategic hardware, espionage, and whatever else seemed to fit. Pulp writers such as Emile Tepperman, Walter Gibson, Norvell Page, and Lester Dent, working under real and "house" names, began to produce what some consider to be the pulps' most exciting hours.

The era of pulp heroes had arrived, heralded by atmospheric, colorful paintings by artists such as N. M. Baumhofer and John Howitt.

Almost no genre went untouched. Fran Striker dressed the West with the Lone Ranger. Edmond Hamilton spaced out the planets with the adventures of Captain Future. Gibson, Page, and Dent put crime on its toes with the amazing careers of the Shadow, the Spider and Doc Savage. Tepperman predated Ian Fleming with tales of Operator 5. Robert E. Howard went back into time and found a home for his violent swordsman, Conan. Robert J. Hogan upset the skies over Europe with tales of G-8 and his Battle Aces.

Kids caught in the unsure wartime years were reassured by monthly contact with the Man of Bronze, the Wizard of Science, America's Secret Service Ace, and the Man Who Knew What Evil Lurked in the Hearts of Men. For the poor, the young orphan, and the lonely soldier abroad, the pulps were a world of epic adventure where the end was always certain and justice would always triumph.

For the older reader, the pulps held the lure of excitement and tight writing. In pages of such magazines as *Black Mask,* readers could find recurring stories by the likes of Dashiell Hammett, Raymond Chandler, and Tennessee Williams. The Continental Op, Sam Spade, and Phillip Marlowe made their earliest deductions on pulpwood paper and continued to do so into the late nineteen thirties.

Some pulp heroes continued their exploits into the early years of television, when changing tastes and competitive mediums took their toil on the remaining few. Some genre pulps continued to survive in one form or another and some are still around today. *Amazing* and *Fantastic,* the science fiction/fantasy pulps, retain a scaled-down pulp format and appear bi-monthly under the editorship of Ted White. *Black Mask* was revived for a short time by Lopez Publications. *Black Book Detective* has become *Ellery Queen's Mystery Magazine* and *Argosy,* Frank Munsey's old dime novel publication, continues its metamorphic existence as a slick magazine, with "male-oriented" subjects such as outdoor sports and crime.

The old pulp heroes have not been forgotten, either. Paperback companies have picked up the rights to many of the pulps' most popular characters. Doc Savage moves toward his twelfth anniversary with Bantam. Pyramid Books is releasing unrevised novels about the Shadow. Operator 5, Nick Carter, the Spider and Captain Future have all seen paperback publication.

The work of many pulp writers, such as Hammett, Chandler, and Max Brand, have been recognized as classics of fiction, prototypical stylized interpretations of their respective genres. Each style has had lasting influence on literary descendants of the old pulp writers.

The influence of the old pulps extends to many other forms of popular fiction. Their heroes spawned radio shows, movies, and most recently, a revival film—*Doc Savage, Man of Bronze,* filmed on a million-dollar budget by adventure film expert George Pal.

It can be argued, as Jim Steranko most effectively does in his *History of Comics,* (Volume 1), that it was the old pulp heroes who spawned many of our comic book favorites. Batman, Superman, Spiderman, and other superheroes can be traced back to such pulp characters as the Black Bat, Doc Savage, and the Spider.

The old American pulps were filled with adventure, spectacular, ambitious plots, and taut dramatic stories. At times, they were also filled with hack writing, racism, sexism, and titillation. They were products of their times, and, as such, remain an accurate portrait of tastes and attitudes of America in the first forty years of this century.

To new readers, an old pulp is wonderment, fun, and adventure rolled into one book.

Now we have ten new characters for you. If there's anything of the old pulps we want to retain, it's that feeling of wonder—and entertainment.

On to the stories!

QUEST
OF
THE
GYPSY
TM

Quest of the Gypsy
by Ron Goulart
Illustrated by Alex Nino

Remember an unusual television program starring Patrick McGoohan as a spy trapped by his own resignation? It was called "The Prisoner" and, more than any other show in recent memory, it took on proportions of an epic adventure. Not only was it exciting to watch McGoohan's attempts at escape from a mysterious village, it was equally as exciting to match wits with the paradoxes of the show in an attempt to figure them out.

I very much wanted to include a story in this book which would present readers with a mystery, a collection of clues, which, if correctly unraveled, would reveal the entire story behind the focal character.

The focal character I had in mind was to be called Gypsy and the basic elements of the mystery behind his identity were rooted in contemporary America.

With a character portrait by Marvel artist Richard Buckler and a basic outline for the mystery behind the quest, I approached noted science fiction author Ron Goulart with the proposal for an epic adventure.

Perhaps it would be fair to say that Ron is best known for his light fantasy stories about people and their machines, but the qualities that made him a prize catch for *Weird Heroes* are his qualifications as a pulp author and historian. His *Informal History of the Pulp Magazines* is an easy-going study of the Western, weird, and heroic pulps and the business behind them during the mid-nineteen hundreds. His novels for Warner Paperback Library, starting with *The Avenger . 26, The Man from Atlantis,* are among the few new prose adventures of an old pulp hero to be written since Walter Gibson and a few others scribed six *Shadow* novels in the early nineteen sixties.

When Ron agreed to pen "Gypsy," the matter of selecting an artist became a special pleasure. Alex Nino was an exciting candidate for interpretation of Ron's mechanistic fantasies and when he showed up in San Francisco from his native Philippines, I made an effort to attract his interest to the book. Alex is a science fiction illustrator with imagination and draftsmanship of the highest calibre. He is also a wonderful and giving individual. All of these qualities are reflected in his work. His interpretation of Ron Goulart's Gypsy is a window to only a partial sampling of Alex's many styles. From the smallest rivet on a machine to the overall composition of a fantasy mural, the touch of Nino can be readily seen—and appreciated.

The "Quest of the Gypsy" on which you are about to embark is the fruition of Ron Goulart's dynamic and delightful concepts. He has created his own Gypsy, placed him in a wildly enchanting world of cyborgs, robots, and Dickensian settings, and moved the quest fifty-eight years into the future. This episode is your first opportunity to look for clues. They are present in the story, the art, and even the logo. Enjoy.

There's Coming A Time

The Bastille fell.

The clatter and tumble made him sit up on the bench he had apparently been resting on. A tall, broad-shouldered young man, seemingly.

"Liberty! Equality! Fraternity!" they were shouting across the dirt road.

Gypsy, which was probably the young man's name, blinked. He rubbed at his eyes, as though he'd been sleeping.

"Fraternity! Equality! Liberty!" They were jumping up and down on the remains of the Bastille now, stomping on the boards, smashing the neon tubing, flinging the ancient stones.

Standing, Gypsy shook his head.

"It's only a revolution," said a raspy voice behind him.

Perched on a stone gargoyle some ten feet above the dirt road was a medium-sized vulture. Its hunch echoed that of the gargoyle. Directly below the vulture's clawed foot a neon tube flashed *Notre Dame Cathedral* into the waning day.

"Down with all monarchs!" shouted the little aluminum men across the road, jigging on the remains of the Bastille. "Down with all presidents! Down with all prime ministers! Down with all prefects, procurators, mayors, governors, and first selectmen!"

"Feisty little bastards, aren't they?" said the vulture.

"What are they?"

"The working class."

"They look like . . . robots."

"Very perceptive, Gyp."

Turning his back on the robot revolution, Gypsy strode over to stare up at the vulture. "And where are we?"

The gnarled bird chuckled. "You're doing very well, Gyp.

You've adjusted to this situation with a minimum of dislocation. It doesn't seem to bother you that you're standing in the middle of Paris having a chat with a bird. Very good."

"If they've got robots, politically oriented robots, here," replied the young man, "then a talking vulture isn't that unusual. But this isn't Paris."

"Ah, Gyp, but it is. Look over there. You can see the Louvre, the Arch of Triumph . . . "

"That's the Louvre? It's made out of plywood and vinyl, and it's lopsided."

"Times change. A couple wars, a plague, few dozen revolutions, two or three famines, and so on and so forth. They all take their toll."

"Okay, so this is Paris. What year is it?"

"Good question. This is, in New Paris time, the year 26. However, by the reckoning you're used to, it's 2033. Welcome to the future, Gyp."

The robots were slowing down as twilight drifted through the dirt streets of New Paris. They were trampling with much less enthusiasm, sloganeering hardly at all.

Gypsy put his hands on his hips, watching the vulture through narrowed eyes. "The last year I remember is . . . 1976."

"Some nap you've had, huh?"

"I can't have been asleep all this—"

"But you have, Gyp, old pal," the hunched bird assured him. "Actually, see, a few things went wrong. You know how it is, with every technological breakthrough there are bound to be kinks to work out." The vulture arched on its perch, extending its wide wings and flapping them twice. "No reason, far as I can see, not to resume the game."

"The game?"

"See you in London, Gyp." The bird rose up into the descending darkness.

A few memories of a white room.

All the light, glaring circles of light, high above him.

A circle of men around him. Pale blue robes, faces hidden.

Whirring, pumping, rattling. Sounds not connected with any actions he could see.

"Nearly completed."

"Excellent piece of work, but—"

"We're not going to argue about—"

"Wait a few weeks. He ought to have a—"

"He has no say at all. If it weren't for me, he'd be dead and gone after . . . "

Nothing else.

The lanky young man would have outdistanced the pursuing black landvan if it hadn't been for the dead man.

In the thick fog of the twisting London street he didn't notice the corpse sprawled at the intersection. He tripped, went smack into a brick wall.

"Citizen Walpole," spoke a voice through the speakers mounted on the roof of the black van, "we ask you to surrender peaceably. I am one of His Majesty's duly authorized Newgatewagons and I have a warrant for your arrest and detention as a suspected dealer in contraband. You are charged with skulking about the streets and byways of London 3 and environs and—"

"Not so loud, old man," cautioned the lanky Walpole as he eased to his feet. "Don't want the whole bloody neighborhood to know what a bad 'un I am, do we?"

"Don't say bloody," said the voice of the Newgatewagon, "it's not nice." A door in its side opened to let a long, jointed metal arm come snaking out. "Come along quietly, m'lad."

"Watch out you don't touch that dead bloke and pick up a good dose of plague for yourself, old—"

A different hand took hold of Walpole, grabbing his shoulder. He was yanked into a narrow alley.

"Run," suggested Gypsy. "That truck can't follow us through here."

"Right you are, gov."

After the two of them had covered a jogging mile through the mist-thick alleys and lanes, Gypsy halted and put out an arm to stop his companion. "Safe now," he said.

Walpole took several shallow breaths, panting. "You're in excellent shape, old man" he said finally. "I often regret a life of crime commenced when I was but a babe in—"

"You know London," cut in Gypsy.

"That I do."

"I've been looking for someone to show me the town," said Gypsy. "You came along at the right time. When I heard that truck outlining your past accomplishments I decided—"

"Lies, bloody lies most of those charges," said Walpole. "Which isn't to say I ain't the best ruddy guide you could have put your hand on." He took a step back, surveying Gypsy. "This ain't the height of the tourist season, I might as well tell you. What with the plague and the Ripper convention and—"

"Ripper convention?"

"Bunch of blokes fancy they're Jack the Ripper. Meet here in London 3 once a year and prowl around, must be a hundred of them," explained Walpole. "Would you mind my asking, gov, where you acquired your togs?"

"A long time ago."

"Not that it matters. In London 3 life is what you call eclectic. Have you noticed?"

"Just arrived this morning."

"Where from?"

"New Paris."

"Those frogs. You can't run any kind of stable society with a bunch of little tin blokes doing all the ruddy work," Walpole said. "Still, I'd like to pop over there sometime and see that Louvre. Hear they've got some smashing pictures."

"Too late, the robots burned it down right before I left."

"Shame." Walpole shook his head, then grinned. "Well now, how can I help you?"

Gypsy told him.

The innkeeper's hand fell off into the punch bowl. "Blimey," he exclaimed. "Life is damn hard for a cyborg." Using the ladle, he fished out the mechanical hand. "Wager it'll be on the damn fritz again now for sure. Last time I got it all soaked it wouldn't do nothing but flash the blooming finger at the clergy."

Walpole led his new friend into a back dining room of the inn. "Let me see that wad of money again," he said as he sat at a neowood table.

Gypsy, once he'd seated himself opposite the lank young man, took a folding of bills out of the inside pocket of his black leather vest. "It's good enough currency, I've discovered. And enough to live on comfortably for a month or more."

"Marialice, love, fetch us a couple pints of ale," Walpole called to the cherub-cheeked barmaid. "You couldn't have had that money on you when you started your snooze back in 1976. Somebody planted it at a much more recent date."

"Yeah, obviously. Probably the bird."

"The bird, yes." Walpole poked out his cheek with his tongue. "I tell you, mate, it's a good thing you've got such a believable face. Otherwise I'd not have bought anything you've told me so far."

Marialice placed two pseudopewter mugs on the table and

proceeded to fill them from her right forefinger. "How've you been, Walpole? I heard the bobbies was hunting you."

"I remain at large, love." He leaned toward Gypsy. "You wouldn't have guessed her for an android now, would you?"

"The ale coming out of her finger gives it away."

When the android girl moved to another table Gypsy said, "I've been remembering a few more things. About this game the vulture talked about."

Walpole sampled some of the foamy ale. "Must be some game, old man. Since it seems to have been going on for fifty, sixty years."

"The game isn't between me and the vulture," said Gypsy, a frown touching his face. "No, there's a . . . I can't quite get it, can't remember."

"Something happened to you, gov. Well, I guess that's obvious. A chap don't usually snooze through one century and into the next."

Gypsy smiled slowly. "Yeah, I'd have to agree with you," he said. "There is one other thing I've remembered, which is why I need you. When the vulture told me he'd meet me in London, I remembered a name. The name of the place where I'm supposed to go . . . to find out something."

"So what is it you've recalled, gov?"

"Name of a place . . . Thorne Hill Hospital."

Walpole finished his ale, wiped his mouth with the back of his hand. "That's not much to go on."

"Why not? There has to be a Thorne Hill Hospital somewhere in or around London."

"Might have been sixty years ago, mate. You weren't able to find it on your own, was you? No address in any of the directories."

"You know more than any directory. Okay, so maybe the place has changed its name. We still should be able to find it."

"Well, I never heard of Thorne Hill Hopsital or of just plain Thorne Hill. Most likely the place is a heap of dust," said Walpole. "London hasn't had it as bad as Paris; still, a good lot of it simply ain't here no more."

"I want to look; I'll pay you to help."

"We'll hunt for the ruddy place. I don't want you to be disappointed should we find nothing."

"We'll find something," said Gypsy.

The next day he remembered something else.

It was a hazy brown day, and he and Walpole were trudging

along a road which led beyond the jagged outskirts of London 3.

A large black shape hummed over them, floating some thirty feet up.

"Must be getting worse, the plague," observed Walpole. "That's the fifth deathwagon in the past hour."

"Can't anybody do anything about the plague?"

"Well, as you've no doubt been noticing, mate, society ain't what she was back in your day. We got some heads-up scientific blokes, but none of them's been able to come up with a cure. Some sort of new strain they say. Kills you within twenty-four hours, bam. Very selective, too. Only knocks off men."

"What?"

"Plague. It hasn't killed one female since it popped up two months ago."

Gypsy had slowed. "That sounds like . . . no, can't get it.

"Remembering?"

"Trying to." He shook his head.

"Maybe things'll come flooding back when we get us a look at this Thorne Hill Hospital."

"If this Fairlegh Academy really is the hospital."

"When I ask around, I usually get the truth," said Walpole. "Your hospital went under in 1999; two years later the academy blokes took over the estate. They folded in 2026 and the buildings and grounds've been rusticating since." He tapped Gypsy's arm, pointed at the crossroads they were approaching. "There's the road we want, old man."

The heavy fog was thicker, filling in the spaces between the trees, spilling out on the climbing road.

"Maybe we won't find anything."

"You've got to be optimistic," Walpole told him. "Here I am, hunted by the law, a potential plague victim and the only girl I've so much as touched in a week is that pudgy andy at the inn, and yet I don't—"

"Quiet a second."

"Hear some . . . ah, I hear it too. Horses."

Gypsy nodded up at the fog to their right. "Coming down across the hill over there, least a half dozen of them."

"Might be a wild herd, though it's a bit too civilized hereabouts for that."

The sound of galloping hooves grew louder. Then the first horseman showed. The mount was a silky black stallion, the rider was dressed in an old-fashioned fox-hunting outfit, scarlet coat and white breeches. He carried a stungun in his gloved right hand, and on his face he wore a grinning death's mask.

"Don't like that mask touch, gov," said Walpole. He pivoted and ran across the road, away from the sound of the approaching horses.

It was evident the man meant to attack them. Gypsy ran too. He leaped over a collapsing rail fence, began to jog uphill across the misty field.

Looking back over his shoulder, he saw that there were at least five horsemen in pursuit. Each dressed in a fox-hunting costume, each masked with a skull.

Walpole went scurrying away to the left. The fog closed in around him.

The lead hunter was narrowing the distance between himself and Gypsy.

"Keep running, lad," he urged, voice muffled by the death's head mask, "it adds to the sport."

Gypsy increased his pace, the fog rasping into his lungs. The thud of the pursuing horses' hooves was the only sound he was aware of as he ran.

Then he stumbled, his foot caught in a twisting tree root. He fell, hit against the trunk.

The black horse snorted, reared up.

"We may as well end this," said the huntsman. He aimed his stungun.

Then Gypsy remembered.

The gun spun out of the rider's grasp, rose up, was swallowed by the mist.

Easing to his feet, back against the tree, Gypsy now concentrated on the man in the saddle.

The hunstman jerked the reins, kicked at the horse's flanks. They both wanted to get away now.

Gypsy again made use of the ability he'd remembered.

The rider was lifted from the saddle, thrown to the ground. "Get away!" he shouted as he hit, shoulder against turf. "He's got some kind of . . . power!" He scrambled upright, went chasing after his horse.

The fog dropped in close.

Gypsy waited. No one else came near him. The sound of the horses faded away.

"Walpole?" he shouted after a moment. "Walpole?"

No answer.

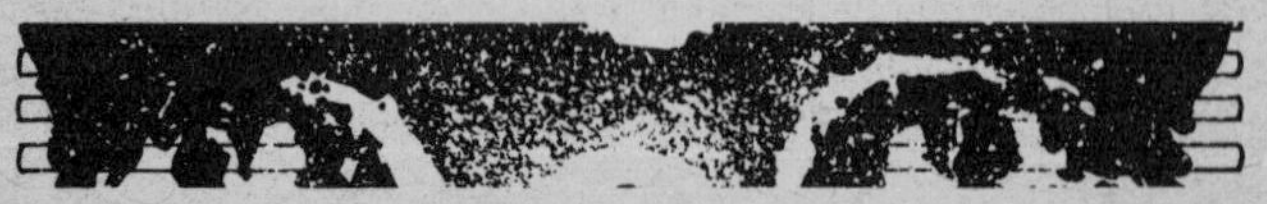

A woman's voice, talking back there in time.

" . . . because it amuses me."

"You must have some reason beyond that."

"No, none."

"But building these abilities into him. Don't you—"

"There is no other purpose. He's designed to play the game."

Then the past was gone.

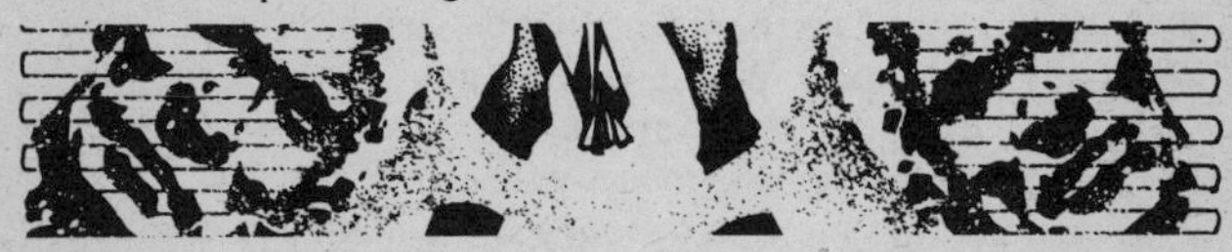

Gray stone walls sticking up through clouds of gray fog. A gabled roof beaded with mist, its copper trim stained an underwater blue.

Halting on the flagstone path, Gypsy watched the building. Several dark birds huddled on the roof; none of them the vulture.

"I was supposed to come here," he said to himself. "Something to do with the . . . game."

The windows of the big gray building had once been shuttered. A good many of the shutters stood open, some hanging by one hinge.

"But what is the game? And who am I playing against?" He walked to the wooden door. "They must all be dead anyway, the ones who started the whole business. If not dead, very old."

He pushed at the door; it swung inward.

Something in the long musty hallway went skittering away into the shadows at its far end.

Gypsy stepped across the threshold of the building which had once housed the Thorne Hill Hospital.

"None of this looks familiar. I don't think . . . don't think I've been here before."

There was a faint noise to his right in the room which had once been an office. Its door was a few inches open.

Moving silently, Gypsy went to the door and booted it open.

"Hey, that's some entrance."

"And who might you be?" he asked the slim girl who was crouched beside a venerable chesterfield.

She was dark-haired, about twenty-five, dressed in gray trousers and a plain gray shirt. "I'm a tenant, more or less," she said as she rose up. "As such, I'm not too happy about the way you kicked in my parlor door. Who are you, if it comes to that?"

"My name is Gypsy and—"

"Not much of a name. Who stuck that on you?"

"I . . . don't really know."

The girl shrugged her slim shoulders. "I'm Annabelle," she said. "Why are you here?"

"Could be I'm looking for a place to live," he answered. "How many others are staying here?"

"None but me. This is not a popular neighborhood."

"Not a friendly one. Who are those guys in the red coats?"

"Oh, the Hunt Club." Annabelle sat on the chesterfield. "They're basically highwaymen, with a flair for dressing up. Never much bother me, since money is the main object of their little jaunts."

"Been traveling with a friend of mine," Gypsy told her. "Could the Hunt Club have grabbed him?"

"Don't you know? I'm glad you're not my friend if you're that careless."

"We got separated in the fog, when your Hunt Club friends attacked."

"You can't find him now?"

"Not a trace."

Annabelle twisted a finger through her hair. "Doesn't seem like something they'd do, unless . . . "

"Unless what?"

"Well, once in awhile the Hunt Club lads hire out, do a job for somebody else," the girl said. "Might be somebody paid them to make off with your friend."

"Where would they take him?"

"To whoever hired them, I don't know."

"Do they have a hideaway, a meeting place?"

Annabelle jumped to her feet. "They do, Mr. Gypsy," she said. "I could take you there."

"I'd appreciate it."

"Okay then." She crossed to a dusty desk. "Wait till I get my knapsack strapped on." She picked up a gray backpack from the desk top, reached into a flap pocket, took out a stungun and shot Gypsy.

Walpole was saying," It says something for my basic character, I think, that I can make friends no matter where I—"

"They got you, too?" Gypsy asked, sitting up and rubbing at his stiff arm.

"Several hours back, gov. You been out a few yourself," said

the lank young man. "But listen, I want—"

"Any idea what it's all about?"

They were in an underground room, the only illumination coming from a cross of light strips on the low ceiling. Storage bins, crates, discarded office equipment, and rows of old filing cabinets covered most of the floor space.

"They decided we was getting too close," said Walpole.

"Too close to what? Information about me, about the—"

"They don't know nothing about you, mate," Walpole said. "What's aggravating them is our trying to nose around in the academy here."

Massaging his neck, trying to shake off the last effects of the stungun, Gypsy said, "Is that where we are, under the Thorne bill building?"

"And a good thing, too, because—"

"If this doesn't have anything to do with me . . . what is going on?"

"This is where they're turning out the plague, gov. It's the headquarters for the group."

Frowning, Gypsy said, "The plague . . . something about it is familiar. I remember from back then . . . "

"You're thinking about Dr. Laurel Stayne," said Walpole. "She developed this particular male-attacking virus back in 1975, while before you began your nap."

"Where are you getting all your information?"

Walpole grinned, reached out to pat a three-foot-high aluminum cabinet. "Been trying to tell you. I made friends with Faxo here."

"Pleased to meet you," said the cabinet out of its third drawer speaker grid. "Or possibly *boa tarde, god ettermidag, dobro pop—*"

"English will do, Faxo," said Walpole. "He's been down here five years."

"Put out to pasture, tossed on the scrap heap, given the gate," said the file mechanism. "Been vegetating ever since, but keeping up with events as best I could."

"He's chock full of facts," explained Walpole. "Knows the history of the hospital, the academy, not to—"

"I'm also good on nineteenth century British novelists," added Faxo. "Not much call for that sort of info down here, but if—"

"Does he know anything about me?"

Walpole made a face. "Not much. Tell him, Faxo."

"You were supposed to report here at Christmas, 1975," said

the machine. "Would you like to hear a little something about Dickens' Christmas books? I've—"

"Report to who?"

"To whom," corrected Faxo before continuing. "To a Dr. F. E. Anmar, he was from America, a colleague of Dr. Stayne. He's the chap, working with her, who made up the first usable batches of the plague virus."

"See," said Walpole, "the hospital wasn't a hospital. It was a cover for an Anglo-American research project."

Faxo said, "Clandestine, it was."

"What do you know about the game?" asked Gypsy.

"You mean cricket?"

"The game I'm supposed to be playing."

"No facts on that, except that Dr. Anmar was to give you the next clue," said the machine. "Apparently you were to have become involved in some sort of elaborate paper chase."

"What was the clue?"

"Madrid."

"Madrid?"

"Name of a city in Spain, or was. That's all I know. You see, when Dr. Anmar was killed by the plague it put a damper on a good many of the activities."

"What about . . . do you know why I've been asleep since then?"

"No info."

Walpole patted the machine's top. "You've been a big help, my boy."

Gypsy paced on what little clear floor space there was. "This group who's got us . . . they found the secret of the plague and are using it."

"That's the setup," said Walpole.

"Defore had some interesting things to say about the plague which—"

"Quiet for a bit, mate," cautioned Walpole.

"Who are these guys?" Gypsy wanted to know. "Is it the Hunt Club?"

"They only work here," answered Walpole. "No, there's a group of ladies who are running this thing. I gather they have a strong anti-male bias and are planning to eliminate a good chunk of the male population of the isles."

Faxo said, "We have had instances of similar stands taken throughout the history of—"

"Where's their supply of the virus?" asked Gypsy.

"Here," said Faxo, "stored in the old lab wing on the second floor."

Gypsy ran his hand across his chin, left eye narrowing. "They don't know who I am," he said. "And they don't know what I've been remembering . . . the things that have been coming back to me."

"What sort of things?" asked Walpole.

"Things like this." Gypsy concentrated on the heavy metal door of their prison room.

Five seconds passed. Then the door exploded out of its frame, went clanging against the wall of the corridor outside, and settled on the floor with a bang.

"Pity he doesn't have legs," said Walpole in a low voice.

"Who?"

"Faxo, I rather took a liking to him. Hate to leave him behind, but he's much too stout to haul around. Reminds me of my Uncle Burt's bloodhound who—"

Gypsy motioned for silence.

The second floor corridor was dark. Its only window had been boarded up. You couldn't see the faded word "laboratory" until you were quite close to the double doors.

Gypsy said, "Six of them in there, including the girl who flummoxed me."

"How do you know that?"

"I . . . just know." He moved away from the lab door, beckoned Walpole to follow him to a dusty alcove. "We don't want to have anything to do with the law right now."

"Indeed not, gov."

"I'm going to have to destroy the lab, burn everything in there."

Walpole swallowed. "You can do that . . . like you did the door?"

Gypsy nodded.

"About the ladies . . . I wouldn't like to see nothing done to them, even though they—"

"Nobody'll be killed."

"It ain't that I'm . . . look out!"

There was a girl in the corridor, ten feet from them. Dressed in gray trousers and tunic. She held a blaster rifle aimed at them. "How'd you two—"

All at once the rifle wasn't there. It was hovering near the shadowy ceiling.

The girl opened her mouth to cry out.

Then she was gone. Not in the corridor at all.

"Um . . . where'd she get to, gov?"
"I moved her."
"Moved her, did you. Where to?"
"Outside in the woods, a good distance from here."
"That's a very handy trick. How'd you happen to acquire—"
The lab door swung open, two more women dove out, each armed with a blaster rifle. One of them was Annabelle.
"It's Gypsy!" she said.
He looked at them for a second, eyes half closed.
Then they were no longer in the corridor. The surrounding air made an odd sound when it filled the space where they'd been.
"Makes a sort of a pop," observed Walpole.
Gypsy went running for the open doorway. He headed into the laboratory without hesitating.
A blaster crackled.
Walpole ran, took a careful look into the long narrow room.
There was only one woman left. She was nearly forty, with close cropped blonde hair. She wore a jacket of military cut, with the name "Queen Bess" across the left breast pocket. She was facing Gypsy with a pistol in each hand.
For a few seconds. Then the guns vanished. Followed by Queen Bess herself.
"Over the hills and far away," murmured Walpole, glancing around the lab.
"Get outside now," Gypsy told him.
"What about my chum Faxo? I wouldn't like him to burn down."
"The fire will only touch this lab," said Gypsy.

Walpole saw it first.
Perched on a dry branch above the country roadway. "Doing very well, Gyp," said the vulture.
Gypsy looked up. "Listen, I want you to tell me what—"
"Nope," said the great hunched bird. "That's not in the rules. I'll see you in Madrid."
"I know some of what I can do. And I can stop you from—"
"That's not in the rules either, Gyp." The vulture made a dry croaking sound before taking off into the dusk.
Gypsy discovered the bird was right. He had no power over it. After it was gone, he said, "I'll be moving on, Walpole. So I guess—"
"No, gov, it ain't time for goodbyes yet. London'll be a lot safer now the plague's no more. The Newgatewagons, though, are after me yet," said Walpole. "I fancy I'll be much safer

across the water in Spain."

"Okay, come on then." Gypsy started down the darkening road.

Afterword

The last of the real pulps were tottering and collapsing when I began my writing career back in the early 1950s. I was barely able to collect a rejection slip apiece from *Planet Stories* and *Thrilling Wonder* before the pulpwood era ended. I'm pleased, therefore, to have another chance at working for the pulps. Gypsy is not quite the sort of hero I would have concocted back in those distant Fifties and THERE'S COMING A TIME is not the kind of stuff I was submitting then. This may be a sign of progress.

TM

Stalker
by Archie Goodwin
Illustrated by David Sheridan

When I was in public school, devouring *Creepy* and *Eerie* horror comics at a suspiciously voracious rate, I began to notice that almost every story contained the same byline: "Script by Archie Goodwin." A quick look at the bold indicia on the first page revealed that the role of this Archie Goodwin expanded beyond the scripts to the whole magazine; he was editor, too.

A few years later, heavily into my *Marvel*-reading days, I began to see "Archie Goodwin" on a number of superheroic stories. *The Hulk*. Perhaps others. Certainly this was the same man, but was it the same writer? The scripts were weak, they lacked the style and firmly established characterizations of the *Creepy* and *Eerie* days. The byline soon vanished.

After a brief passage of time, I witnessed the return of this Archie Goodwin to *Marvel*. Ah, this was more like it. These adventures were *stories*, not just a tied-together group of fights. Alas, the byline vanished again.

By the time I next saw "Archie Goodwin," I could associate the name with a face. Both Archie and I were members of ACBA, the professional society of graphic story artists, writers, and production people. The byline was on *Batman* and Archie had become editor and author of *Detective Comics* magazine.

In the back of *Detective Comics*, Archie began a short feature with artist Walt Simonson. Entitled "Manhunter," it was the revolutionary saga of an old super hero revitalized for a seventies-style epic of conspiracy and counter-conspiracy. It won the best short story award for the year 1973; Archie won for best writer; and Walt was bestowed with the award for most promising new talent. In 1975, Archie and Walt continued their coup by winning best writer, best short story and best full-length story awards for tales featuring the same character in 1974.

"Manhunter" died when Archie became a major editor at Marvel Comics, but the manhunter concept lived on.

In the spring of 1973, I discussed with Archie the possibility that he might create a nonviolent new hero for this book. His answer was Adam Stalker.

The story you are about to read is highly entertaining. Stalker is not a Superman, or a Dirty Harry, or a Doc Savage. He is a person with problems and talents, a human being who witnesses injustice and seeks to expose it to the victims.

Violence repels him; he has seen it at its worst. Yet his hand gropes for a gun in times of stress. Stalker's past shadows his existence.

The Darkstar File is the first episode in Stalker's effort to overcome the influences of his past. It is a story of conflicts, internal and external. It is also a study of illusions; both public and personal.

This isn't the story of a character who condemns violence, then does his best to exploit it. It is the story of a man, imperfect and striving to find peace.

Archie Goodwin has put a long time into this story, perhaps more than he has into any story in recent memory. From a writer with an acute sense of detail, a sharp eye for surprises, and a solid style of exposition, it means we have a lot to enjoy.

As for the drawings which accompany this adventure, they are the sum total of an experiment between myself and David Sheridan. Dave is a cartoonist. The majority of his published work has appeared in underground comics such as *Mother's Oats* and *Slow Death*. He is presently doing commercial art, such as a record jacket for *Papa John Creach*. He maintains a steady connection to the underground field by illustrating "Fat Freddy's Cat" for each installment of Gilbert Shelton's *Fabulous Furry Freak Bros*.

The experiment here was to see if Dave's tight black-and-white cartoon style could be applied to realistic drawing. The result is a stylish, pulpish set of plates that fit nicely with the atmosphere and characterizations of Archie's tale.

Stalker: The Darkstar File

There were two of them, moving on hands and knees along the ditch beside the road. One wore a mummy mask, the other a Phantom of the Opera number. The Phantom was giggling; soft, muffled under rubber, excited. I could hear him before I saw them. To make it really easy, he had smoked a joint just before taking to the ditch. Even if there hadn't been a full moon, I could have found him by the smell. But the boy and girl in the parked Maverick weren't alert to sounds or smells, only to each other.

They came out of the ditch, keeping low. Mummy took the driver's side, Phantom the passenger side where the girl was. It was hot; the windows were down. Mummy came up fast, jerking the door open with his left hand. Something glinted in his right. It might have been a knife, but the account in last Thursday's *World* of the rape and torture in Mohawk Park had said he used a straight-edge razor. By the time the kids in the Maverick began screaming, the razor was at the boy's throat and Phantom was tearing at the girl's clothes.

I had used the sound of the car doors opening to cover my own movement out of the stand of horseweed on the far side of the ditch. The pair in their rubber fright masks had passed close enough for me to touch. I could have had them then, but it would have been like the guys who'd been trashing Ed's Garage. Ed kept my five-year old International Scout running. I'd nailed them in the alley out back, all set to wreck Ed's place for the third time. When the police found them in the morning, tied up the way I'd left them, they'd taken them in, questioned them for a while, but finally let them go. I spent another two weeks finding them again, but I made sure they were obviously into

Sheridan·74

the act before I came down on them. And I've been making sure ever since. Like with Mummy and Phantom.

By the time the razor was poised at the boy's throat, I was coming up behind Mummy. The fingers of my right hand kept opening and closing reflexively. It's been four years now. More. But there's a part of me that still wants to be gripping that M-16, triggering it. Despite the village. Despite the grenade. Despite all the time I put in trying to bury that end of it. If I couldn't put the hunting behind me, maybe it's stupid to think I could the killing. But I try. I don't own a gun, and the only knife I carry is the Swiss Army model. Great for the woods, but getting past the saw, the scissors, and seven other gadgets to the blade limits it as a weapon. Still, I have my hands. Sometimes, that's enough.

I clamped my right hand onto Mummy's wrist, not jarring the razor, but keeping him from moving it. As I went for the nerve center by the carotid artery on each side of his neck with the fingers of my left hand, I dug the fingernails of my right into the nerves of Mummy's wrist, just the way the tough little sergeant major from Northumberland had shown us at the Royal Malaysian Tracking School. Mummy's fingers flew open. The razor dropped. But the rubber mask was slowing my effort on his neck. He was over his surprise and starting to struggle. I jabbed with the stiffened fingers of my right hand at his kidney. He gasped loudly and I ripped off the mask, left thumb and forefinger sinking into the nerve centers on each side of the neck. Mummy sagged, something dying in his throat. Probably the beginning of a shout. Let's hear it for Northumberland.

Phantom bolted up from the seat where he'd been clawing at the girl, eyes bright behind the layer of rubber, uncertain as to what had happened just across from him. I sank down with his falling partner. I couldn't be certain if he had seen me, but neither could he. While he took a beat to stare and try to decide, I was snaking under the car. He reasoned it the way I wanted him to. If something was going wrong, the car was a trap. Mummy jumped back from the girl onto the shoulder. That's when I grabbed his foot and twisted hard.

He landed in the ditch and before he could get up, I landed on top of him. There was little more to it after that, but nothing that any of my instructors at Bragg or Benning would've cheered about. But those bastards weren't much on cheering anyway.

I stood up, and the couple in the car, beginning to come out of the numbness and shock, stared. What they saw couldn't have been too encouraging. Around Berkeley or the East Village, I might have been one more dude on the street. In Tulsa, Oklahoma, at going on four in the morning, the long hair, the beard, the flak vest and dark clothes blended into basic Hells Angel. The dirt and mud I'd rubbed on my face and hands to cut any shine from my skin probably didn't help. Crazed hippie freak. Charlie Manson rides again.

Time for the command voice. "It's okay. You're safe. Drag the other one around to this side of the car. Move it. Fast. Before they wake up."

NCO training. Get 'em moving, keep 'em busy, don't let 'em think. You can't beat it. Until you're in a spot where you *need* someone to think.

Using Phantom as my model, I showed the boy and girl how to tie them, using their shoe laces. Arms behind the back, bind the thumbs together, then the big toes. The kids weren't much on knots, but they got it done.

"Okay. Fine. Number one," I said, "now you're going for the cops. This road will lead you right onto Southwest Boulevard. Soon as you turn, you'll see the Pig-in-the-Pen Café just beyond a Paxco station. A patrol car team will be inside having coffee. Go!"

They did. Not even a "thank you, Masked Man." I checked the area to make sure I hadn't left any traces, then went over Mummy and Phantom's trail, making it obvious for the patrol car team so they wouldn't miss where the pair had hidden their car by the empty house. Phantom's dope was stashed under a seat. The pair might talk their way out of assault and attempted rape charges, but possession of a bag of the killer weed would hang their asses for sure.

I double-timed over toward Skelly Drive where I'd hidden the Scout on one of the sewage plant's private access roads near the bridge, and minutes later I was driving down Southwest Boulevard myself, heading back to Uncle Carl's trailer camp. As these things go, it had been a good night. The hunting's the thing, but until I find someone, I get edgier and edgier. Sleep comes harder and harder.

Still, good night or not, when I looked down at my right hand on the steering wheel, the fingers were opening and closing. Reflexively. Adam Stalker and the Hand That Wouldn't Forget.

At least I'd be able to get a decent sleep.

I was wrong. At nine-thirty, Bethany Cord, owner and chief operative of the Cord Detective Agency, knocked on the door of my trailer.

Once in high school Bethany and I had gone out together. For me, it was on a dare from my fellow jocks on the football squad. Her father was a detective sergeant on the Tulsa police force then. It intimidated quite a few prospective suitors. For Bethany, I suppose it was curiosity. Nothing much came of the evening. As Webster High School's hell-raising, all-star halfback, I expected to get laid when I went out. Bethany didn't. Though we both went on to the University of Oklahoma, we were never more than nodding aquaintences. Sometimes, even the nods were a little forced. One November day in my junior year, I looked around at the crowd cheering as a Colorado tackle I'd gone through was carried off field, and decided I didn't want to play anymore. Not long afterward I left O. U. for the army, and never saw Bethany Cord again.

Until she woke me up at nine-thirty.

"You don't seem to answer the messages I've been leaving with your friend Leon and his wife," she said, as I peered through the screen door at her, still zipping the jeans I'd slipped into at her knock. "I decided I'd visit."

Ten years sat very lightly on her. Ten more probably wouldn't make all that much difference. She had the kind of lean body and good bones that take age well. The pants suit of faded denim she wore emphasized that leaness, just as her short-cropped hair emphasized the long, graceful curve of her neck. It was a neck that invited nuzzling. Her eyes, behind the blue-tinted lenses of her glasses, didn't. They were strictly business.

"As I understand it, you wanted to talk about me going to work for you. I don't need a job," I opened the door and gestured expansively at six trailers and four vacant plots, "All this is mine. The Stalker Trailer Court empire. Legacy from my Uncle Carl. Plus my monthly disability pension. Legacy from my Uncle Sam. When the V.A. doesn't fuck up."

Like any good bill collector, Jehovah's Witness disciple, or, I suppose, private investigator, Bethany accepted the open door as an invitation and stepped in past me. While going through the motions of setting down her shoulder bag, she gave the place a quick but thorough visual check. Not that there was a lot to see. The trailer was small; bedroom, bath, and kitchen-living area. It was built when they still thought people wanted to hook the things on the back of their cars and actually move around with them. For a widower like Uncle Carl, it had been just right. For me, after six years of mostly tents or wrapping up in a poncho, it was like the Waldorf.

"Very neat," Bethany said, "Somehow, I expected it to be sloppy."

"It's the hair and beard. Everyone knows us wild-eyed radicals can't plot the overthrow of Christian democracy in anything less than total squalor."

She smiled a little. It looked good, but didn't last long. Whatever had brought her wasn't really a smiling matter. "No, I was thinking that if I'd spent the time you have in something regimented as the army, I'd react against it once I was free. I'd *want* to be messy."

"Not much regimentation out in my part of the boondocks," I said, "Moving fast was the important thing. There's no way to pull a mess together fast."

Bethany sat down at the built-in table and looked up at me. She sat quite still and was given to very few gestures or excess motions, but I could almost feel her fingers ticking off points as she spoke. "It's been four years since your discharge. You've got a small but adequate income, and since your neighbor, Leon, runs the trailer camp for you, nothing but leisure time. I wouldn't think moving fast would be important anymore. Old habits die hard?"

My right hand was doing it again. Opening. Closing. Searching for that goddamn M-16 stock. Bethany's eyes took it in briefly, moved up to the scar tissue on my neck and shoulders, then settled on my own eyes, studying for further reaction. When she didn't get it, she pulled a folded copy of this morning's *World* out of her bag and handed it to me.

"I was fishing," she said, with another brief smile that made me wish I could be treated to a full-length version, "leading up to this."

Bethany had circled an article. It wasn't exactly a piece of investigative reporting. Someone had taken the cops' version of what happened last night and rendered it into basic English. Like other times, their version didn't mention me.

"They do know about you," Bethany said when I looked up noncommittally. "Not *who* you are yet, but they're hard at work on it. I've been talking with some of my father's old friends in the department, from before he quit to start the agency. They want you in the worst way. You're making fools of them. Next to killing a cop, it's probably the worst thing you could do. So far they've kept the lid on what you've been doing, but some reporter they don't have in their pocket is going to connect the string of incidents soon. They know that, and they mean to have you stopped before it happens."

I laid the paper down on the table. "Aren't you making a lot of assumptions about me?"

"Yes, I am," Bethany said. "I'm assuming that those are the same pants you wore last night because the little stains around the knees look like they could be from horseweed pulp. There was a large stand of it where the police found your latest catches. Chemical analysis could probably tie you to the scene much better. That side of the road is public land. It was sprayed by the city two days ago. They use a cheap—and ineffective—weedkiller commerical firms wouldn't touch. Some traces of it are bound to be on those jeans."

There didn't seem to be much to say, except to ask her how she liked her eggs. But she'd already had breakfast. At six. Before driving to West Tulsa to look at horseweed. As I stood at the stove, Bethany took a packet of index cards held in a plastic sleeve out of a side pocket on her bag. She removed several covered with writing and referred to them from time to time as she went on talking. I remembered in high school she was the one whose notes everyone wanted to borrow.

"Of course, I have an advantage. I know all about you and your record. The police don't. *Yet*," Bethany said. "Our agency hires a number of veterans as security guards. We've an in at the V.A. who keeps us informed of new arrivals. That's how I first learned you'd come back to Tulsa. I remembered you from high school and college, and went into your background pretty thoroughly.

"Basic and advanced infantry training at Fort Bliss, Texas. Airborne jump school at Fort Bragg. Ranger and Special Forces training at Fort Benning and Dalton Air Force in Florida. Something called recondo school at Na Trang, South Vietnam. And the Royal British Jungle Tracking School in Malaysia. Then, you served on something else I'd never heard of, a Special Mission Team. For over four years, except for leaves. I thought one year was a tour of duty in Vietnam?"

Bethany looked up at me from the index card as I sat down across from her with a plate of scrambled eggs and a large glass of orange juice.

"I got gung-ho," I said. It didn't come out as funny as I meant it to. I guess I was moving ahead of Bethany and her index cards. To the village. "They wouldn't have invested all that training for just one tour. No, I was what they call motivated.

At first, it was a carry-over from the football thing. I liked being good. Being best. And in Nam I wasn't doing it for a bunch of cheering assholes. But finally, I think I came to like it because it was just *me* and *them*. Basic. Simple. Like things ought to be but almost never are. We'd have assignments, specific missions, sure. But in the end it'd boil down to the same thing. Moving at night. Hunting. Being hunted. Never thinking about who 'they' were, who 'I' was. At least not until—"

"The grenade business. Someone from your own unit threw it into your tent. What's that word they have—?"

"Fragging."

"That's where you got those scars."

"Uhuh. The beard hides a lot. So does the hair." I pulled it back on the left side and let Bethany see the pitted, red nub that used to be an ear. It's a cheap trick. I usually save it for rednecks in bars after they've been coming on for a while about the length of my hair. But sometimes, like with Bethany, I seem to test people with it. I've never quite decided just what the test proves or the exact response I'm looking for. Maybe when I know, I'll give it up.

Bethany wasn't having any. She didn't quite yawn, but there was a touch of impatience in the way she looked. Why was I bothering with this? Obviously, it was already down on the note card. "And when your hair grew back in, it was gray?"

I nodded. "But getting fragged wasn't what started my questioning Nam. Something happened before that. Brought on the fragging. Your sources seem pretty good, but I doubt if this made it into your notes."

"I knew there had to be something. All that training, all that experience. And they let you just slip back into civilian life. Not even an offer from the C.I.A."

"You go to a hell of a lot of trouble picking a security guard." I got up and began washing off my plate and glass. Bethany slipped the index cards back in their sleeve and tucked it into her shoulder bag.

"I don't need a security guard, Adam. There are things to be done that no one else in my agency has the particular skills to do. *You* have them. Instead of staying on a collision course with the Tulsa police, I want you to use those skills for me." Bethany stood up and walked nearer. I was wrong earlier about her eyes being strictly business. It was something colder, harder, than that.

"About a month before you came back to Tulsa," Bethany said, "a file was stolen from us by a former employee, Floyd

Riggs. He's now chief of security at the Paxco refinery. I need you to steal the file back."

"Doesn't sound like a big swerve from that collision course. What is this file? What's it deal with?"

"An organization that should be familiar to you. The Darkstar League. I believe they had my father killed for keeping the file."

And I believed it was possible. After all, the Darkstar League had me cover up the murder of twenty-five people. Men, women, and children.

"Well," Bethany said, "will you do it?"

My impulse was to say no. Instead I said I'd think about it. Bethany left it at that and went back to doing whatever private detectives do at ten-thirty on a Thursday morning. I went back to scrubbing a plate that was already clean. And thinking about it.

The first thing I thought about was lying inside a cocoon of bandages at Zama Army Hospital in Japan, listening to the soft gurgle of various tubes running in and out of me, watching the light show on the back of my eyelids. Then I heard the voice.

The doctors, the nurses, I always heard coming long before they spoke. I'd spent too long in the bush, in the dark, to miss anything moving near my bed. But I missed the voice. It just began right beside me. A slow, measured whisper, distorted through the guaze and tape, impossible to identify. The voice wanted me to do what everyone at the base camp before the fragging had wanted me to do, what Hugh Dunsford and the Darkstar League wanted me to do, what Lieutenant Kenneth H. Chalmers wanted me to do. Forget about the village. In return, the voice would forget about tearing out the various tubes it now was pinching for effect.

Lost beneath the bandages, I found the one thing I never had in the years in Nam, in the months of training. My breaking point. I had never been helpless in my life, but there on that hospital bed, I was. Maybe that's what broke me. My jaw was wired, so I couldn't even scream. But I could cry. And I could nod my head a little. Enough to agree to anything the voice was asking. The voice was very reasonable. Fragging me had been messy. It would be much neater for everyone concerned if I didn't die, if I just lived and got discharged and kept my mouth shut about the village. So I cried. And nodded my head. And paid back the Darkstar League everything I owned them with interest.

The Darkstar League was an organization of wealthy men who had gotten their start in Oklahoma's oil fields. The name came from one of the state's biggest strikes, make in 1923 near Cromwell by Billy Sam Arnett, a wildcatter from the California fields. "Oil's the star I follow," Billy Sam was said to proclaim on occasion, "My dark star." His strike became known as the Darkstar strike. It also became the foundation for the Arnett Petroleum Company, which was second only to Standard in the area until overtaken by Phillips and Paxco just before World War II. Like Billy Sam, who served three terms as U.S. Senator, the men who formed the Darkstar League wanted to help the state and the industry which had made them rich. Most of the league's activities were promotional, but some were philanthropic. Whenever and wherever possible, they liked to help fellow Oklahomans who showed potential.

At least that's what Hugh Dunsford told me the first time we met.

He arrived at Uncle Carl and Aunt Marian's house in the Carbondale section of West Tulsa on a January day in 1961. The whole neighborhood took notice. Carbondale was not the kind of place where you saw many new cars. At least not Lincoln Continentals; particularly not ones driven by a chauffeur. I could see heads in all the windows as I let him in our door. My senior class advisor at Webster had said to expect the visit, that it might be "very important to my future." Which was fine because my future at the time didn't seem wildly promising.

My mother and I had come to live with Uncle Carl and Aunt Marian when Dad was killed in a barroom fight while waiting to be shipped overseas to Korea. Like his tries at professional football and professional wrestling, his career as an army lifer was cut short by the bottle. Only this time it was the glass, not the contents. I was ten at the time. Just right to never quite get over it. The drinking, the moving from place to place that wore my mother down, hadn't touched me yet. The man died in time to leave my illusion intact, and nothing I learned later seemed to crack it. At least not on the surface. But you could probably make a pretty good case for most of the things I've done with my life being an attempt to complete what Dad kept starting and failing at.

Uncle Carl and Aunt Marian took Mom and me in. They'd closed in the back porch on the three-room house in Carbondale. Mom settled there and I got the foldaway couch in the living room. Aunt Marian was the nucleus of this small universe, perhaps its prisoner. The rest of us were comets, trailing through it at various times but never really staying. Uncle Carl was more or less a mechanic, working at an irregular procession of gas stations, repair shops, and garages. Mom, who'd been a waitress when Dad met her, became one again, working nights, odd shifts; growing tireder, thinner, harder. I moved between school, part-time jobs, and practice for whatever sport was in season. On holidays we all gathered around the kitchen table for dinner and the awkward conversation of strangers. We'd probably still be doing it, except in my last year of high school, Mom found she was dying of cancer. And the rest of us found she couldn't afford to. By Christmas, I'd decided to forget a football scholarship to O.U. and drop out to find a full-time job.

Instead, I received the visit from Hugh Dunsford.

Standing in our living room, giving his velvet-collared overcoat a quick, neat fold as he handed it to Aunt Marian, Dunsford looked as out of place as his Continental parked outside. He was a tall man in his forties with well-toned, lightly tanned skin that suggested sun lamps and rub-downs. He wore his salt and pepper hair combed straight back, making a virtue of his widow's peak by emphasizing it. He looked in good condition and wore clothes well. Maybe a little too well for Oklahoma where being "just folks" was the state fetish. The membership of the Darkstar League probably regarded him as something of a dude. But in a society of good ol' boys, Dunsford was impressive. And, when his pale blues eyes settled into a stare and his radio announcer's voice took on an edge, intimidating.

Of course on that day in Carbondale he restricted himself to being impressive. Mostly it was overkill. With what he had to offer, he could have been a delivery boy riding up on a Cushman Eagle and still impressed us.

"You mustn't feel you're accepting charity," Dunsford said, "the Darkstar League sees any help we extend to you, financial or otherwise, as more of an investment. All the people we talk to think you've got a big talent, Adam. A talent sure to carry you beyond college football into professional athletics. Jim Thorpe. Mickey Mantle. Those are proud names in this state. And the Darkstar League wouldn't mind a bit giving Oklahoma someone else of equal stature. That's the kind of potential we see in you. And with that kind of potential, we're certain the future will see you able to repay us many times over."

It wasn't unlike the kind of speech the football team got at Kiwanis and Lions Club lunches. Only the delivery was better and the benefits went well beyond roast chicken with gravy. It took Nam and the village before I saw how little was hype. Particularly the repaying part.

But I got a hint the second time Hugh Dunsford visited. He showed up at my dorm the day after I let O.U. know they were short a starting halfback. The tone this time was intimidation. Dunsford even wore a darker suit for the occasion. He was disappointed. Some members of the league were angry. My behavior seemed irresponsible. Dangerously irresponsible. Particularly in view of all that had been done for me. The medical expenses. The funeral costs when my mother died in my freshman year. The convenient summer jobs which left me with tidy amounts of cash to see me through the school year. The new cars donated each fall for my use. The fixed speeding tickets. The squelching of publicity on a brawl in one of Oklahoma City's better-regarded whore houses.

The last two didn't seem to fit the league's promotional or philanthropic activities. I said as much. Dunsford turned from his disinterested study of paperbacks crammed into a shelf above my desk.

"Members of the Darkstar League are men with connections, Adam. They are also men used to protecting their investments. They are *not* used to having investments fail. Whether or not you play football is your decision, but I guarantee you won't be on this campus by the end of the week if you fail to show up for practice tomorrow."

"Dunsford, you ever knee anyone in the balls or gouge somebody in the eye for no better reason than a few thousand dipshits have paid money to see you run a ball from one end of a hunk of grass to another?"

"I play tennis for the exercise, Adam. I've always tried to avoid contact sports." Dunsford reached for his overcoat carefully draped on one of my chairs. "I could afford to. You can't. You've a talent for violence and a profitable channel for it. What will you do if you give it up? Spend your life picking fights in bars?"

"Whatever I do it's going to be because *I* put my ass on the line. And for something better than a stadium full of weekend blood-sniffers."

Dunsford was already at the door. He sighed with the resignation of someone who's heard just what he expected to hear, and looked back. "Try to remember what I said about the league's help not being charity. You're no longer as useful as you might have been, Adam, but don't count on being written off."

Before the week was out, my scholarship was withdrawn and an application for a student loan turned down. I decided to join the army before I was drafted. And the next time I saw Dunsford was in Nam. Just as I was beginning to push hard about the village.

It was a little south of the DMZ, too small to even have a name. Or at least a name we bothered learning. It wasn't much more than four hooches and a well. I came there because of the well. For something over a month, our team had been up north. Officially it had been to scout NVA troop movements; unofficially, it was to pay back infiltration of our line units. Grunts had been waking up to find their foxhole partners with throat cut and penis and testicles stuffed in their mouths. Morale wasn't worth shit. So someone decided the NVA should wake up sweating too.

It should have been a clear-cut mission. No hassle with outside factors beyond our control as when we had to bring out a downed airman or some CIA spook. Only the lieutenant, or team leader, got tired and did the worst thing you can do in the bush. He fell into a pattern. Moved the same way once too often. He and two others bought the farm for it. Three of us got away. My wounds were superficial. The others' weren't. Still, we finally crossed the DMZ. But it took a week of moving without water, surviving by chewing bamboo shoots.

When I saw signs of a village ahead, I hid the others and went to check it out. The place was clean. Peaceful. Beginning to stir. I could smell rice cooking, hear a hungry baby starting to cry. Daylight was almost full as I moved back to get my men. The sun had already burned off most of the mists when I heard the first shots. Plenty more followed. M-60s and M-16s. Grunts or Marvin the ARVN. Not the NVA. At least a platoon. Moving in on the village from the south.

They already had their Ronsons out setting the hooches aflame when I got there. I think most of the villagers were already dead. Twenty-five people taken by surprise don't last long under full platoon fire power. But the shooting hadn't slacked off; the grunts were charging wildly around like they had the whole 17th NVA division in their sights. Near the well a first lieutenant was waving a .45 and screaming, "Don't let any of 'em get away! Don't let any of 'em get away!"

He didn't hear me come up beside him. He was big, more than half a head above my six feet. He had handsome features, but appeared almost baby-like because they seemed too small for his open, ruddy face. More so because they were squinched up in anger. Tears ran across his red cheeks. The Campbell's Kid learns war is hell. I wasn't sure what I was going to do when I approached him. But as soon as I was close I struck his wrist with the barrel of my M-16, then knocked him down with the butt as the .45 fell from his hand. So far, his platoon hadn't even noticed me.

"Tell them to stop," I said, "or I'll blow your fuckin' head away."

He began yelling and a couple of non-coms took it up. Meantime, I noticed something he seemed to have dropped earlier. A map. As the firing died out, I looked at it. "Christ! The wrong village! You led 'em into the wrong damn village!"

"I know, I know," the Campbell's Kid said, as though being forced to tell his teacher that he hadn't done his homework, "but if they're all dead, nobody has to find out. There weren't many of them and—"

He shut up. After a month in the bush, I was mostly hair, dirt, and shredded tiger suit. I don't know exactly what he saw looking up at my face, but he shut up. The rest of his platoon was coming close and they were silent too. But it was a sullen kind of quiet, dangerous. I kept my M-16 leveled at the lieutenant's head. "Take your men out of here. Take 'em out fast."

As he stood up, I ripped off his dogtags. He rubbed his neck where the chain had broken and looked at me blank-faced, no longer crying. Then, he and his platoon got the hell out.

I counted the bodies. Twenty-five. There might have been more in the burning hooches, or everyone could have run outside when the shooting started, hoping to get away. But at least twenty-five. I stared at the dogtags I'd taken. His name was Chalmers, Kenneth H. He had blood type A. I filled my canteens with water from the well and went back to my own men. I didn't want to bring them to the village anymore.

Nobody at base camp really wanted to hear about it. Some officers fingered the dogtags uneasily and talked vaguely about how these things happened, how it was that kind of a war. Some got indignant, demanding to know how I could be on a Special Missions team and still get upset over someone *else* killing gooks. I hadn't really thought it through, but that brought it home. Up north, it was *me* and *them*. It wasn't women and it wasn't kids. But boil it down and I was doing pretty much the same as Kenneth H. Chalmers. Just killing gooks. We didn't give a shit for Nam. Anyone leaving it talked about "going back in the World." At best it was a place where you could prove you were a good soldier. At worst you proved you were First Lieutenant Chalmers. But either way you were killing gooks and nobody cared. I hadn't seen it before, because I hadn't bothered to look. Until the village, when the Campbell's Kid showed me the war. And myself.

So I made up my mind about two things. I was through killing, and I was pressing charges. Nobody at base camp could talk me out of the last thing. Nobody bothered about the first. That's how it stood when Hugh Dunsford stepped off a chopper up from Saigon for his third chat with me.

He dressed just as well for Nam as for the States. No safari jacket like the CIA spooks favored, just regular fatigues. But they were perfectly tailored and weathered to just the right shade, and his boots came from a sporting goods store, not Clothing Maintenance. The story seemed to be that he'd been meeting with Thieu's government officials and members of our embassy. Something involving off-shore oil. How he parlayed that into a trip in-country wasn't clear, but his reason for doing it was. The time had come for me to pay back the Darkstar League.

Only I welched.

"Surely it's clear, Adam, that the league has interests and influence considerably beyond what we show the public," he said when we were alone in one of the command bunkers. "You're placing yourself in the way of both. Kenneth Chalmers has a bright political career once his army service is complete. It's a career we have reason to promote."

"I hope so. He's going to have a hell of a job campaigning from Leavenworth."

"Any charges you bring, Chalmers will be cleared of. Understand that. We have the power and the influence to guarantee it. That's not at issue. But we prefer not to have it in his background at all. A political opponent could capitalize on the accusation alone. So the accusation won't be made. And you'll have squared your account with us, Adam."

I told him to go back to Saigon. He did. Two days later, someone rolled a grenade into my tent.

I almost got clear. It tapped something as it rolled. I woke up and instinctively twisted away. Into canvas and tent pegs.

A dust-off got me to 12th Medical Evac. They saved my jaw. The left ear was long gone. After that, it was Japan. And skin grafts. And metal to replace missing bone. And transfusions. And a whispering voice to take up where the grenade left off.

I decided to get some more sleep before calling Bethany Cord and turning down her offer. The copy of the *World* she'd brought was still on the table, so I took it in with me to leaf through before nodding off. Only the society page woke me up. It had the article Bethany might have been better off showing me. If she'd known.

Essentially, it was a wedding announcement, but since it involved prominent Tulsans and a minor national celebrity, elephantiasis had set in and swollen it to feature-article size. The Tulsans were Jared Paxton, of Paxco Industries, and his family. Their daughter was marrying a freshman congressman whose television appearances while serving with the House Judiciary Committee had made the charisma calibrators take notice. Being the son of an old New England family (whose discreet patronage in charity, the arts, and politics had eased them into the position of American royalty), as well as being a much decorated veteran of the recent Vietnam conflict, hadn't hindered him in the "force to be reckoned with in '80 or '84" sweepstakes either. There was no mention of the boost he'd gotten from me and the Darkstar League. In the three accompanying photos, Kenneth Hadley Chalmers looked pretty much like the same overgrown Campbell's Kid, only his crewcut with white sidewalls had flowered into one of those carefully sculpted jobs sported by the fiery young second bananas on all the TV doctor, lawyer, and detective shows. Also, he no longer seemed to have anything to cry about.

So I called the Cord Detective Agency and told Bethany maybe I *was* the one to get back the file that seemed to have landed Floyd Riggs his job at Jared Paxton's refinery.

The Dodge Dart was pulled over under some trees along the side road just beyond the trailer camp. It was robins' egg blue with a black hardtop and had rental plates. Nothing happened when I swung out of the camp drive, but as I went into my turn from the side road onto Southwest Boulevard, it started up and carefully kept one car behind me as I drove toward town and Bethany's office. Traffic was light. It has been ever since they rerouted U.S. 66 onto Skelly Drive, which made it rough for a lot of small businesses looking to the boulevard for drive-in trade. Like Uncle Carl's trailer court. But it's nice when you're being tailed.

I checked my watch. 11:43. I goosed the Scout a little without trying to be too obvious about it. 11:44. I could see the Santa Fe crossing ahead and no cars in front of me. I slowed down as the red lights and the bell started. Trees and a billboard for Jax beer on my side of the road made it impossible to see where the train was. I glanced at the sweep of the red second hand. The left hand lane was clear. The Dart was holding its one-car interval, matching my crawl. I slammed the Scout into second, hit the gas, and went leaping across the tracks. I didn't bother glancing to my right because I knew what the train would look like. Very big and too fucking close.

I hooked the wheel to the right and nosed into the drive of the Paxco station just beyond the tracks. Nothing seemed to have stayed on the train. I cut left, pumped the brakes, and stopped hard by the inside pumps. The attendant stood in the doorway staring at me, shoving his tongue in and out of his cheek. "Damn, you sure as hell musta needed gas."

"No," I said, getting out of the station wagon, "the john. But you can fill it up."

I looked at my watch, then over at the train moving through the crossing. "11:46. Right on time."

"Hell, no," the attendant said, "that sonuvabitch is always fifteen minutes behind."

"Same difference." I said and headed into the office, past the latrine, to the lift and grease pit area, then out the overhead doors on the side of the station nearest the tracks. I trotted quick over dirt and gravel into the weeds by the track bed, about twenty-five yards from the crossing. Once the caboose passed, I meant to run across, low and fast. I'd reach the Dart before it was moving. Meantime, I kept down in the weeds, waiting. That's how I saw the blurred motion of a figure taking cover by one of the trees on the other side of the track. Through the flicker of the train wheels, I saw his head come out briefly again, probably making certain he'd grabbed the best possible cover. He had. He was Black, with a moderate Afro and a heavy moustache. Today he wore a jacket and pants of what seemed to be green leather. The last time I'd seen him, he was wearing a black suit and a chauffur's cap and was leaning against Hugh Dunsford's latest Continental, while his boss peered through the screen door of my trailer and told me how unhappy I'd made the Darkstar League by coming back to Tulsa.

"As far as we're concerned, Adam, Japan was the finish," Dunsford said, squinting, because I wasn't standing close enough to the screen for any reactions to be read well. Or for any sudden moves from him or his chauffeur out in the drive to be effective. "If you've returned with notions of revenge, or some such, that would be foolish. Pure and simple, we can crush you. In the Orient, you had a glimpse of what we can do if necessary. And it was just that. A glimpse. A hint.

"The gentlemen who founded the league were quite foresighted. They saw that as the need, the demand, for oil increased, so would the conflicts, the controversies, over its use and control. From the beginning, they worked to stay ahead of any problems, to remain in control of any situation. We're still doing that, Adam. The scope has grown from this state, this country, to the world. We're subtle, we stay behind-scenes, but we're *there*. Create any kind of trouble and you'll learn that. Quickly. Permanently. And in the way you undoubtedly understand best. Violently."

Having given himself an exit speech, Dunsford turned and marched back to his chauffeur and his Continental before I had time to top it or dilute the effect by prolonging the exchange. Stagey. But he had my memories of the Zama hospital and a whispering voice to make certain it still came off. But they were bad memories to stir up, to play on, because that makes you want to lay them to rest. Which means confronting them. And whatever caused them. Like it or not, Bethany Cord was offering that chance.

The caboose clattered past, and my first confrontation with the Darkstar League was underway. I flattened into the red clay soil of the weed patch, waiting to see what reaction Dunsford's chauffeur would have when I didn't come charging across the tracks the way we both originally had it figured.

There was a moment of silence; then, there was a laugh. It was deep, but burst out fast and short, almost like a sneeze. It didn't make me think of confrontations but of a case of Johnny Walker Black from the Da Nang Officers' Club and the three-day bender that followed.

"You're still *bad*, Indian."

It was something I rarely got called in Oklahoma. With the hair and the beard, too many more obvious things seem to spring to the local mind. In the army, once they got curious about the story behind my last name, it was inevitable. Great grandaddy was a Yankton Sioux named Horse Stalker. Great grandma was the wife of an Indian agent. Family history is vague on just who raised Grandpa, but at some point when he was making his way through the world, the name got shortened to Stalker. With that out, I was "Indian," and usually deferred to on woodlore and survival techniques. Nevermind that Horse

Stalker's contribution was watered down to a sixteenth, or that anything I knew about woodlore or survival came from the same sources as everyone else: Uncle Sugar and experience. At least, they didn't call me "Chief."

"Hey, Stalker. I ain't carryin'. Step out an' talk to an ol' buddy." I let him do the stepping out first. He really wasn't carrying and he really was an old buddy.

"Jesse," I said rising out of the weeds. "You've changed."

"We both have, stud. Hairier. I just didn't get as carried away." He smiled as we met on the tracks. Jesse Long had been sergeant of the first team I was assigned to in Nam. The fact that he was from Oklahoma City gave us a bit in common. By the time I made sergeant and was switched to another team, we were friends. We'd been celebrating my promotion the time we stole the Scotch. "Would you believe, Indian, I didn't even know it was *you* that day Dunsford came to your trailer camp?"

I nodded. "If you hadn't laughed, I'd still be in the weeds wondering who was behind that tree. Not like you to slip up, get spotted."

"No slip up, my man! Think I'm gonna go snakin' in the dirt just 'cause you might be peekin' under the train? That'd ruin all these *fine* clothes." Jesse snorted out his laugh and spun around on red and gray alligator boots to show off the whole outfit. He was about thirty-five now, heavier than in Nam, but none of it looked like fat. Even with high wooden heels, he was a bit shorter than me, but his shoulders and upper torso were broader, beefier. Working for Hugh Dunsford hadn't hurt him a bit. "Shee-it," Jesse went on, "I ain't on maneuvers. Just wanna rap."

"This is the place for it," I said. "No more trains for half an hour."

"Won't take that long. Left my wheels illegally parked to play these games. Besides, you don't wanna be late meetin' with the lady, right?" Jesse was smiling as he said it. Then he just stopped, like a curtain had come down. "Thing is, man, when you *go* to that meetin', I gotta get on the horn to Dunsford. He's sittin' in an air-conditioned office over in Oklahoma City in a boxy-lookin' building, all bronze metal an' smoked glass, the Darkstar dudes call home. When he hears what you're doin', he's gonna say, 'Jesse, move on it.' An' I'm gonna move. Not on it. *You.* That's my job."

"You got a shit job. I'd quit."

"Same hardnose Indian. Ain't learned to *roll* with nothin'! Someone says push, you gotta pull. How many people, me included, told you to back off reportin' what went down in that village? Every-fuckin'-body, right? Army had *one* Mylai. That's their quota, man. They weren't takin' on another one. No way. You were *beggin'* to get your head handed to you! An' now look. Doin' it again! Wasn't bein' blown up enough? What you think the Darkstar people gonna have me *do*? Slap your wrists?"

"Thought you were a lifer, Jesse. How'd you wind up being Hugh Dunsford's hired badass?"

Jesse let out a long breath, slowly. When he spoke again, some of the hardness was gone from his voice. He spoke quickly, but deliberately, as though saying something he'd been waiting for a long time. "While you were out on that last mission of yours, I had me a last mission too. Didn't know it when I went out, but comin' back I decided. Stepped on a fuckin' mine. Years in the goddamn boonies an' I step on a fuckin' mine like the greenest grunt ever set down in-country. It was one'a those pressure-release dudes. I kept my foot on it while the rest'a my team eased some M-60 ammo cans on the detonator plate 'til the weight was right for me to step off without that mother blowin'. End of war, end of career, baby! I wanted out. Fastest way possible, long as it wasn't through Zama Hospital like you."

His brown eyes studied mine for a moment, making sure I understood. I did. Maybe a little too well.

"I had plenty of R & R due me, Stalker. I took it *all*. That's why I never got around to lookin' you up after the fraggin'. When I came back, I hustled the cushiest spot I could. No more Special Mission shit. Just played Mr. Cool 'til my hitch was up an' I could go back in the World.

"Only this recession crap was goin' down in Okalahoma City, goin' down hard. No jobs, 'especially if you were Black. So I fell into doin' a little boostin', breakin' an' enterin', sometimes steal a car. Kind'a puttin' my army trainin' to work. Nothin' fancy, but it put me next to brothers who were into heavier stuff. Word comes around 'bout a job. Equal opportunity employment. Someone big wants muscle. They don't care what color it is, long as it's the best. Someone big turns out to be Dunsford, lookin' even more impressive than that day he stepped off the dust-off to see you in base camp. Everybody figured him for State Department at least. Kinda pleased him when I told him that. Anyway, he knows my record an' likes what's in it. That was it," Jesse managed a smile. "First in my neighborhood to break into the oil business."

"But for payroll purposes, they carry you as a chauffeur."

"Uhuh. An' it's pretty good cover for when I have to move in white sections. But it's *just* that, man. Cover. I got but *one* job with the Darkstar people. Got its drawbacks, but it's better than anything else I ever had goin'."

"I can dig it. Very few mines in Tulsa or Oklahoma City. But it's still a shit job, Jesse."

"I don't have a trailer camp to fall back on, Indian. Even if I did, this ain't the kind of thing you quit. An' I ain't been at it *long* enough to retire." Jesse started moving up the tracks toward the street. I walked along. "Gonna go see the lady now, Stalker?"

"You don't think you talked me out of it?"

"Anyone *ever* talk you out of anything?"

"Once. I've never been too pleased about it."

"Twice wouldn't set any better. Just thought I ought'a make the try." Jesse stopped. We were at the street. He stuck out his hand. I fumbled the grip. It wasn't any of the old ones from Nam.

"What's that?" I said. "I'm at least three years behind on the latest handshakes."

Jesse shook his head. "Red power. You always were a piss-poor Indian."

He started up the little path worn in the ground beside the curb. Sidewalks had never really caught on much beyond the downtown area of Tulsa. But then, neither had walking. Oil, the internal combustion engine, and inertia were too much competition.

"See you, Jesse," I called. He glanced back.

"No. Not if I'm good as I'm supposed to be."

His Dart was just up the street by a No Parking Day or Night sign. I watched as he got in, made a fast U-turn, and disappeared down Southwest Boulevard the way we came. Probably looking for a phone. Or maybe he was driving back to Oklahoma City to tell Hugh Dunsford in person.

Downtown Tulsa is disappearing, moving out to the suburbs and giant shopping centers with its citizens. A new Living Arts Center, library, and post office don't seemed to have helped. A lot of tearing down and rebuilding is being done, but it's a lot like cosmetics on a corpse. Lately, Main Street's been remodeled to look like a shopping center mall. That hasn't helped either.

West of Main is Boulder. Named after the city in Colorado.

All the north-south streets west of Main are named for western cities. Everything on the other side for eastern cities. They're also in alphabetical order. It's a pretty simple system, but it's shot with exceptions. Beyond three or four alphabets it gets dumped entirely.

Much of the wrecking and erecting downtown is happening on Boulder, but the block between Fourth and Fifth streets has escaped so far. The Cord Detective Agency was in one of the escapees, a tan brick job trimmed in white stone and red tile to suggest Spain or maybe Mexico, if either place went in for twelve-story haciendas. Apparently, it had been some kind of residential hotel and failed. Now, judging by the empty slots on the lobby directory, it was failing as an office building, living on borrowed time until the city planners came up with a modern, worthwhile, and duller replacement.

Cord's offices took up the rear half of the eleventh floor. The reception room was dominated by twin portraits of the Tulsa skyline—one view by day, one by night—and by a fiftyish lady with light purple hair who, after a disapproving look and a confirming phone call, led me to Bethany's office. We passed through a large, open room. Most of it was given over to a bench-lined area where uniformed security guards gathered; the rest, separated by a railing, contained desks for field operatives. The walls needed paint and almost everything made of wood seemed to have cigarette burns. Bethany's father may have moved from the police force to private investigation, but he had carried the look and feel of the squad room with him. Bethany had obviously inherited his office. It was brighter and cleaner, but had the same feel as the big room. She was trying to counter this with plants and a small aquarium. It didn't completely work, but it helped.

"You've been playing in the weeds again, Stalker," Bethany said once we were alone. "Near a railroad track. The Santa Fe. I'd say someone followed you, and you doubled back on them, using a passing train for cover."

I checked myself out. This time it wasn't the pants. They'd picked up a little clay and sand but Tulsa had miles of both. But there were three green sticktights on my flak vest where I couldn't have felt them and a bit of tar and gravel on one boot. All of which could give you weeds and possibly railroad tracks.

Bethany smiled. Another of the quick ones, unfortunately. "There's a smudge on your forehead. Diesel soot. It might have been a truck, but combined with the other two things, I opted for a passing train, particularly since you had to cross the Santa

Fe tracks on your way here."

"And why would I get out of my Scout to go crawling around in broad daylight unless I was doubling back on a tail? Elementary, my dear Stalker. They must love you at parties."

"I usually save it to impress new clients. Makes them feel they're getting a real detective, just like in the paperbacks. Otherwise, they're a little uneasy about putting their trust in a woman. Or maybe I'm too sensitive. After school, I tried police work. It wasn't a happy experience. My beat kept turning out to be at the switchboard or typewriter, while men I could outthink and outperform got the kind of assignments I'd joined the force to have."

"So you got Dad to take you into the family business?"

"First I had to prove I was a real professional. He would tolerate almost anything else in a person as long as they were professional. But it wasn't easy convincing him. While I was growing up, he thought my interest in his work was cute. He wasn't prepared for me to make it a career. Most people react the same way when they hear what I do. So I overcompensate with a little warmed over Sherlock Holmes."

"It works," I said, and gave her the details of my encounter with Jesse. And because she listened very well and asked just the right questions at just the right times, the details kept expanding until I was into Nam, Kenneth Hadley Chalmers, and the village. And finally Zama Hospital and the voice. "I'm staking a lot on your missing file, Bethany. I'm hoping it can hurt the Darkstar League enough to make up for my keeping quiet about twenty-five dead Vietnamese, maybe even enough to stop Kenny Chalmer's blossoming political career. He's come too damn far in four years, even for a Campbell's Kid."

Bethany had been making minute notes on index cards as I talked. She slipped a rubber band around the pack and stuck them in a drawer, then opened a folder already out on the desk. Along with other material, it contained another pack of notes. I don't think she really needed them, but she glanced down from time to time anyway, just to be certain.

"It's a habit I picked up from my father. He was a great believer in keeping records, taking notes. 'Always get it down in writing, Beth honey,' he used to say, 'you never know what's worth looking back on.' When he quit the force after twenty years, he had quite a set of private files to 'look back on.' And in nine years running the agency, he added to them considerably. All of Dad's information could keep a large number of important Tulsans squirming.

103
PRIVATE
DAVE SHERIDAN-74

"I don't think he used the files for blackmail, Adam. Not in the technical sense. But he didn't keep their existence a secret. Consequently, the agency never hurt for business. It was a success right from the start. Jobs that might have gone to larger, national firms found their way to us instead. But Daddy wasn't greedy, he didn't milk the situation. And he delivered. Any case he received was well-handled. No one got cheated or less than their money's worth. By and large, it seemed to be a happy enough arrangement."

"Until the Darkstar League got fed up with it and had your father killed."

Bethany got up and walked to the window. She motioned for me to join her. Directly behind the building was a parking lot and some two- or three-story buildings, allowing an unobstructed view of what older residents call the new City Hall, though it's been there about fifteen years and up close shows more cracks than any good fifteen-year-old building should.

"If you crane your head a bit, you can see where it happened," Bethany said. "There, at Fifth and Cheyenne, shortly after midnight. Daddy had been working late. Whenever he did, he'd stop at the Cheyenne Lounge before coming home. It's close enough to police headquarters that he could always find one or two old friends having beers after coming off-duty. A car hit him as he was crossing the street. The medical examiner estimated that it must have been doing at least fifty. The impact broke one of its headlights. Some hangers-on in the lounge heard the whole thing. They came out in time to see a black Continental disappearing around the corner onto Fourth Street."

I looked at Bethany. "Did it have Oklahoma City plates?"

She walked back to the desk and the note cards. Referring to those three-by-five pieces of paper seemed to give her words distance, and enabled Bethany to keep it cool and professional. "No one saw the plates. It's been seven weeks, and the police haven't found anything. The case is in the "open" file, which means they've given up the investigation. Some of Daddy's pals claim that word came from higher up to give the case standard treatment. Fulfill all procedures, than file and forget."

"That kind of influence would come easy to the Darkstar League. But it might to others your father had dirt on as well. You can't be *certain* it was the league."

She smiled, but this one wasn't real. Just a cold thing the eyes never got behind. I didn't miss it a bit when it was gone.

"I can't *prove* it was the league. There's a difference, Adam."

Bethany took something else from the folder on her desk. It looked like a police mug-shot, but up close proved to be a Cord Detective Agency ID card. The man, full-face and profile in Polaroid color, looked to be in his fifties. The card said he was forty-six. It was a pleasant face, probably handsome in its day, but that day had been about twenty years ago. Even then, the chin would have been weak. Now it was losing further ground to a set of folds. His temples and modest sideburns were nicely splashed with gray. The rest of his hair was reddish-brown, dipping thickly and gracefully across his forehead. Maybe too thickly and gracefully.

"Floyd Riggs," I read from the ID. "He wears a rug?"

"And the gray comes from a bottle. Floyd's vain. He's also gay. The detective squad forced him to resign seven years ago. As long as it wasn't obvious, they looked the other way. But Floyd made the mistake of becoming too open, moving in with a boy friend. It wasn't an image the force could live with. My father knew him and was happy to hire him. As I said, all he cared about was that his people were professionals. Floyd was that. Possibly the best investigator we ever had. Daddy was considering making him a partner."

"Your father must have badly misjudged Floyd."

"I think he badly misjudged how far the Darkstar League would go to get the file from him. I believe he felt that as long as he wasn't pressuring them, they'd accept the situation just like anyone else he ever had a file on."

"In the meantime they must have been making offers to Riggs until he got one too good to turn down."

"The day after Daddy was killed, Floyd told me he was quitting, even after I assured him I'd honor my father's intention of making him a partner. I thought he was genuinely upset by my father's death, perhaps even regarded it as some kind of writing on the wall. At any rate, he obviously, seriously, wanted out. I didn't even attempt to hold him to the usual two weeks. But then, Floyd didn't appear at the funeral. It made me suspicious. When I arrived home, I found I had a right to be. The house had been broken into and the Darkstar file taken."

I started to ask a question, but Bethany anticipated it.

"There'd been attempts to lift the files before. That's why Daddy had them moved from office to home. Whoever broke in circumvented the main alarm system as well as the back-up, and was able to find where the files were hidden without disturbing the rest of the house. Two people had the knowledge to do that, Adam. And the skill."

"You and Floyd Riggs," I said. "You were at the funeral. What was Riggs' alibi?"

"A job interview. Floyd met with Jared Paxton to discuss becoming chief of security at the Paxco refinery. The police were very impressed. Evidently Jared Paxton was too. Floyd started the job one week later."

I stood up, stretched, and paced the room a little. Normally, I'd have been up for less than an hour, probably about to treat myself to a chicken-fried steak at the Pig-in-the-Pen. If I didn't get anything going with one of the waitresses, I'd be starting to think about the night's hunting. Basic. Simple. Just like Nam. Before the village.

"What's in the damn file, Bethany? What made them want it so much?"

"Most of the material I never saw. My father seemed to prefer it that way. But I worked on one case that went into file. One of the local truckers' unions hired us to track down an official who'd run off with some funds from the union treasury. We found our man in Dallas, sharing an apartment with two topless dancers and a lot of Jack Daniels. Apparently, he'd filled a suitcase with everything he could grab from the union safe. That included some checks. One was from the Darkstar League. The amount was impressive, but, since it was in with the other checks, I didn't think too much about it. My father did. Enough to slip a xerox copy into the file before the material was turned back to the union. Shortly afterward, the truckers went on strike against the local oil companies, refusing to haul gas to any stations. Big places, like Paxco, weathered it fine, but a number of independent stations and chains went out of business, including one whose president had been trying to organize the independents against crowding out by the major firms."

"Doesn't sound like anything that will knock the pins out from under the league. They surely had a cover reason for the check. Donation to the Truckers' Relief Fund for Hardship Hemorrhoid cases. Something like that."

Bethany nodded. "And there was a cover reason when that runaway union official died just before the strike ended. It was called hit-and-run. I never realized it happened until I decided to check back on that type of accident when Daddy was killed. Perhaps there's no connection. Totally different cars were involved. But the thing is, Adam, these are possibilities from *one* item. The Darkstar file has *many* of them. Investigating is usually a matter of accumulation. You don't often find the dagger with the bloody fingerprints on the handle. It's more like pulling threads, until little by little the whole ball begins to unravel."

"And your father had a big package of loose ends just begging to be tugged. Okay. I can see the league getting itchier and itchier over the file that stayed with your father. Still, it seems like they lived with it for years without having to do anything. You *sure* he didn't turn up that dagger with the bloody prints after all? What was the last thing he was working on?"

It was in the set of note cards Bethany had out, which meant it was a possibility she'd already considered. But Cord's last case was apparently a pretty standard one. The wife of a dentist in Southern Hills who thought her husband was playing around. He was.

"Our field men were very happy with the photos they got," Bethany said. "There was a lot of anguish when Daddy turned all the prints and negatives over to the client."

"The dentist wasn't important enough to have a private file."

"Some of his patients may have been. But this wasn't the kind of material Daddy would use against anyone. At least I like to think it wasn't. Shortly before he was killed, he seemed to be having regrets about having kept the files at all. 'Too much temptation for one person, Beth,' he said one night when he was putting some material away. 'Should've burned them when I still knew I could make it without them. Now I can never be sure.' I decided that if I inherited them, I would do what my father couldn't. Burn the lot."

"Can you be sure Riggs or the league haven't already given you a start toward that?"

Bethany looked at me levelly from behind the light blue lenses of her glasses. "Yes. Because Riggs is still alive. If the Darkstar file had been destroyed after it was stolen, Floyd wouldn't have a thing to keep him from winding up just like my father or that runaway union official. Instead, he's dividing his time between a comfortable office right at the heart of the Paxco refinery security system and a cabin cruiser that he and two muscle-heavy friends keep shifting around Keystone Lake."

"Floyd sounds like a hard man to visit."

"That's where you come in, Stalker."

There was a lot I had to be briefed on first. Bethany had most of it on her index cards, but that and the planning took the rest of the afternoon. As I stood up to leave, Bethany began to reorder her notes, integrating new material with the old.

"I'll go over it later alone. There's always something you

miss the first time."

"Here. Might as well add this to the collection," I said and handed her the society page I'd torn out of the *World* this morning. "Guess I don't need to psych myself up by carrying around a picture of the enemy."

From the way I'd folded the page, a photo of Paxton, his wife, Kenneth Chalmers and his bride-to-be stared up at us. Jared Paxton was a dark man, square and solid-looking. He seemed to have better things to do than smile for the camera. Kenneth Hadley Chalmers more than made up for it. His fiancée had inherited her mother's thin but heavy-breasted body, and she shared her father's reluctance to smile. Or perhaps, marrying a Campbell's Kid was just plain serious business. Or just plain business.

"She has a sensuous mouth," Bethany said. "Chalmers may be getting far better than he deserves."

I studied Ken Chalmer's practiced smile for a few seconds longer, then started for the door. "Not if I reach Floyd Riggs."

Gravel flashed beneath me and sprayed up like a claymore exploding. The flak vest took most of it, but several pieces hit my face.

The fuel truck swung onto the Paxton refinery road without slowing down. Late at night, coming off Southwest Boulevard, there shouldn't have been any danger. *Except* with all three gas tanks empty, the rear end bounced like hell as it came off the concrete, almost shaking me from where I hung, braced between the truck's two spare tire racks.

I slipped down another inch. Pushing harder with my legs and back, I checked the slippage, fighting back a cough from dust raised by the truck as it headed for the rear gate of the refinery.

Climbing in rock clefts during my training around Fort Benning, I'd found I could usually hold such a position for half an hour or more. Of course, no one had been blasting me with dust or gravel. The ten minute trip from the all-night Paxco station where I'd mounted the truck felt more like ten hours. And once we were through the gate, the job would just be started.

The driver chatted briefly with a security guard at the gate. It gave me a chance to check my watch. Blood trickled from a gravel cut above one eye. The scent might put the Dobermans onto me faster when I hit the inner grounds. *2:03*. I looked at the burlap bag on top of the spare tire at my feet. No sign of movement and it seemed to be riding fine. Bethany had gotten [illegible] don't know what kind of story she used or the bag about nine; I do[illegible] [illegible]ative was estimated to last five what it cost to swing it. The sedat[illegible] [illegible] been on top of the or six hours. Bad. To be safe, I should have be[illegible] [illegible]eet storage tank already, but the driver had taken his own swe[illegible] time checking the truck's tanks and putting away hoses before leaving the Paxco station.

Now he sent the truck lurching forward toward the storage tanks in the yard beyond, ready to pick up a fresh load of fuel. With a good percentage of all-night stations, Paxco made round-the-clock deliveries. *That was in my favor.* It also meant the refueling yard was christmas-tree bright any hour. *That wasn't.*

I got down when the truck finally halted, but didn't move until they were actually pumping gas, and the driver and the yardmen were laughing, talking up by the cab. Then I moved out on the side by the tank. *2:20.* The burlap bag was tied by its drawstring to the left-hand side of my web-belt. I thought I felt a movement inside. I elected to consider it as nerves, and edged toward the ladder that ran up the nearest storage tank.

The main grounds were separated from the refueling yard by a twelve-foot cyclone fence which encircled the whole refinery. Topping it were three strands of high voltage wire. Armed guards were always on duty by all gates. That was what you could see. There were no traces of the alarms, of course, until you set them off. According to Bethany, most of this grew out of the 1974 energy crisis, when the hijacking of several gas trucks seemed to justify increased security all around. Once in effect, it was never relaxed.

But, like anything, there were weak spots. Of sorts. From plans Bethany had furnished, I picked out the four storage tanks. Each seventy feet tall. Regular. Ethyl. No-lead. Diesel. Paxco fed their gas stations from these. And they bordered the main grounds, replacing the fence where they did.

Reaching the ladder of the regular tank, I slipped in between it and the smooth, metal surface. With the flak vest and web-belt, solidly hung with equipment as well as the burlap bag, it was tight. But climbing this way, I'd create no silhouette to attract attention. I started up, moving awkwardly, the bag overbalancing me. Ordinarily, I limit equipment to exactly what I think I'll need. For average forays, like my run-in with the pair in the fright masks, that's next to nothing. Around buildings, rooftops, a coil of nylon climbing-cord comes in handy. But reaching Riggs involved too many factors neither Bethany nor I could be sure of. So I carried my whole bag of

tricks, such as it was, plus a few extras
burlap bag. we doped out. Like the

"Aw, damn!"

I fr-

roze. One of the yard-men had come scrambling up onto the truck. I was almost level with him. He seemed to be staring straight at me.

"Joe Don, you got fuckin' *no-lead* runnin' in here! Order calls for two regular, one ethyl!"

He bent down to the tank compartment being filled. Joe Don joined him. I began climbing, wanting to go fast, knowing I couldn't.

"Hell," Joe Don said, "make the rest regular. Half the shit-birds drivin' around don't know what they should be usin' anyways!" The driver climbed up too. All three talked at once. No one seemed to have stopped the flow of no-lead. Or looked up. Yet.

Not far above me was darkness. The top of the storage tank rose higher than the lights that beamed on it. I swung out to the proper side of the ladder and began scaling it quickly. Down on the ground on the far side of the truck, a huge shadow figure was suddenly doing the same, begging someone to notice.

Then I rose above the light and the shadow-giant was gone.

2:30. There was, a definite twitch from the bag. I stood still, took several deep breaths, felt better. The cut above my eye seemed to have dried. I decided to skip any first-aid. Undoing the nylon cord looped onto the right side of my belt, I crept to the center of the tank where there was a small cluster of valves and pipes. I tied the cord to one of them and moved to the tank's far side, dropping the rest of my line over into seventy feet of darkness. It was short by.about thirty-five. Gripping the cord, bracing my feet against the side of the tank, I went into descent. There were more twitches from inside the bag.

At the end of the cord, I dangled full-length by one hand, gathering the bag up against me with the other. Then I dropped. Jump school all over again. It's a long way to fall, especially in darkness. You keep expecting to hit, then don't But when the impact came, my actions were reflexive. The training all came back. I doubled over, hugging the bag close, shielded from the shock, and rolled. The ground was soggy, yielding. Oily mud sprayed around me. But nothing broke.

Ahead were more storage tanks, much bigger around, if not as high as the one I dropped from. Floodlights at their bases played up on them, but the areas between, such as where I was standing were dark. Beyond the tanks, the refinery proper rose

DAVE SHERIDAN·74

in the air, its Erector-set structure covered with lights. They seemed to flesh out the towering, twisting metal, giving it the appearance of a city of massed skyscrapers lit against the night. Then I heard the dogs.

They weren't barking. It was a strained, eager snarling. From three directions, which confirmed Bethany's information. Three teams patroled the grounds. Two Dobermans, one handler each. All coming toward me amid the storage tanks. Using my Swiss Army knife, I cut the bag's drawstrings free of my web belt. Grabbing the bottom of the bag, I jerked it away from its contents and ran low and fast for the protection of one of many pipelines that snaked over the grounds. For a moment I was afraid the sedative was still working. Then, as the dog teams heaved loudly into view, I saw movements. Wriggling streaks of white.

The handlers' flashlights picked them out also. When it was too late. They'd kept their animals leashed, but given them their head. They came converging fast on two skunks, neither happy over being rudely awakened.

"Oh, Christ," someone yelled. A lot more followed. But I was already moving along the pipeline in a fast crawl. There wasn't much chance any of the Dobermans would be picking up my scent. The skunks moved as I had hoped. They got away as planned.

Past the storage tank area was a small, tin-roofed building, exactly as Bethany's map had shown. A sign stenciled on its door read: QUALITY CONTROL STATION 4. I picked the lock. On hooks inside near the door were hard hats and what looked like lab coats. I took one each and left the burlap bag. Until I reached Floyd Riggs, I didn't want anyone finding out that the skunks hadn't come in by themselves. For the same reason, I'd kept my climbing cord short so it wouldn't be left dangling down in easy view.

My watch said *2:51*. From one of the pouches on my belt, I took out a length of slow fuse and cut it for what I estimated would be the time I'd need. When everything was set, I lifted a clipboard that hung near a complex of dials and pipes, lit the fuse, and stepped out. After relocking the door, I jammed the lock so anyone showing up with a key still couldn't get in.

With my hair tucked up in the hard hat, wearing the coat and carrying the clipboard, I was able to walk freely to the Paxco refinery security offices. They were in a whitewashed concrete block building. The windows at the rear had bars. That was where I'd find Floyd Riggs. But the only way in was through the front door.

Two brown-uniformed security guards rushed out past me as I entered. There was a counter across the front of the room. Two more guard were behind it. One was at a radio mike, talking to the boys in the field. The other, who should have been at the counter, was drinking a Pepsi and listening. Squawking that didn't quite reach me as words occasionally came out of the radio receiver to interrupt the men at the mike.

" . . . just sent out our last two men, Arvie. Auntie Riggs is havin' a hissy. Wants every inch of that fence checked. He says those polecats weren't born in here. Gotta be a break somewhere, he says. Well, I wouldn't do that, Arvie. Don't think Auntie wants to see you or them dogs. He's locked up in his office to sulk. You know he comes in nights cause it's cool an' quiet an' nobody can bug 'im. You an' them skunks have upset his whole evenin'. Say again, Arvie? Well, you know Auntie's got broader tastes than most folks. He may have already tried that, Arvie."

The radio man turned to wink at the dude with the Pepsi and saw me. A nod of his head brought his partner around. According to the name tag on his freshly pressed shirt pocket, he was Seevers. Beards made him scowl a little, but apparently he had seen them before inside the Paxco gates. I kept the clipboard up high to cover the blank spot where my ID should have been.

"Like to see the security chief."

"Chief's a little busy now, pardner. You better talk to me."

"Well, I think he might want to hear this personally. See, I was making the quality check down at Station 4 tonight. You know? Near where the watchdogs were doing all the fussing earlier. Found something pretty odd. Could be the chief'll want to call Paxton himself about it."

Seevers frowned, but went to a door at the rear and knocked. After a moment, someone opened it. Then he disappeared inside. The radio man was still talking with Arvie.

"Diesel fuel don't cut it, huh? Ol' boy I knew up in Oolagah used to swear by tomato juice. Say again, Arvie?"

The door opened. Seevers stepped out and Floyd Riggs, looking very much like the pictures I saw at Bethany's office, curtly waved for me to join him. Once I was in he locked the door after us.

"Otherwise those boys outside poke their heads in every five minutes over some fool thing or another." Riggs leaned back against the edge of his desk. He didn't ask me to sit down.

"Now *this* isn't a fool thing, is it? I've already had my patience tried this evening."

"You know Quality Control Station 4?"

Riggs looked annoyed. "I know the whole refinery. Part of my job. You can see station 4 from the back window."

His wall clock ticked off *3:09*. "Would you take a look out there now?"

He did it, acting like a man who's humored a child and is beginning to regret it. As he looked, I laid the clipboard on his desk and began taking out what I needed. By the wall clock it was 3:10. Riggs was just starting to turn back and ask me what the hell was going on when he saw the explosion. It didn't make much noise, but it looked bad, taking out the little building's one window, lighting up the whole interior.

Riggs spun around, mouth open to yell something, when his eyes fixed on the pink, rubbery wad I was kneading with the fingers of my left hand. "I don't know how much you know about plastic explosives, Mr. Riggs. They gave me a course in Special Forces. Funny stuff. You can twist it, break it, slap it around like Silly Putty." I slammed the wad up against the side of Riggs' desk. He winced. I pushed a small metal disk into the pink mass as it clung to the desk. "But nothing will happen unless you explode it with a detonator cap. They've got some interesting ways of doing that."

I held up the little black box in my right palm. Someone began knocking on the door. Probably Seevers. "Newest way is with an electronic charge, radio-transmitted. Of course, you need a special kind of cap as well as the transmitter. But if you've got both, you can explode something from far away as, say, here to that quality control station. Or from close as, say, here to that desk."

On the other side of the door, Seevers began shouting as well as knocking. "Shout back, Riggs. Tell him you're on the phone with Paxton. Tell him you want every available man down to find out what's happened at Station 4."

Floyd did it, without taking his eyes off the black box in my hand.

"Who are you?" Riggs said, once Seevers was busy again.

"I'm the man you're going to give the Darkstar File to, and whose time you're not going to waste by saying you don't know what I'm talking about."

Riggs seemed to relax, perhaps comforted that I had some purpose beyond pointless terrorism. He even smiled and moved for the first time since turning from the window. "You're not from the league. They surely know better. But . . . Bethany! She didn't have any luck using agency people, but I should've known she wouldn't just let it lay."

His voice was smooth, with more of a Deep South accent than Oklahoma drawl. Combined with the artfully gray temples, Floyd almost came off courtly. Even if he'd been straight, I doubt the detective squad would ever have loved him. He came closer to his desk, smiling more. "Am I right? *She's* hired you."

I stepped around and opened the desk drawer he was approaching. It contained a .38-caliber Smith & Wesson Terrier and a checkbook. I wasn't sure which he meant to use, but I removed the Terrier. "Let's say Bethany and I are in it together, Riggs. I've a personal stake in seeing the Darkstar League do some big hurting. And before you get too comfortable with the idea that I've been bluffing, consider this: To stay alive, you must have arrangements so that if something suspicious happens to you, the file goes to someone who can use it against the league. I'd much rather be able to use it myself, Floyd, but if it comes to the crunch, that'll do. The Darkstar League needs you alive. Not me. Not Bethany either. Not after you set her father up to be zapped in exchange for a cabin cruiser and a cushy spot here in Paxton's Playland. Think about it."

Riggs patted his hairpiece and did just that. He was just a little too old and a little too overweight to make jumping me worth considering. And without knowing more about me, my nature, everything else had to keep coming back to my losing patience, tying him up or knocking him out, then strolling outside and pushing the button on my little black box.

Floyd licked his lips and gave the hairpiece one last pat. "You won't be able to get the file yourself. I'll have to take you to it."

"And that's where?"

"The cruiser. In case I die, there's arrangements, just like you figured. But something my life depends on I don't care to keep far from my hands."

He moved to a coat tree in the corner and removed the police-style hat that went with the rest of his uniform. "I suppose you'll want me to tell the boys outside that we got to go *see* Mr. Paxton now."

"Fine. With one addition, Floyd." I ripped the pink wad off his desk and dropped it into the unturned hat in his hands.

We reached the company parking lot just outside the

maingate without any problem. Riggs had a current model LeSabre, complete with radiophone and white Naugahyde interior. "You plan to switch to your own vehicle someplace," he said as he opened the door, "or shall I drive us all the way?"

My Scout was parked way over in the northeast section of town, near a wooden area off Dawson Road. It was the kind of spot where kids parked and more than once got raped or robbed, which also made it the kind of spot I picked for my nightly forays. Except I had left the woods on foot to be picked up by a friend of Bethany's and dropped off at the all-night Paxco station as prearranged. If the Darkstar people were still having me watched, it was being wasted on a parked International. And anyone spying on Bethany would find her spending a quiet evening at home.

"You can drive all the way, Floyd," I said, stopping him as he started to slide under the wheel, "after I easy my mind about something."

I found a Browning .25 automatic clipped under the dash where a hand appearing to use an emergency brake could pull the gun instead. It slipped nicely into the pocket of my jeans. The Terrier I had thrust in my web-belt. After I tossed the hard hat and lab coat into the rear seat, we both got in. Riggs put his hat on the arm rest between us. He had carried it carefully all the way to the car without putting it on. Before starting the engine, he stared down at the soft, almost fleshy mass with the shiny, metallic disk at its center.

"You know, up close, under the dome light, that special detonator cap looks a lot like one of those little batteries some camera flash attachments take."

"Uhuh. And plastique is more of a blue-gray color. The clays I tried were pretty close, but most of the effect is in the way you manipulate the stuff and slap it around. Silly Putty did that best."

Color came up in Riggs' face. And anger.

"The damn explosion in Station 4 was real!"

"But mostly flash powder. And a pre-set fuse." I pushed the button on the black box. Nothing happened. "Pocket alarm. Needs batteries."

"I'd say you went to a great deal of trouble just to play me for a fool."

"No, Riggs, just enough. Enough confusion to keep all your security force occupied, but nothing so messy that Tulsa's tac squad would come piling in every gate. And enough threat to make you break down fast, but still be in shape to get us out of your office and off the grounds nicely and quietly."

Through the anger, Riggs still managed a tight, faint smile. "Now that's fine. Only you're some distance shy of getting the file, and completely through the hoax that would make me take you to it."

"I don't need a hoax now, Floyd. I've got all these guns. And Seevers and a radioman aren't right outside to make me prefer not to use one." I drew the Terrier. It wasn't an M-16, but it felt very comfortable in my right hand. Maybe too comfortable. "Let's go to the lake."

In the night stillness, the launch's outboard motor sounded like a 707 as it came across the water from where Riggs' cabin cruiser bobbed at anchor. But this finger of the lake was an isolated one, not likely to attract campers in the middle of the week. Whatever happened here would only bother the fish.

Riggs had phoned ahead as we drove. It seemed to be a nightly procedure. "One of the problems with living the way I do. But it makes it hard for us to be taken off guard. At least, it did until now."

Contact was good. I could hear both sides of the conversation. Someone named David took the call. Floyd told him he was bringing a guest and gave an estimated time of arrival. David expressed regret that Jason was spending the night in town and would miss a party. Riggs glanced over at me.

"No party, David. I don't believe the gentlemen swings that way." The call seemed to leave Riggs feeling talkative. "Does it bother you that I'm gay?"

"I knew a few homosexuals in the army. Some were all right dudes, some weren't. None of them ever used it as an excuse for getting a buddy chopped."

"You think that's what I was leading up to?" His words came faster and he began patting at his hairpiece as he had at the refinery. "I don't need to make excuses. Not for Cord's death. He was one of the few people in Tulsa who knew I was a good detective and was willing to let me go on being one. I liked him. And I warned him the Darkstar file was trouble. Many times. He thought he could handle it and the people it involved him with. He was wrong. It is *not* my fault he was killed."

"No. You just ripped off the only thing between him and staying alive."

"I didn't do anything until *after* he was dead. There was no helping him then so I helped myself. Jared Paxton had felt both of us out about the file. It seemed like the moment to do business. Bethany's a bright girl, but she left the police force too damn soon. She's still got an idealistic streak, as well as some illusions that her father kept his hands a little bit cleaner than your garden-variety blackmailer. Types like me. Once she saw the Darkstar file, I *knew* what she'd do. Declare war. And that was going to be fatal. For her, and anyone who partners with her."

Riggs nodded his head as if agreeing with himself and gave the hairpiece another pat. The dash lights underlit his face, weighting each wrinkle and fold with shadow, making them look like lines etched in stone. "The gay world's no place to grow old. Maybe the straight isn't either. At least not if you have my tastes. Not if you find most of your pleasures in the young and *their* pleasures. Time comes when you no longer attract or interest those who attract and interest you. Instead, you pay. Taking the Darkstar file made it possible for me to pay very well."

"Cord couldn't handle it, but you decided you could."

"Cord left people wondering where they stood with him. I made it plain what I wanted from the start. The boat. The car. An easy job that enables me to afford friends like David and Jason. I made it all very plain. And it worked."

"Uhuh," I said, "For almost two whole months." Riggs looked over at me, and at his revolver in my hand. Then, his eyes went back to the road, and he didn't talk anymore. Not until we stood at the edge of the lake, and he pointed out the obvious.

"Here's David with the launch."

David was a big boy, hair bleached white, surfer-style, wearing a tank-top shirt which showed off his weightlifter's body. He looked at me and the gun expressionlessly, then glanced to Riggs. When Floyd told him just to take us out to the boat, he seemed satisfied. The cruiser was a thirty-six-foot Kings Craft, big enough to sleep six. Lights were on, and I could see easily into the empty galley as we approached. David brought the launch alongside a ladder at the stern and started to tie up.

"He returns to shore, Riggs," I said. "We'll signal with the flashlight when I'm ready to go back."

Neither of them gave me an argument. When the launch was well away, I turned to Riggs. "All right. Where's the file?"

Floyd opened the door leading into the cabin. "In the galley. The refrigerator."

He went ahead of me, down three steps into what the promo pamphlet Bethany had provided called the master stateroom.

From there, you could look past the closed door of the head on the left into the large galley, complete with dinette and bar. Beyond, I could see the forward cabin with its twin bunks forming a V into the bow. Other than a transistor radio and two used cocktail glasses left sitting out on the bar counter, everything was practically showroom clean.

"David's a very neat boy," Riggs said, suddenly talkative again as I prodded him forward into the galley. "Keeps everything—well—shipshape."

He turned around, smiling. But I was turning too. Hard and fast, kicking out at the door to the head we'd just passed.

It had opened up just enough for a thick-wristed hand to thrust a 9mm Browning Parabellum at my back. Just the way I'd expected it to. Behind the door, someone screamed as it slammed on his wrist. I threw my shoulder to the door before it could come open, and the Browning dropped to the floor. Then I jerked the door open. A young man who'd pushed weights with as much dedication as David came tumbling out. I slashed at the mass of black curls atop his head with the barrel of the Colt, hard enough to be certain that he'd hit the floor unconscious, but not hard enough to do any real damage.

I whirled and yelled at Riggs, who'd reached the refrigerator and was about to open it. He froze with his fingers on the handle. "Those damn glasses," he said. "They handled everything else well. Why couldn't they have put away their glasses? Or at least *one* of them?"

"Probably too busy feeling good over being clever, Riggs. You tip them off to trouble with the 'bringing a guest' phrase. David camps up the bit about Jason being in town for the night just enough to be convincing. Clever. I imagine you've had it all worked out ever since settling on the boat. All right. Time to stop being clever. I want the file. No more tricks."

"I know, I know," Floyd said, patting at his hair. "I'm getting it for you."

"No. You're playing fucking games. Jason had the big Browning. The little one was in your car. They make boxed sets of three. Middle one's a .380. Used in Europe a lot. *That's* in the refrigerator, isn't it, Riggs?"

He didn't answer, just got up and let me remove it. It felt like I'd spent the night taking away guns. While Riggs watched and Jason made soft, moaning noises on the cabin floor, I dropped all three Brownings out the window. Then Floyd took me to the Darkstar file.

It was in a styrofoam buoy floating on a line off the stern.

Using a screwdiver, Riggs cracked the buoy along its seam, which had been opened once before and resealed. The interior was hollow, the file within—a blue manila folder thick with papers—was sealed in plastic. I opened it to check the contents, and had Floyd signal David on shore. While the approaching outboard buzzed in my ear, I flipped through well-thumbed notes, xeroxes, and occasional photostats. Something fell out onto the deck. I was about to reach down for it when the launch came alongside.

Instead of David, Jesse Long was at the tiller. An automatic rifle was cradled in his free arm, aimed up at Riggs and me. "Just chuck the piece back over your shoulder, Indian. Far enough to get it into the water. Then you can toss that file down here in the boat."

The Colt Terrier made a big, hollow splash. I began missing it right away. A lot more, at the moment, than I missed the Darkstar file when it landed at Jesse's feet.

There was nothing left for Riggs and me to do but stare into the barrel of Jesse's weapon, an Armalite AR-10, and wonder how soon he'd start using it. Floyd began saying, 'Oh, Jesus, Oh, Jesus,' over and over to himself. For a while, I listened to him and other night sounds. Then I decided to see if Jesse felt like talking. "I thought hit-and-run was the league's official assassination method, Jesse."

He smiled, but the AR didn't waver. "Whatever suits the occasion, man. I did one dude that way. Union man. But if you're fishin' to find who nailed the detective lady's Daddy, forget it. Far as I know, that was a *real* hit'n'run. Darkstar people weren't happy about Cord's file, but he'd gotten his fingers in shit a few times when he was a cop an' they knew about it. So it was sort'a live an' let live. They could even *deal* from time to time.

"But when the blackmailin' little flit beside you there grabbed hold of the file, everyone got nervous. Paxton claimed he could keep 'im satisfied, but the main men over in Oklahoma City kinda figured different. Them two factions are always a little at odds anyway."

"Listen! The Oklahoma City people are wrong!" Riggs moved excitedly to the rail, one hand going at the hairpiece. "I've got everything I was ever going to ask for! Keeping the file was just insurance—"

"Tonight, my man Stalker *cancelled* it, baby. League couldn't go after the file, so Dunsford came up with the idea of leanin' on Stalker here. Pushin' him enough that he'd go right after it once the little Cord fox put the bug in his ear."

My right hand began doing its reflexive trip. Opening. Closing. Jesse seemed intent on his rap, the position of the Armalite more relaxed in his grip, cradled almost carelessly. "So you watched the refinery until I made my move and then just followed us out here."

"Shit, Indian. I sure wasn't gonna be over in Dawson watchin' that beat-up station wagon of yours."

And that's when Jason came leaping off the cruiser's bridge. Just like something from a movie. Beautiful. Rippling white muscles tensed; body arcing through the air toward Jesse and the launch.

He was dead before he hit the water. Ugly.

Jesse looked up at me over the smoking AR. "Guess we were both stallin' for the same thing, only for different reasons, huh, Stalker? If he'd broke for shore, you probably could've jumped me when I turned for the shot. I was sweatin' it some when I heard that forward hatch same as you. But those muscle-bound boys, seems they always gotta prove somethin', right? Kinda thought if I played it a little careless, I could get 'im to grandstand. His playmate on shore showed a bit of fight too."

"You animal," Riggs shouted. "You fucking animal!"

Jesse ignored him and kept staring at me. "Damn it, Indian. You should've backed off when I gave you the chance there at the railroad tracks."

Then he started shooting. Full automatic fire.

The Armalite 10 is a lightweight weapon, made mostly of aluminum with few steel parts, making it handy to carry. But the lightness also induces muzzle-climb on automatic fire. It rides up and to the left. So I tried to twist and drop in the opposite direction. Bullets stitched up through the back of my flak vest, almost parallel to my body, raking one shoulder with fire. The force sent me crashing back against the cabin and down to the deck.

Floyd Riggs fell on top of me, his hairpiece gone and too much blood in its place. I was trying to move him when the grenade dropped lazily over the rail and bounced across the hardwood. I think I screamed. But my hand closed on it and flung it awkwardly.

It cleared the bulkhead and exploded somewhere in the air. Riggs' body and the flak vest saved me from what shrapnel sprayed the boat. When my ears finally stopped ringing, I realized I couldn't hear what automatically should have followed the blast. The sound of the outboard revving up. I crawled to the opposite side of the deck from where I would have been seen falling, then peered quickly over the side.

The launch was still afloat, but beginning to take on water. Bits of flame danced on it in places, but they were quickly going out. The grenade must have blown almost directly overhead, sending some fragments toward the cruiser, but most into the water and the launch. And Jesse Long.

I caught hold of a line floating in the water, and pulled the launch close enough to climb in. Jesse was breathing, but not too well. He opened his eyes a little.

"You could use a Med Evac," I said.

"Wouldn't help. Even if they had 'em here." His voice was little more than a whisper. A whisper I could almost imagine coming to me through a layer of bandages. Just the way it had at the hospital in Japan, only caused this time by approaching death instead of the need for disguise. It shouldn't have been a shock. Bethany had picked up on the possibility when she went back over all the notes. Jesse had said at the tracks that he hadn't had time to look me up after the fragging, yet he knew I was at Zama. Even though the army has two *other* hospitals in Japan to which I might just as easily been sent, Jesse said Zama. It was just a possibility. Sometimes they aren't easy to accept.

Something must have shown on my face. Jesse read it and nodded.

"Yeah. The fraggin' too." I had to lean very close to hear him now. "I wanted out. Remember? Just like I told you there at the tracks. Wanted out *bad*. Day ol' Dunsford showed up at base camp, I figured *there's* a dude with connections. Able to *do* things for a man. Or against 'im. He didn't get no help from you? Maybe he could use a little from me."

"So you went in with them then, not Oklahoma City like you said. And when the fragging didn't do it, they set it up for you to go play games with me there in Zama. Christ, Jesse."

"Once you're in, you're in for the whole ride. But I tried, Stalker. There on the railroad tracks. Tried to make up for some of it by warnin' you away. I tried, but—"

"But I'm a hardnose. Sure, Jesse. I know," By the time I said it, he couldn't hear me anymore.

I picked up the Darkstar file and started to nurse the launch to shore while it would still float. Then, I remembered that something had fallen out just as Jesse appeared. It was still on the cruiser's deck. A photo. One that hadn't gone back to the wife of the dentist in Southern Hills. The figures in the

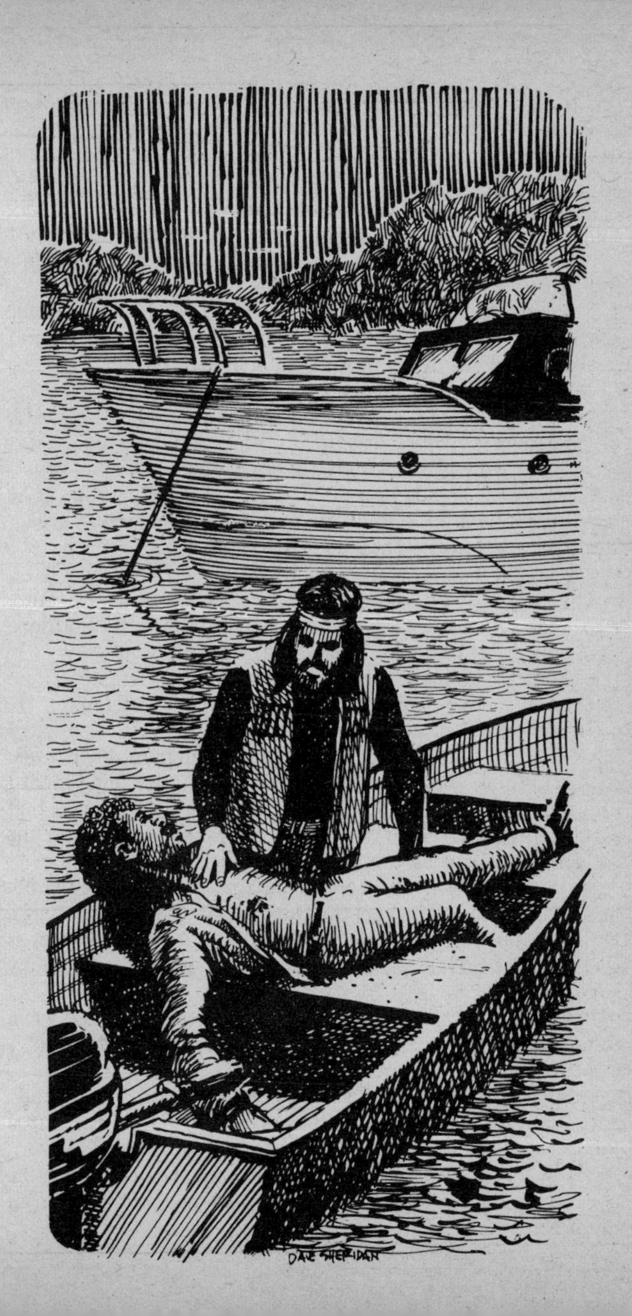

foreground weren't important. One in the background was. Enough to be circled in white when the print was made. Enough to make me pretty certain who killed Bethany's father.

In the proper moonlight, Adam Stalker can be quite a shock. I did my best to make this a dramatic performance. Having just about run out of night getting to Jared Paxton's home, I didn't want to waste what little time was left to me.

Kenneth Hadley Chalmers woke up quickly. He had trouble breathing the way my hand was clamped on his mouth. When I could tell he wasn't going to scream, I removed it.

Instead of listening, the Campbell's Kid decided to fight.

I pinned him quickly to the mattress and stared into his eyes. The pleading look of surprise on his face assured me that he was more than willing to take me to Jared Paxton.

Paxton was slipping his square, stocky body into a robe as he opened his bedroom door in answer to Chalmers' urgent whispers and knock. Then he saw me.

"What the hell is this about, Ken?"

The congressman looked uncertainly from me to his future father-in-law and back again. He wore only pajama bottoms. "He says he's Adam Stalker, Jared, The one who—"

"The one who made all that trouble over in Vietnam." Paxton said it the way Lyndon Johnson used to. Vee-ET-nam. He scowled and pulled at his large, blunt nose. "Well? Ken and I have a wedding to attend tomorrow. You must have *some* reason to think you can get away with this without being shot or dragged off by the police. So I'll save time and *give* you that much. Now, the sooner you get to the *point* of this visit, the sooner the two of us can get back to bed."

"I think you're done sleeping, Paxton. And I doubt there'll be a wedding. Tonight I got the Darkstar file from Floyd Riggs. Do you want to stand here in the hall and talk about it or is there a more private place we can go to watch you and Kenny squirm?"

Paxton stared. There probably weren't many times when things happened for which he wasn't prepared. "My study's right behind us. We can talk there."

Inside, Paxton and Chalmers headed for the brandy decanter. The Campbell's Kid poured and drank. But Jared Paxton decided to ask a question first. I cut him off.

"How do you know I'm not lying?" I took the photo from the pocket of my flak vest. "Congressman, get this for the father of the bride."

Paxton started forward too, but I made sure Chalmers was the one who got it. "God, Jared! That's—"

"It's your daughter, isn't it, Paxton? And it's the same picture Riggs must've shown you when he asked for the car, the boat, and the lifetime job. Before that, Cord probably flashed it so you'd stop nosing around Riggs about the Darkstar file. It could leave you up shit creek with the league, couldn't it?"

Chalmers waved the photo in front of Paxton incredulously. "Jared, I'm *Presidential* material! Any wife of mine has to be . . . well, *clean!* You can't expect me to saddle myself with anyone capable of *this*. I mean, look! She's *enjoying* it, for Christ sake! If it's happened *once*, you can't tell me she wouldn't do it again and—"

"Shut up, you stupid son of a bitch," Paxton exploded, shoving Chalmers and ripping the photo from his hand. "Sit down and shut up. You're *going* to be President. Just like I promised on that day we set up the engagement. With that fine ol' Eastern establishment background and Darkstar money and leverage, you can't miss. That's how I *sold* you to those bastards over in Oklahoma City. And I guaranteed they could push you all the way and there'd be no problem 'cause you were marrying *my* daughter. I'd always be right there, a power behind the throne. And they *bought* it, didn't they, Kenny? Just like I promised. Even after you fucked up in Vietnam. So don't you make noises about running out, boy. I've kept the lid on this so far and I'll keep on doing it."

Chalmers had sat on a black leather overstuffed chair. He perched on the edge of the seat. "But the league doesn't have anything to worry about now, Jared. After what they did for me in Nam, how could I ever turn on them? It's just the *marriage* I'm questioning. Why jeopardize my chances with a less than *perfect* wife? I mean—"

"The congressman's a little slow, isn't he, Paxton? He doesn't understand that *that* way it'd be just the Oklahoma City crew in charge. *Not* you. But if he's slow, you're too damn fast. You didn't solve very much by rushing to run Cord down with that big, black Continental out in your garage. The one with the newer headlight on the right-hand side."

Chalmers got to his feet and started toward Paxton, who had set his untouched brandy down and was shredding the photo, letting the little pieces fall into an ashtray. "Jared, he's talking about *murder*. If you're in some manner of power play against the rest of the league, that's *your* business, but I won't be dragged into a killing."

"You're still twenty-four people up on me, Ken. Or don't you count gooks? Sit down and be quiet." Paxton was pouring his brandy over the shreds in the ashtray. "Cord had too many dealings with the Oklahoma City people, Stalker. After he showed me that picture, I couldn't be sure he wouldn't pass it along to them like he had with other information. They've hoarded the power long enough. I mean to shift it back to me by being the one with direct control over the Darkstar candidate. Once those bastards saw that photo, they'd have the excuse to shut me out. So I removed Cord to have someone I knew *I* could deal with. Floyd Riggs."

Taking a match from a nearby holder, Paxton set fire to the content of the ashtray. "It's a big file, Paxton. Do you think Cord had only one copy of that photo in it? And, thanks to your associates in Oklahoma City, you don't have Riggs to deal with anymore. You've got me. And I'm partners with Bethany Cord.

Paxton looked at me and did something that must have been very difficult. He smiled. "Floyd was a partner of Cord's, Stalker. Open the drawer of the writing desk."

I did. It reminded me a lot of the drawer in Riggs' office at the refinery. There was a checkbook and a gun inside. This gun was a .25-caliber Beretta Jetfire. "Take out the checkbook, Stalker. There's a pen by the desk lamp. You write out your own price, son. Whatever you want. Just write it out."

I stood there. I stared at Kenneth Hadley Chalmers, who could live with being responsible for a massacre, but not with a wife who had sex in groups. And I stared at Jared Paxton, who wanted to control the Darkstar League and a President of the United States. Both stared back. Eager. Expectant. Waiting for me to name my price.

"Forget it, Paxton. I've already got what I came for." I dropped the checkbook back in the drawer and didn't bother to close it. Then, I started out of the study.

Chalmers was on his feet talking before I was through the door. "What *else* is in that file, Jared? You kept after Riggs for it in hopes of getting something on the *others*, didn't you? If it implicates the rest of the league in anything as serious as you've gotten *yourself* into . . . well, I mean . . . look, we're talking about total *ruin*! If I can't depend on you *or* them for help . . . then, I'll have to find *some* way to get myself out. I mean . . ."

I left by the same second-floor window I came in. The gray morning half-light was already spread over the large, rolling backyard of Jared Paxton's home. I crept across it quickly, using trellises and shrubbery hung with decorations for the coming wedding reception as cover.

All the way, I thought I could hear the two men in the study shouting. Then I stopped when I reached the protection of a thick stand of cottonwoods which bordered the property.

If there had been sounds, the house was silent now.

I looked down. Instead of opening, closing, in reflex action, the fingers of my right hand were still and steady.

The *World* gave it big headlines. WEDDING MORNING TRAGEDY. *Wealthy oilman shoots intended son-in-law, kills self.*

Bethany and I read it together over coffee in her office. One thing particularly pleased me. In the accompanying photos, Paxton's daughter seemed to be taking it well. Maybe now she'd have some choice about who she married, And her past sex life would be her own business again.

"You think Chalmers was ready to go to the authorities to make it easier on himself?" Bethany was bringing her notes up to date.

"That's the way it was headed when I left. Having gotten into this because of what he staked on Chalmers, I don't think Paxton was about to let him just walk away. And killing himself only beat the league to it. He had to figure they'd blame him when all the Darkstar file info came out."

"Only it's never going to come out." Bethany poked at the Darkstar file where it lay on her desk. A pile of charred scraps, flaked ashes. All that I had been able to gather up from the bottom of the launch after the grenade exploded. All that was left.

"Maybe there's a little Jared Paxton in me," I said. "But I couldn't see him and the Campbell's Kid getting off clean because of that. Not when five other people died over the damn file, your father included."

And if the way things worked out, Bethany was left with one or two illusions about her father and the way he used the file, that didn't seem so bad either. Probably she didn't need them. She was cool and intelligent enough to handle whatever she had to handle. But I kept thinking about Jesse Long. Once that meant laughing and drinking Scotch. Now I couldn't think of him without also hearing the whisper at Zama hospital or the grenade going off in my tent in Nam. I liked the first memory by itself, and I wouldn't have minded an illusion or two about Jesse to still have it that way.

Maybe it'd be the same for Bethany.

Hugh Dunsford and the rest of the Darkstar League were still out there, still in business. I didn't see them letting what had happened pass. We were just getting started with each other. Anything Bethany and I had to help us along, we could probaby use.

Even an illusion or two.

Afterword

I write comic books. Usually about people who wear fancy costumes and capes and fight against mysterious groups or individuals bent on ruling the world. The people are called super heroes and they're fun to write about. And there's a fair reason for their fancy costumes and capes. They look very good when drawn and reproduced in four colors on pulp paper.

But, maybe because I'm a little perverse, or maybe because I was never much of a fancy dresser, I've always pushed for a more "realistic" super hero. One who doesn't have to wear longjohns or save the world every issue or so. It's hard to get away with in the comics because they tend to get lost amid the flashier competition, and that's the last thing most editors want—something lost amid the competition.

When Byron asked me to contribute a story to this book, it seemed like the perfect opportunity. So I did *Stalker*, who wears a costume and fights against a mysterious group bent on ruling the world. Of course, it's a costume he could at least walk down the street in and not have everyone think he was on his way to a David Bowie concert. And he doesn't have a cape to trip over. And the mysterious group is bent on ruling the world from Oklahoma, which is quite a ways from the giant laboratories at the earth's core or on the dark side of the moon, where my villains are usually planted.

It was a nice change. And it was fun. It gave me a chance to inject a little of the love-hate I have for the city where I spent my teens, and to make one very small protest about the people who have the balls to make me pay 69.9 cents per gallon for gas. And rising.

It was also agony. A confirmed comic book writer without an artist is a pretty uncomforable figure. I'm glad Dave Sheridan's illustrations are in evidence here and there. If only I weren't so uncertain about the spaces in between.

TM

Guts
by Byron Preiss
Illustrated by Steranko

This is my entry in the book.

The story of Guts, the cosmic greaser, involves Judaism, holography, time travel, soul music, synaptic energy and radiofrenetic material.

To learn more, you will have to discover the contents of the three sections that await you. The first lays a base for Guts' story. The second is the introduction of Israel's time-shuttle program from Guts' point of view. The third is, well, you'll see.

The illustrations by Jim Steranko are a departure from his slick comic book days. These drawings are highly illustrative and the portrait is a good example of Steranko's ability to subtly blend two themes.

For those of you unfamiliar with Jim's work, he is the winner of the Prix de Saint Michel, one of the highest awards bestowed by Europeans on their favorite graphic storytellers. He grand-slammed the 1968 Alley Awards for Comic Art, being nominated for his writing and his art (his short story and his novelettes about a spy character, *Nick Fury, Agent of Shield*).

In 1970, he founded his own publishing company, Supergraphics, to independently produce material related to visual fiction. He has written and published two volumes of his massive and invaluable *History of the Comics* under the Supergraphics imprint.

In 1972, he began *Comixscene*, a bi-monthly magazine about comics. Broadening the scope of the periodical in 1974, he changed the titled to *Mediascene*. It is one of the handsomest periodicals currently in production.

Jim Steranko is a painter, an artist, and a designer whose work has consistently excited readers of adventure fiction. Asked about his best work, Jim replies, "It's yet to be done."

I sent a copy of an earlier draft of "Guts" to Phil Farmer, who wrote back to say that he thought the story was good and even funny in some parts. That, and concurring opinions from close friends and family are enough for me.

I hope you enjoy it too.

Introduction

> Asser Martin said he was an atheist so they sent him back into time.

It read well. A tight passage. But it was a distortion. The government copywriter pressed "V-E" and the screen was erased. She pressed "R," started again. On the video screen appeared the words:

> Asser Martin said he was an atheist. From this contention stemmed his desire to be sent into time.

Rather stungy, but at least it was accurate.

The teacher entered the store. It doubled as Urban Practice Center 3 (Secondary Level 5). The students were learning about Bureaucracy and Progress. "Progress—what's that?" "Something you read about in the encyclopedia." (Old Joke.)

"Good morning. Today's discussion relates to the brief history of the Chronos Program. I think I have enough styluses for all of us.

Mr. Earl at the Center tells me that a new videotape has come in on Chronos, so please tell any of your missing field partners to talk to him if they want an at-home presentation."

The Chronos Program was the official name for the time shuttle. The time shuttle was the technicians' name for the Time Machine. The Time Machine was Asser Martin's name for the device that he thought would help him test the existence of G-d.

The time shuttle was an exciting playtoy not unlike the Gemini probes of the last century. Yet the time shuttle was T.R.T. (the real thing). Whereas Gemini was a steppingstone to longer, more fruitful explorations, the time shuttle was a root from which time travel would grow.

Gemini got off the ground and was completed as a government-funded program. The time shuttle got off the ground and was changed. Public resentment (stemming largely from the outcome of the last economic conference) resulted in a senatorial thrust for a redirection of funding.

> ra´´di-o-fre-net´ic: adj. radiating energy in a manner that defies calculation—rad´´di-o-fre-netic´ity, n.

Radiofreneticity made its public debut in Texas with the ruination of the Yuba Desert (formerly the Dallas-Ft. Worth Airport). In areas of high radioactivity, material was becoming unstable and unplottable. Nobody knew for sure when it was going to blow up.

"Could we see it now?"
"Sure."

"This is Steve Cambell for Midtown News. Senator Keystone of Massachusetts had proposed that the orientation of Chronos, the government's time machine program, be changed from neo-historical to ecological. The senator is with me and he is going to comment on his proposal. Senator?"

"Why, ah, yass. Thank y'Steve. Whut I propose, is that the government's Chronos Program be changed from a neo-historical endevah to an eco-logically oriented endevah."

"Thank you, Senator."

"Shit. We can't use that."
"What are we going to do for a spot!"
"Run the Chronos film."
"Again?"
"How about Marcy Brent?"
"I'll call her."

"Marcy, can you do a minute on Chronos tonight?"
"Will it get me dinner?"
"Dinner, a hologram, and my company."
"That would be nice, Steve. Could you send over a tape?"
"Thanks, Marcy. I really appreciate it."

8-7-6-5-4
"You're on, Rachel."

"Now here with an insight on Senator Keystone's proposal is Marcy Brent."

"Essentially, the senator wants to turn the government's long-range time-travel program into a more practical, immediate tool for dealing with the radiofreneticity problem. By focusing their attention on the transportation of radiofrenetic *objects* instead of *people*, the senator hopes that Chronos researchers will be able to find a way to send the dangerous materials back to a time and place so long ago that their half-lives would expire before they could become a menace.

There is little Senatorial opposition to Keystone's proposal. Since the death of the much-publicized Asser Martin, Chronos has been plagued with experimental snafus and widely-echoed charges of overspending.

The lack of any new secondary funding for Chronos makes for likely passage of the Keystone proposal, clearing the way for a public referendum.

Although Chronos administrators express a deep hope for the support of the people, they confide a low expectation for acquiring the nine-figure funding they will need over the coming five years.

The people passed Keystone's proposal. Several staff changes took place at Chronos and within two weeks, the program was busily planning for the development of a system that would time-transport radiofrenetic material.

Departing researchers described the action as "turning their exploratory research into a quest for a new garbage disposal." Two departed for long sabbaticals. Five entered academia. Three went into firms doing research. Forest Stone took a position with Walt Disney Productions.

A year later, eight of the ten were on their way to Jerusalem. The Israeli government offered to fund a refinement of the original time-shuttle mechanism and all but Stone and Joan Ferris accepted. Ferris and Stone were a team of physicists. Their work had been a crucial component to the original time-shuttle research. Their theories had beat the clock in ironing out the return capacity problems in Dallas. Asser Martin had made the as-yet unduplicated return trip and Ferris and Stone could take the scientific credit. Now they were gone. Israel knew the chance they were taking on Chronos sans Ferris-Stone. The remaining team felt they could do it. Ferris-Stone offered help from the sidelines.

April 24th
21:00 hrs.

Dearest Shalla,

Today we examined the research facilities to be provided by the Israeli government. Your father was a happy man today! I am amazed by the sophistication of the equipment and the willingness of the technicians to be of help to us. My thoughts on the future of the time shuttle have brightened even more. I suspect that we will be able to reach our primary goal earlier than we had imagined.

I'm off to dinner now with Jane McAllister and Marc Silverstein. Please call when you are sure of your arrival date. See you soon.

Love,
Poppa

Ten months passed.

The Chronos Program and the Israeli time shuttle program completed their primary research within two weeks of each other. The Israeli government immediately started a program to prepare individuals for participation in time travel. The American government immediately started a sampling program to determine priorities for transportation of radiofrenetic matter.

"Gutstein! Shalom!"

"Shalom, Peter!"

"I hear you made it."

"That's true."

"When does the training start?"

"Right after Tu B'ishvat."

"Are you excited?"

"Yes. Very."

"Is it safe?"

"I'm rather sure they're taking precautions. Besides, the program isn't ready to send us anywhere."

Construction of the Israeli time shuttle paralleled construction of the American Chronos Slide. The Americans finished first. On December first, in a test situation, a small piece of radiofrenetic material was transported by the Chronos Slide. The test was declared a success and a schedule for completion of three Chronos Slides, with monitors and capacity for three tons of material, was developed.

Israeli law forbade the use of animals for test purposes. Time shuttle researchers had to develop a piece of matter possessing the kinetic, proxemic, and physiological properties of an "average" human being. The result was a fluid block which technicians jokingly referred to as "Al."

The time shuttle staff was faced with another major problem. Retrieval. This didn't bother the American program. Who wanted the radiofrenetic material back? But the Israeli time shuttle dealt with human beings.

BASIC STATUS (Skeletal Summary)

To: David Morra
From: David Weinstein

re: Shuttle Progress (General)

To date, we have developed a system capable of transporting material of human dimension into time. Also development of a monitoring device. Main problems: Return capacity and energy source for transients.

REQUEST GREEN LIGHT FOR EXPLORATION OF BOTH.

MEMO

To: David Weinstein
From: David Morra

re: "GREEN LIGHT"

Go ahead, fuzzy.

DM

Five months later the researchers were faced with three final systems from which they were to select the portable energy source for time shuttle users (transients). The first alternative was a solar backpack. The mock-up was rejected as unwieldy.

The second alternative was called a "false neck." It was a thin, flesh-colored collar to be worn around the neck. It proved erratic under varying weather conditions.

The third proposal was the most daring and most flexible one presented. It called for the channeling of electrical energy which crossed the synapses of the human body. More than that, it called for the channeling to be done without the aid of any mechanical device. Each transient would undergo a two-year training program during which he/she would learn how to channel the "synaptic" energy in his/her body to a nexus in the center of the chest. This channeled energy would be enough to turn on a light bulb or recharge a battery.

The only device included with the presentation was a set of fourteen paper-thin metal bars with the capacity to amplify the channeled energy up to five thousand times. It would be worn on the chest and held in place electromagnetically. As so:

The main problem foreseen with this system was a reduction in human sensitivity to recepted temperatures and pressures. Disadvantages were weighed. Shuttle researchers were especially pleased with the amplifier's safety mechanisms. The potential for electrocution was impressively below their standards.

MEMO

To: David Weinstein
From: David Morra

re: Training program for transients

If it will help insure the safety of the transients, take two years.

DM

"Asser Martin said he was an atheist. From this contention stemmed his desire to be sent into time."

The woman with the aching feet continued to read the pamphlet. Two stops from Newkirk Avenue. Time enough to finish the page.

"The government's Chronos Program had been in existence for one year when Asser Martin approached the directors with his offer. Asser Martin is best known as the man who first made holographic motion pictures for general theatrical release. He was secretary of media under President Wilson (David) and liaison to Korea under President Davidson. At eighty-six he had a reputation as a self-confirmed atheist. His offer to Chronos was $500 million to develop a system with two-way travel capacity for human beings. Contingent on the donation was an agreement from Chronos that Martin could be the first person to use the system and that he could select the time period to which he wanted to go.

The offer and terms were approved by Congress."

A chime rang. The woman placed the pamphlet in her shopping bag and left the car. She lost it outside of DeMato's Pizzeria. The pamphlet dropped to the ground and found a resting place between an IVC Porta-Player lid ($2) and the cheese from a slice of kosher pizza (6¢). Two days later it was picked up by an elderly man with a short, frazzled Afro and a pocket full of newspaper clippings. He sat down in the morning sunlight to read.

Most of Martin's remaining days were spent in anticipation of the results. Five weeks before his death, Chronos physicist Joan Ferris announced a prototype system which Martin would have the opportunity to test. It was dubbed the CHRONOS SLIDE.

Asser Martin announced his intentions in a short press conference in the White House Blue Room: "Before I die, I wish to travel to the time of Moses to hear G-d speak."

Media reaction approached computer speed. Before Martin had left the air, vids were shuffling material to make room for the story.

The government copywriter paused. "Am I getting too literary? I wonder if they'll take that out?" She continued, determined to keep her style intact in at least two paragraphs.

There were many treatments of Asser Martin's announcement. Much play was given to the theory that if Asser Martin heard G-d, it would be proof of G-d's existence.

The man with the frazzled Afro lowered the pamphlet and closed his eyes. Oh how good the sun felt. Warmmmmmm. He remembered the day Asser Martin held his press conference.

Where was he working then? He remembers the fuss. Silly. Why prove something you already know? You don't need proof to believe in G-d.

They shot Asser Martin back into time while 500 million people watched on video.

In layman's terms, time traveling takes up very little "real" time. The only time lost is that which is covered by the physical movement of the traveler. Hence Asser Martin returned thirty seconds after he had left.

His first words upon returning were: "Adoshem hu haadoshem."

Translated: The L-rd, he is our G-d.

Asser Martin died three weeks later, convinced of the existence of G-d. He became an Evangelical hero. Self-declared atheists rebuked Martin's activity as an elderly man's scheme to bring faith to skeptics.

Martin's death left the Chronos slide short of funding. Rumor began to spread that the Martin "time trip" had been a hoax. Within scientific circles the reality of the "trip" went unchallenged. However, the prolonged withholding of Chronos Slide research on all levels caused widespread alienation between the Chronos researchers and their associates in the field. Editorials on major scientific cassettes and in academic journals began to view the Martin "trip" as a "ffluke," a qualified success under an uncontrolled situation. In the face of mounting costs and controversial results, public support wained. A spirited core of "sliders" urged continuation of the program, but within two years legislative action was introduced to change the Chronos Slide into an experimental device for recycling of radiofrenetic material.

To date, the government has not approved any new program for human time travel. An Israeli program, largely developed by members of the original Chronos research team, is in the experimental stage.

The man looked at the picture and closed the pamphlet. A little girl and her mother walked past. The girl smiled and shook the string of her balloon. The man hoped.

Guts!

Shema yisroel adoshem eloheinu adoshem echod.

Sunny.
Amplifier tests today.
If they're operative, maybe we'll have some shuttling before the year is completed.

GOOOOOOSH. Water's hot.
SST.
"Good morning!"
"Good morning, Guts!"
"Mark."
"Mark—Guts—same person. We're friends, aren't we?"
Crazy programmers.
"I'd like the morning feed."
"Amplifiers in C-14 at 8:00 AM. Interpersonal sheets—Feed RS 20/55 662."
"Thank you." 662.
"SMACK! You're welcome!"

Umf. These shades. Nice to have glass walls.

Clothes. Clothes. Clothes.
Blue Jumpsuit. Red jumpsuit. Yellow jumpsuit.
Yellow.
Blinds up for the plants.
Amazing. Like living in a garden.

BOOM!

What was that?
"Guts! That came from the Center!"
Run!
Jesus, the place is on fire!
"Get those people out of here!"
I hope nobody's inside.

3:30.
Here comes Weinstein. He looks worried.
"We're in trouble."
"Damage to the amplifiers?"
"No."
"Worse?"
"MUCH."
"We were running a test with "A!" this morning. Chronos America was doing a major sendback at the same time. Their radiofrenetic material wound up shuttled to the time period we had cued for "Al."
"When?"
"Your era."
"BACK TO THE NINETEEN-FIFTIES?"
Nod.
Jesus, that's fuel for a war.
"YOU KNOW WHAT CAN HAPPEN."
Nod. "Mark, we have to do a shuttle immediately. Prevent any conflict."
"I thought we weren't prepared to shuttle?"
"Not within the safety margin we wanted, but the shuttle is operative."
"Without return capacity?"
"Without return capacity."
"What about the Chronos Slide?"
"Americans say it's inoperative. It would take at least two weeks to get it operative."
Dave wants to have me shuttled.
"Mark, I'd like you to take the job."
YEAH. I realize HE WANTS ME TO GO. what a burden LEAVE FAMILY AND it is to be asked, even on a FRIENDS non-official basis, BE A HERO Mark. PERHAPS GET STRANDED IN THE 20th/55-60.
"Are we meeting on this?"
"I was going to call for an immediate."

We're all here. Eight bananas and an orange. The orange stands up.

"As you know, the accident resulted in the material being shuttled to the 20th/55-60. For those of you unfamiliar with the period, political stress predisposed the United States and the Soviet Union to terrible sensitivity about nuclear attack. We want to send one of you to monitor the material—and if necessary, prevent it from causing conflict. Before coming into this meeting, I spoke to one of you and specifically told him that I'd like him to take the job."

Well, there go the women.

"The transient was Mark."

There go the men.

"Are you sure you want to do this, Mark? I told you—I don't have any close family to be worried about—I'd take your place."

"You're terrific, Jerry."

"Dave wants me because I've been doing the interpersonals for the period. He thinks I'll be able to live in the nineteen-fifties if necessary."

"So do we."

"Thanks."

Is the rush justified, Mark?

What do you mean, Stephanie?

Is it really necessary to send you back to the fifties *now*? Why not wait until the shuttle is approved? Couldn't they send you back to the same time period later on? What difference does it make when you go if you're going to the same time?

I understand what you're saying. It does make a difference. David is worried about funding. You know what happened in America. David thinks we must do it while we can.

"How do you feel, Mark?"

"Hungry."

"Ha. Get some fruit on the way to Reconstruction."

"I'm starting there?"

"Yes. Look at this."

PRIMARY PRIMARY PRIMARY PRIMARY
PRIMARY PRIMARY PRIMARY PRIMARY

To: David Morra

From: David Weinstein

re: Mark Gutstein

Even with his functional knowledge of the twentieth century, Mark should get an intensive diet of supplementals before his period of transience begins. As for RECONSTRUCTION, the sock hop tapes Warren was getting together should help. If there are no major objections to Mark, I will proceed with orientation and preparation for shuttling.

(Will make sure to include "Dobie" in video orientation.)

Dave

"If you are going to live in the nineteen-hundred-and-fifties for any length of time, you're going to need an identity."

"I have an identity."

"Yes, but we want you to be able to function with a set of era-related characteristics."

"Why not my own?"

"Mark, you were part of the talks on interaction. The consensus was that we should make an effort to interact with any era on their own interpersonal level."

"I can manage with my own identity."

"Perhaps—but your shuttle is an exception to our discussions."

"Because of the radiofrenetic material or because I'm the first to be shuttled?"

"Both. Since we don't have return capacity as yet, we may not be able to shuttle you out if there's trouble."

"What's the chance of help from the Chronos slide?"

"I hope positive. We're pushing for help."

Have to get home.

"We also want you to have the tools to interact conspicuously."

"Conspicuously? What do you mean, Dave?"

"How would you describe the role of media during the era?"

"Growing."

"Exactly."

"You'd want me to gain media status?"

"We want you to have the option. If there's no information

on the radiofrenetic material, you may need help in locating i Media status could make it easier for you to gain unnatur mobility and accessibility to security-oriented people."

"Would you shuttle that again, Dave?"

"Ha. How familiar are you with the clothing of the era?"

"Much of what I've seen comes from our library–periodicals, video, books. Then there's the music. Also som things from secondary."

"We're having Max tailor a suitable set of clothes for you Typical of the period, but bolder. It will be a lot heavier tha what you've been wearing at the Center."

A change from jumpsuits.

"Perhaps with your knowledge of the music and the distinc tiveness of Max's clothing, you might find it easier to attai some type of entertainment status."

Elvis Gutstein.

PRIMARY PRIMARY PRIMARY PRIMARY
PRIMARY PRIMARY PRIMARY PRIMARY

To: Mark Gutstein

From: David Weinstein

re: Preparation for Sendback

Mark, could you look this over and let me know if any changes are necessary to suit you?

We're running on a very tight schedule. Sendback is scheduled for 8:00 AM tomorrow morning. In order to familiarize yourself with much of our remaining data, we have set up the following orientations for you.

6:00 VIDEO Period video pieces (I think you'll enjoy these)

6:45 PUBLICATIONS Some new supplementals

7:30
9:00 Your time, Mark.

9:30 RECONSTRUCTION
Sock hop, commerical store.
PROXEMICS EXERCISES

10:30 INTERPERSONAL DATA

12:00 INTERPERSONALS

1:00 RECONSTRUCTION

2:30 INTERPERSONALS

We'll be testing your amplifier at 3:00 AM. I'm sorry for the predesigned situation. Let me know your considerations. We've weighed some of the data to relate to some of your focal interests, especially music.

6:00 Shuff!
Hey, this is funny. Dobie
Dobie Gillis—Dwayne Hickman
Bob Denver—Maynard
6:45 Sniff Sweet/sour Sickening: Old newsprint.
There's my material.
TV Guide—I've seen this issue. *The New York Times*, Sunday, September 20, 1959: "KHRUSHEV THREATENS TO RETURN HOME; WARNS COAST AUDIENCE OF SOVIET ROCKETS; PUTS QUESTION OF WAR OR PEACE UP TO U.S."

War or peace. That's where the radiofrenetic material is. Trapped in the cold war period. Unstable, unpredictable, unsafe, and I'm supposed to watch it.

A lot for one man.

Collier's Treatise: An Analysis of Social Mores in the Late 1950s. This book is theory.

Looks like a pile of clippings.
It is a pile of clippings.
From "The Fifties Story" (Cooster):

Dick Clark

Host on the famous American music-dance video, "American Bandstand," Dick Clark was one of the foremost figures of rock and roll over a three-decade period. In the fifties, his efforts pushed the careers of tangential rock and roll singers such as Frankie Avalon and Fabian. In the nineteen-sixties, Clark promoted groups such as Paul Revere and the Raiders from his new base in California.

In the seventies, Clark became involved in late-night video and commercial video game programming.

Behind the scenes and before the public, Clark was a significant figure in the development of rock and roll. (Comments of friends and associates follow.)

"It was bad enough in our time, Mark. People traveling all over—relationships lasting for a few months—letters that stopped coming—unanswered, unspoken questions—relatives going away—long distance calls from my brothers—. But you, our son, we won't even be able to write to you."

"Momma—I'm—"

"They're looking into a shuttle for things like letters."

"I don't want a shuttle, Isaac. I want our son here!"

"I didn't plan on doing this my whole life, Momma."

"But what you say—"

"I hope I'll be able to come home. This will always be my home."

"Then stay with us!"

"Momma, you raised me to help people. Could I turn down the people at the shuttle?"

"Couldn't somebody else do it?"

"Maybe—but I'm prepared for that era, Mom. What if somebody else went and there was trouble? I would feel sick."

"It hurts me Momma. I'm sorry. Dad"

IS THIS NATURAL?
IS THIS NATURAL?
IS THIS NATURAL?
IS THIS NATURAL?
IS THIS NATURAL?

"Her folks were always putting him down. (Down Down)
They said he came from the wrong side of town. (Town Town)"

"Leader of the Pack" by the Shangrilas. But wasn't that early sixties? Mom will be all right.

Time to see what Rico, Warren and the Reconstruction people have come up with for me.

Amazing! A hologram projected within four walls. Looks like an old lyceum gymnasium.

There's Janie.

"Like, what's shaking, Guts, Baby!"

"Janie, how did you get your hair that way?"
"Wig, baby. Want to twist?"
"You're on, honey!"
"23-Skidoo!"
Rico gives Janie a jab.
"Different era, Janie!"
We twist.

Interpersonals at midnight.
"How do you feel, Mark?"
"Tired."
"How was the sock hop?"
"Fun, I'll admit. But I need practice with the dance."
"Ready for some interpersonals?"
"I think we're supposed to do the data interpersonals first."
"That's what David told me."
"Shuttle."
"Destry was fantastic! What did you think of the guy who played him?"
"Audie Murphy?"
Calle has a nice smile.
"Fella! You got a union card? Ain't enough room inside for anybody tonight. Hoffa's gonna talk."
"More."
"Who are you?"
"Guts."
"Don't get smart with me, kid. I got a lot to do tonight."
"I just want to get inside."
"You a teamster?"
"Jimmy Hoffa—head of the Teamsters' Union in 1957."
"Mark, you're supposed to get it in dialogue."
"That was dialogue."
"You know what I mean. This is supposed to be a replication."
"All right. I was just tickling you."
"Did you see that show with the talking dog in it?"
" 'People's Choice'?"
"Yeah! What was the name of that dog?"
"Cleo."
"Terrific, Mark!"
"Thanks."
"You know you walk like a faggot?"
"What?"
"Yeah—and your brother Jack is a Commie."

She's shuttling as a little girl.

"I don't swish!"

"Huh?"

"Swish is a description of a type of walk—waddling your backside effeminately to the left and right."

"I'm sorry."

"What do you think of Richie Valens?"

"Could be a big star."

"No, Mark, he was a singer."

"Somebody can be a star and a singer, Calle."

"I'm just using the information they gave me, Mark. Do you have to be a corona?"

"I'm sorry, Calle. It's not you—it's interpersonals. Sometimes they're so lateral."

"Maybe—but I'm not an expert on this era and the interpersonal sheets have data."

"I know—sometimes I rebel against the approach."

"Could you do a few more? I'll look for a few less lateral exercises."

"Sure."

"President Eisenhower's had a heart attack!"

"Serious?"

"I don't know—it just came over the radio."

I'm falling asleep in this chair.

"First man to be shuttled to 55-60 while asleep."

Amplifier time.

They really *are* small.

Concentrate. Concentrate.

The poles are rising.

Thuk!

Incredible! They're holding magnetically to my chest.

Amazing!

Second pair. All right.

Third pair. All right.

Fourth, fifth, sixth, seventh.

"Turn this way, Mark!"

Hmhh—Charlie Cohen wants a picture of his invention.

"Mark, we're going to start the exercises with the scale."

They want me to supply the energy for that scale.

NN NNN NNNNNN

My lower legs get lightly numb.

Energy flows through my chest.

The amplifiers are moving. Hey!

Paper scraps zip up. The scale is on!

Smiles.
Looks like I travel with an amplifier—if medical doesn't find anything unexpected. I feel healthy.

Shema Yisroel adoshem eloheinu adoshem echod.

Sleep sleepsleepsleepsleepsleepsleepNosleep sleepsleepsleepNo sleep

I'm excited.
Why am I doing this.
No don't think that way. This isn't how I think. I'm going. I want to go. Pain. No pain intended. Dad understands.
I have an identity. Character denotes a set of built-in characteristics functioning as a structure. I have an identity.
How will the girls be? Different applications, same attitudes. Maybe different.
1955-1960.

(Translated)

"Time Shuttle Transient"
Mark Gutstein
Age: 24
Weight 165 pounds
Height: 1.83 meters
Hearing: 16/16 audibles
Smell: 1.2 meters i.s. infra-sensitive
Eyes: 20/20

The first shuttle tag for a human transient.
Time to leave. Quiet.
They came.
Capsule's shot.
Time to leap.
Leap to time.
Mom and Dad.
"Shalom!"

I'm here!

A rock and roll concert.
Sniff. Cannibis Now?

The music—The Coasters!

The clothes-*Different*.
The architecture!

"Excuse me, man, but could you like tell me what year it is?"
"Hey, you're really out of it."
"C'mon, paisan! Lay it on me, all right?"
"1976, man!"

1976.
We missed!
1976!
Dizzy.

Henainee

A sea of denim parts quickly as the red-maned woman rushes to the fainting greaser.

Her name is Barrie Chase. She is modestly famous. Modest because her fame is local. Famous because her locality is New York.

She gets help from a bearded onlooker too stoned to know what is happening. Together they pull Mark Gutstein to the paper-strewn entrance of the Felt Forum.

The woman runs outside.

The transient takes his first taxi ride.

Barrie Chase is home.
Mark Gutstein is in trouble.

Barrie Chase's apartment is furnished in "heavy velvet." Her friend Marshe prefers to call it "contemporary gauche." Her copy editor couldn't give a shit. Barrie is late with her story. She thinks it's worth it.

Mark Gutstein rests on a blue velvet sofa. The handsome, sleeping Semite is a walking hardware store. His simulated leather jacket is lined with a monitoring device and a translator. The zipper is a transient "sender." The black boots hold an amplifier.

Barrie Chase stands above him. If she could see through his pants, she might notice two wide sheaths. They hold religious material, a hologram of Mark's parents, and a peculiar pair of sunglasses.

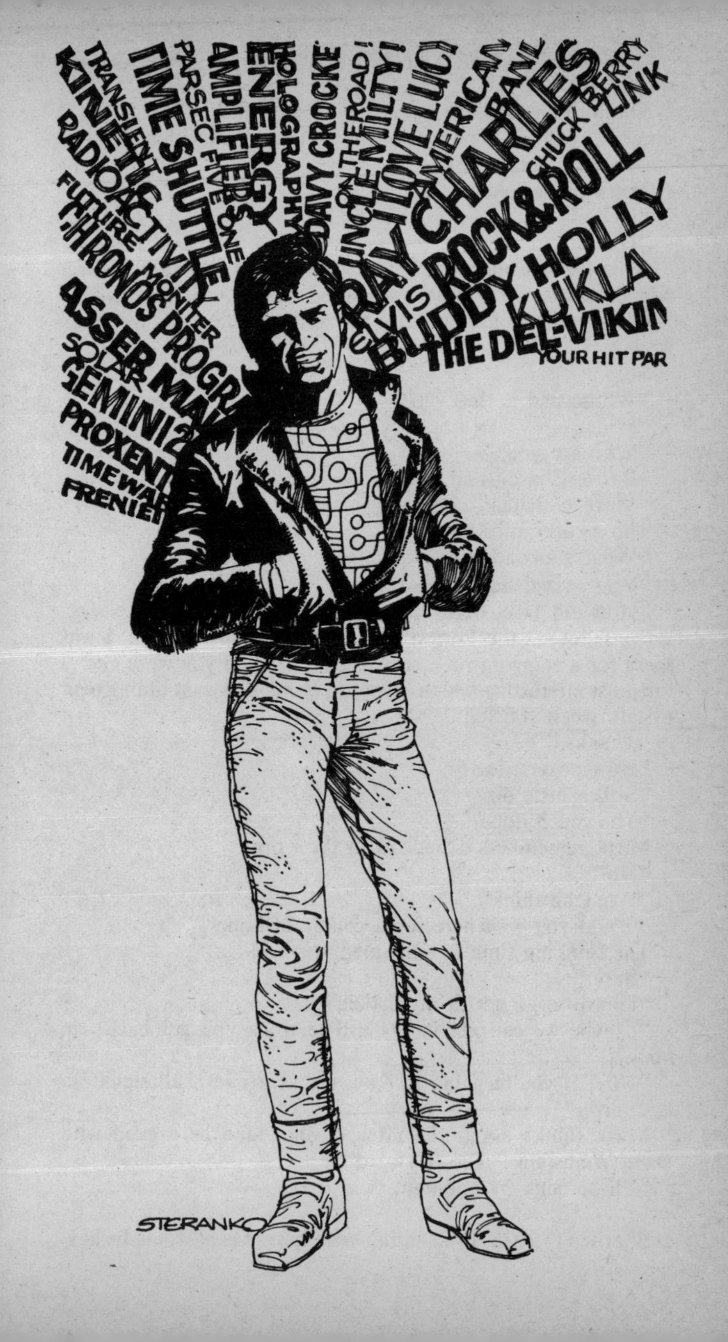

TRANSUENT
KINETIC
RADIOACTIVITY
FUTURE
CHRONOS
MONITER
TIME SHUTTLE
PARSEC FIVE ONE
AMPLIFIERS
ENERGY
HOLOGRAPHY
DAVY CROCKETT
ON THE ROAD!
UNCLE MILTY!
I LOVE LUCY
AMERICAN
BAND
RAY CHARLES
CHUCK BERRY
LINK
ROCK&ROLL
ELVIS
BUDDY HOLLY
KUKLA
THE DEL-VIKIN
YOUR HIT PAR
PROGR
SOLAR
GEMINI 2
PROXENT
TIME WAR
STERANKO

She waits. Her mane, an orange-red verdancy, falls forward on her face, brushing a pair of cheeks that shine with a silkiness enriched by her smile.

Mark has awoken.

"Hello."

"Hi."

Now the big question. What to be? Past? Present? Future? Mark knows the present would be flawed. He hasn't even studied interpersonal tapes for the mid seventies. Future? Risk it? No.

So:

"Whose pad is this?"

"Mine."

"Who are you?"

"Barrie Chase—and you?"

"Mark Gutstein."

The greaser rubs his eyes.

"What happened?"

"You passed out at the concert."

"How did I get here, Barrie?"

"A fellow at the Forum helped me get you to a cab. I was there for a story on rock revival concerts and you were one of the most interesting people I saw all evening. I was coming over to talk when you fell."

"Thanks."

"How do you feel?"

"Still a little dizzy."

"Too much dope?"

Mark remembers a book with the word.

"No."

"Whatcha thinkin'?"

"Could you wait here for a couple of hours?"

The thinking time is welcomed.

"Sure."

"I have to go get in my article."

"Maybe we can get in my article when you get back, eh, honey?"

"*Hey*! If you're going to stay, it's as a *guest*, all right?"

"Sorry."

Mark thinks about the interpersonal tape he argued with Dave Weinstein. "Too 'forward'!"

"I'll be back by midnight."

Shuttled to 1976. If his father were here, Mark would be having a good talk about the negative side of technos. But his father is not here. Nor his mother. Nor the seven other transients who could have wound up nineteen years off goal. But Barrie Chase is here and Mark's "sender" is here. At least Dave Weinstein knows where he is. Hopefully.

Mark looks out of the window at a New York City he did not expect to see. A changing pattern of yellow rectangles dance awkwardly up Third Avenue. A man comes out of a darkened Alexander's. A junkie pursues a pair of moviegoers as they turn down his Swiss-made Phonorite watch for the second time.

"Henainee." Here I am.

Mark hopes for the best.

He will be himself.

In the morning he can do a check for the radiofrenetic material. If nothing shows up on the monitor, he can do some research. Enjoy 1976. Maybe help.

Mark sits down in a blue velvet chair. The furniture is so heavy. The cloth is so rich. Waste.

IF YOU COULD BRING ANYTHING TO THE SEVENTIES, WHAT WOULD YOU BRING?

Mark ponders the question.

Love? No, there is love.

Food? It is not within his control.

Peace. No, not peace. Peace exists.

AWARENESS OF PEACE. Show people what already exists.

No.

Help people to show themselves that peace exists.

BUZZ!

"BARRIE?"

Mark walks to the intercom device. He presses a small white button.

"Barrie is not here."

"Jack?"

"No."

"FREDDIE?"

"No."

Barrie has a lot of friends.

"JIM?"

"This is Mark. Would you like to come up."

"THANKS."

Mark returns to the chair. Should he have

BUZZ!

"YOU FORGOT TO PRESS."

Mark reads the small embossed plastic.

A medium-built black man comes through the white doorway. Brow heavy with sweat, he looks as if he has climbed the twenty flights to Barrie's apartment.

"Roscoe LeJour; I'm a friend of Barrie's."

"We just met tonight."

"Are you in *Grease*?"

"Always man." Mark's grin is partner to the hand moving across his slick-backed hair.

"You're an actor?"

"No."

"A dancer?"

"No. You got any gum?"

"Why do you wear that costume then?" Roscoe is impressed.

"This is no costume, man."

"You're for real?"

"Touch for yourself, baby."

Roscoe eyes the boots, the white T-shirt, the handsome Semetic face.

"You look like the last of the big time greasers."

"Last and best."

"Modest, too."

"Well, y'know how it is—if ya talk big, ya gotta back it up. I back it up."

"Do you work?"

"Looking."

"How well do you know your music?"

"I ain't much on classical, but put a little Platters to me and I'll hit you with the rest."

"Who did 'You Send Me' before Aretha?"

"Sam Cooke."

"'Speedo'?"

"The Cadillacs."

"What year?"

"'57."

"No, '56."

"Nobody's perfect."

"What was the name of the Hilltoppers' big hit in '57?"

"'Marianne'."

"You know your stuff."

"Thanks."

"What did you say your name was?"

"Mark Gutstein."

"Gutstein—*Guts*tein—Guts!"
Mark's smile mixes displeasure with amusement. Not again!
Roscoe continues to play.
"Guts, the Greaser—No—Mark Guts!—Gutsmark! —No—the Last of the Greasers—the Supergreaser—Guts, the Supergreaser—No—the COSMIC Greaser—Guts, the Cosmic Greaser!"
He says it again, pleased with the sound.
"Guts, the Cosmic Greaser! How do you like it?"
"For what?"
"You ever do any announcing?"
"You mean shows and stuff?"
"Radio, television?"
"No."
"How'd you like to make a test tape?"
"You putting me on, man?"
"No, I manage a station."
"You sure?"
"Definitely."
"Then, yeah, I'd like it."
"Tomorrow at WLOC. About ten, all right?"
"Sure."
"You know how to get to us?"
"Can Barrie tell me?"
"I think so—she has an office there."
"Thanks, Mr. Le Jour."
"See you tomorrow. Tell Barrie I stopped up for my piece of cake."
The visitor heads down the corridor to the elevator. As the doors slide open, he hears an afterthought echoed through the hall from Barrie's apartment.
"Got any gum?"
It would be a crazy morning.
WLOC was a progressive soul station.

The early morning breeze gently washes Mark and Barrie as they step onto an abandoned sidewalk. If the windows on Second Avenue could reveal reflections borne on evenings passed, Mark might see himself replaced by Dick Cavett or Murray Kaufman or Fred Astaire. But the windows remain silent. It is Barrie who talks.
"Mark, where do you live?"
"I move around."
"Do you have a place to stay tonight?"

"Not yet."
"You're welcome to my couch."
"You want to catch me if I talk in my sleep?"
"You really are suspicious."
"Are ya just being nice to me because you want to do an article on me?"
"I like you."

They pause at a bookshop.
Mark raises his hand to Barrie's cheek.
His mind flies forward in fantasy.
His fingers touch down on the silk-smooth surface that rises proudly over an almond-shaped bone.
AVOID MAKING LOVE WHILE IN TRANSIENCE.
His fantasy bends under the pressure of a shuttle dictum.
The first kiss is warm and soft and real.
A New York street is only temporarily abandoned.

Cocoa krispies scream under the pressure of Barrie's spoon as the sun does funny things to the surface of her kitchen table. Mark watches as a tailor turns the key to start another day's work. The taxis do their dance. Streak and stop. Weave and turn.
"Those cabs are expensive, aren't they?"
"Yes, do you have enough?"
"Yeah, I'm cool."
He rises and slips on his heavy jacket.
"Later, baby."
"Promise to tell me what happens with Roscoe?"
"Yeah."
"What's the matter, Mark?"
"Got a lot on my mind."
"Worried about the test?"
"Don't bug me."
"You could thank me for putting you up on the couch before getting so angry."
"Sorry. Thanks. Really."
"You're welcome."
Black boots on a blue rug. The door opens.
It's time to use the monitor.

Mark climbs the stairs to the roof exit.
He opens the door a crack. Empty.

The monitor is a network of curved metal rods. Stretched over the skeleton are thin sheets of maleable circuitry. The finished product resembles a kite and a ball of string—with a central impulse cable running from a focal point to a small, flat receiving board which Mark holds in his hand.

Construction of the monitor from the modular set stored in Mark's jacket is not a complex task, but it must be executed with care and near-singular attention. Mark's amplifier provides sufficient energy as he concentrates on the synaptic flows in his body.

When Barrie Chase peeks through the roof door to see why Mark has left an hour earlier than necessary, she sees a man whose face has turned bright red, whose open chest is taut against a configuration of small metal bars and whose mouth is curved upward in a slightly strained smile.

When Mark relaxes, slightly secure in the knowledge that the material is underwater within a 200-mile radius of Manhattan, Barrie Chase is already in her apartment, shuttling three thousand words into a small tape recorder. As Mark worries about the ramifications of the material's presence, Barrie worries about Mark.

"A story is a story, but a man is a man."

Her mother said that when Barrie moved to Manhattan.

The secretaries at WLOC had a pool going. Two dollars a head. Winner take all. The contest was simple: Guess the number of times the word "shit" is used during the board meeting and come out on top. They left the intercom on, of course. That's how they learned about Guts! The Cosmic Greaser.

" . . . But Roscoe, the guy will lead into my show!"

"Exactly, Lamar—since you have a big pull, we're going to punch up his last half-hour, see if we can hold a new audience for you."

"No man, you don't understand."

"Roscoe, if you're going to bring in some jive-ass greaser and break up our programming, you can consider me as good as gone."

"Now wait a minute, Frankie."

"Don't give me any of that fatherly bullshit (16), Roscoe."

"Frankie's right, Roscoe. We have a tight format now. Why break it up?"

"IF YOU'D ALL LISTEN TO ME FOR TWO MINUTES, I'LL EXPLAIN IT AGAIN. First, we need

somebody to fill in for Vi starting next week."
"Then get another sister!"
"ARE YOU GOING TO LISTEN?
"Thank you.
"As I was saying, we need somebody new to fill in for Vi. Now according to ARB, we've held a two share in the market for the last two years. That's hip for a progressive station. But we're at a standstill. No growth. We've talked about moving into TV, true? We've talked about doing our own publishing, true? We don't have the revenue for it, *but* if we could bring up our evening market share—increase the ratings—get some new sponsors—*then* we might be able to move into those things a lot faster."
"But what do we need with a white DJ?"
"This guy isn't just a white DJ, he's a *personality*. I'm telling you just like I did when we hired Bernie away from SOL: This guy can get an audience.
"A WHITE audience."
"Yeah, Roscoe, that rock shit (17) is going to ruin our identity."
"Use your mind for a minute, Jimmy. Who started rock? We did. Chuck Berry, Little Richard—"
"Further back, man—*gospel, african rhythms*—conga drums—"
"True, Frankie."
"But what do we need with a white DJ telling *us* about what we did? I've had enough of that shit (18) in my life already."
"All right. I'm putting it to you. We can either give this man a fair chance and maybe get some of the things that are important to us done faster or we can look for a new woman to replace Vi."
"White man's business, Roscoe. We don't have to do one thing or the other. We can do both." Frankie had the attention of the board.
"We can hire this guy, IF HE'S GOOD, while we look for a new sister to fill Vi's spot. If he helps us enough, then we can consider keeping him."
"What would you do with an offer like that, Frankie?"
"Put it to him straight. Explain our situation. If he wants to check it out, he can take it.
The board's concurrence is punctuated by a message from the program manager's office.
"Mr. LeJour, Mark Gutstein is downstairs for his test."
Eight skeptics watch through a double-glass window as

Roscoe LeJour and morning DJ Jimmy Wax greet Mark Gutstein.

"Is he going right in to do it?"

"No, I think Roscoe is bringing him around to see the station."

"Looks like they're coming over here."

"Mark, I'd like you to meet some members of our executive board. You may have heard them on the air."

"Frankie, Vi, Lamar—"

"Nice t'meet you. I consider it something special to have the opportunity to try out for an R-and-B station with all-Negro DJs." Smiles freeze as Roscoe hustles Mark down to the record library.

"Did he say all-*NEGRO* DJs? Tell me that dude didn't say all-*NEGRO* DJs."

"I'm not going to lie to you, Frankie."

Mark is seated in front of a poster of Roberta Flack. Pasted to the console are the words of Gil Scott-Heron's "The Revolution Will Not Be Televised." There's an audience of twelve in the monitor booth. Mark is slightly tense, but comfortable around a patchwork of wires and machinery. An ON THE AIR light flashes.

"BIG BOPPERS, LITTLE DIPPERS, SOUL-STRUTTERS AND SICK STRIPPERS, HOLD TIGHT AND DON'T FIGHT! YOUR MAIN MAN MARK—GUTS, THE COSMIC GREASER!—IS HERE TO LAY THE FIFTIES ON YOUR HEAD AND IN YOUR BED. GONNA PUT THE BADDEST OF THE BEASTS AND THE BEST OF THE LEAST IN YOUR EAR AND UP YOUR REAR. SO HOLD ON, DON'T BE GONE—HERE'S A SUPPOSITORY OF SOUL TO PUT IN YOUR HOLE—THE COASTERS' 'UP ON THE ROOF'!"

Seven solemn DJs begin to yield. Roscoe smiles and Mark picks up as the song plays out.

"BEAUTIFUL. SWEET. MUSIC FOR THE STREET. DID YOU CATCH THE COASTERS AT THE FELT FORUM LAST NIGHT? LIKE BEAUTIFUL! WE'RE GONNA OPEN UP THE PHONES, FRIENDS. SO

GET OFF YOUR ENDS AND MAKE AMENDS. GET THOSE CHARTS AND GIVE GUTS A CALL AT WLOC 222. WLOC—LOVE, ONIONS, AND CABBAGE—THE STATION INTEGRATION—ROCK AND SOUL IN NEW YORK CITY. BRINGING YOU THE BEST OF THE BASIC BLACK—CHUCK BERRY'S 'MAYBELLINE'!"

The man is *exciting*.
Hands come out and Mark has a job.

The wall behind Roscoe Le Jour's desk is covered with small golden mirrors. They are plaques—WMCA, YWHA, PAL, PUSH, PEPSI. At night they reflect the waterstained shirts which cling to Roscoe's back. He's a hard-working man and a happy man. Today he's particularly pleased. He has a new disc jockey—but more than that, he has a *PERSONALITY*.

"Vi's given us notice, Mark, but I'd like you to fill in for her tonight."

"Sort of a full-length test?"

"If you don't mind."

"No sweat."

"Good. I'm going to have my lawyer draw up a contract tomorrow. While that's happening I'll check with the FCC about your license. Tonight you'll be Frankie's special guest. He'll be there, but you'll do most of the announcing. Just don't touch anything and it'll be cool. You can check with the union in the morning."

"You guys don't mess around, do you?"

"Oh—one other thing. Do you think you can read the news copy tonight?"

"News copy?"

"Our evening woman is at some journalism convention. Do you think you could read the news during your show?"

"Sure."

"Willie will fill you in on the time details and some other things. Anything you want to ask me now?"

"Got any gum?"

Laughter.

Playtime.
Mark pauses on a vacant floor in WLOC's building.
He spots an unconnected telephone and walks over to pick it up.

At the shuttle they call it an electromagnetic communications field.

Mark puts on his amplifier and concentrates. He dials Barrie's number.

"Hello?"

"Hey baby!"

"Mark! Did you get the job?"

"Are my pants tight?"

"You got it!"

"Yeah, but I gotta do tonight's show before I get a contract."

"What time?"

"Eight"

"I'll be at a basketball game. Maybe I can take a radio."

"You want to meet me for dinner?"

"Sorry, Mark. I have to get down there early for some background color."

"Later, then, baby!"

"Mark!"

"What?"

"Can we get together after the game?"

"What ya got in mind?"

"Why don't you stop over to my place around 11:00?"

"That's cool."

"Bye."

The clerk at the microfilm desk watches Mark with the look she usually saves for her TV repairman. The best description she can think of had long been replaced by the word "hippie." Hoodlum. This young man looked like a "hoodlum." But he didn't act that way. Despite his speech, his clothes, and his slick hair, the fellow seemed honest. But just the same, she felt an extra bit of scrutiny wouldn't hurt. It saved her from losing her color TV for a week and maybe it would save the Public Library a few rolls of *New York Times* microfilm.

Mark's mind is far from the green metal stall that surrounds his head. It is in the Gobi desert, contemplating an atomic explosion. Now it is back, rejecting.

He can find no record of the arrival of the radiofrenetic material. For two decades it has been on earth, there appeared to be no notice of its discovery. Of course, recognition could be secreted away in some government file. Still, it was located underwater within 200 miles of Manhattan. A busy area. Likely to be explored if there were any disturbances. Mark plays off some answers. An obvious conclusion was that the radiofrenetic material had been shuttled directly to its underwater location. But where exactly was that? Connecticut? The Verrazano Narrows? The Schulkyll River?

None of the articles provided clues.

Mark wonders about the possibility of classified data. Access to military material might be very difficult to secure.

His attention wanders to an article on time travel. The implausibility of it. Mark reflects on the theory behind the time shuttle. He wonders what the doctor might say about shuttling.

He gets dizzy and falls asleep.

"Young man, you'll have to sleep elsewhere."

Mark awakens.

"If you leave the film too long in one spot, it starts to warp."

"Oh. I'm sorry."

She thought he slept like a baby.

He leaves for the station.

Three members of the WLOC executive board are eating dinner at Romero's. Mark Gutstein's potential is being served with dinner.

"Subway posters cost too much, Roscoe."

"Not if we barter for them."

"You have somebody in mind?"

"U.P. has a running contract with Transit Media. I think they might take twenty spots in exchange for a fifty-percent billboard saturation over one month."

"You have something in mind for the posters?"

"A photo. We'll get Shirley to come up with the captions."

"WLOC DIGS WHITE PEOPLE."

Roscoe is hurt by the resistance.

"Just kidding, Roscoe."

"Hey! Turn it up!"

Six teenagers burden the springs of a '66 Olds in Brooklyn's Bedford-Stuyvesant.

"Are you all right, Cassandra?"

A maid in Westchester prolongs her trip to the bathroom.

"Could you make the stereo a little louder?"

A stockbroker leans over the counter in a crowded New York bar.

Something's up on Frankie's show.

In Romero's Roscoe LeJour asks Ernesto to bring over the tiny AM/FM-radio kept in a drawer under the cash register.

The ON THE AIR light flashes.

Frankie Hollywood goes into his introductory rap.

"Now brothers and sisters, like Frankie promised you—a WLOC SPECIAL. As you may know, Vi Hutchinson will be leaving WLOC next week to take off for sunny California. She'll be here tomorrow night to tell you a little bit more about that, but right now we're going to give you a soulful sneak preview of the man who's going to fill Vi's spot. I'm looking at this dude right now and I can tell you he is *something else*. The man is a flashback, a fastback, a funky fountain of fantastic phrases. Brothers and sisters, I give you Guts, The Cosmic Greaser!

"Yeah! Thank you Brother Frankie. I'm bringing you a hip trip sliding on the strains of Richie Valens, Chuck Berry, Little Richard, Etta James, and Elvis Presley. The Diamonds, the Del Vikings, the Dominos, the Drifters and Dinah Washington tonight—and to all the listeners out there who want to know if I'm white or Negro, I want you to listen to the color of my voice. Dig deep, children. Music!"

"That's All I Want From You" flows into their headphones. Frankie removes his pair while the new DJ gets the news copy.

"Mark."

Four headphones lay on the console.

"Yeah, Frankie!"

"Don't do the color thing, man."

"What?"

"That bit about the color of your voice, don't do that, man."

"Why not?"

"If they're gonna like you, they're gonna like you either way. Don't sell yourself."

"I just thought since—"

"The people are straight, Mark. If you're gonna hold them, it's because of the way you *are*."

The silence is almost as deep as the honest human love that flows between and to each man.

The ON THE AIR light flashes.

"This is a special seven-hour Frankie Hollywood spectacular bringing you a new star on the soulful sea of WLOC. We'll be right back after the headlines and MBN news."

"All right, Mark."

"IN THE HEADLINES TONIGHT, THE MAYOR ANNOUNCES THE APPOINTMENT OF MS. LOUSILLA HICKS AS THE FIRST BLACK ADMINISTRATOR

OF THE CITY'S DRUG PREVENTION PROGRAM . . .

"THE NEW YORK TIMES RELEASED A SURVEY TODAY INDICATING THAT THE JOBLESS RATE IN THE FIVE BOROUGHS HAD DROPPED 1.2 PERCENT SINCE JANUARY . . .

"MINOR ELECTRICAL BLACKOUT ON THE WEST SIDE HAS STRANDED THOUSANDS OF SUBWAY COMMUTERS. MTA AUTHORITIES EXPECT THE LINES TO BE WORKING WITHIN THE HOUR . . .

"SIGHTING OF A BUBBLY SPOUT OF WATER AND INCREASING TEMPERATURES IN THE EAST RIVER NEAR THE UNITED NATIONS THIS EVENING HAS PROMPTED THE ATOMIC ENERGY COMMISSION TO SEND . . .

"What?"

Mark springs up in his chair, finishes the sentence with a speeding look, and nearly knocks over Frankie Hollywood as he whips up his jacket and rushes out of the station.

In Romero's, Roscoe LeJour sits open-mouthed, his spaghetti awaiting a final verdict as Frankie Hollywood reassembles his cool.

Lamar Star talks to the black box on the table.

"Run the MBN tape!"

They run the MBN tape.

Twenty Minutes to Possible Implosion

Now it begins. The long run. Against time. Against space.

If the bubbling in the water near the United Nations *is* from the radiofrenetic material, Guts knows he has but twenty minutes to reach the site and take control of the material's hypercritical mass.

The United Nations is downtown and crosstown. Guts must get to 42nd Street and First Avenue from WLOC's office at 86th Street and West End Avenue. He has twenty minutes. In the rain, heavy traffic, and human overflow from the minor electrical breakdown, an experienced cab driver could make the trip in twelve minutes. Guts hardly knows New York North from South.

RAIN! It pulls the rug out from under Guts' shiny black boots as he bursts into the foyer of WLOC. Sliding across the marble floor, they careen ungracefully into a metal brace at the bottom of the glass front door.

Guts springs up almost instantly, pushes out the door, and flies into the street.

His head spins both ways. He turns east and darts to the corner. The footsteps are more careful, but his pace quickens.

Guts' mind switches thoughts, back and forth from the brain-burning visage of east Manhattan in flames to the logistics of getting downtown during wet weather. He screams internally, *introjecting* blame on his light-hearted attitude.

Yet Guts is a man of spirit. The screams are quieted. The visage extinguished. He *will* make it.

He hits the corner of 86th and Eleventh.

"Taxi!"

"Cab!"

They speed by, loaded.

Guts looks uptown. A bus is coming.

He boards and runs to the back.

"Hey, fella! That'll be thirty-five cents!"

Guts scrambles for change. In his left pocket, two quarters. He runs up to the front, starts to deposit them.

"Exact change only!"

The bus does not move.

"I don't have any change."

"Sorry! MTA rules. Exact change only."

Guts looks around frantically.

A man with a basketball stomach waves from the back.

"Hey! I think I can help you out!"

He comes forward.

The bus does not move.

"Hurry, please!"

"Hold your horses!"

The man's pink sweater is caught on a chair.

Guts rushes back for the change.

"What's the hurry? You late for a fire?"

Guts helps him with his sweater, then gets the change. The bus takes off.

**Seventeen Minutes to
Possible Implosion**

Eightieth Street. Seventy-ninth. Seventy-eighth.

Manhattan is a grid of straight lines. When he hits 42nd Street, Guts will have to span twelve long blocks to reach the East Side waterfront.

He ponders the problem in a momentary rest. The bus stops for passengers, then resumes its trip. Two kids in a tenament window wave down to him. Guts waves back.

Sixty-second. Sixty-first. Sixtieth. Fifty-ninth Street. Without warning, a sudden stop. Guts breaks the forward inertia and ducks his head out of the bus window. Fifty feet ahead a fruit truck has lost its load on the breadth of the street.

Guts spurts over to the man in the pink sweater.

"Is there a subway stop near here?"

"Columbus Circle, but—"

"Thanks, sir!"

"But—!"

Guts is gone.

Twelve Minutes to Possible Implosion

Guts moves east, leapfrogging a newsstand display, knocking into an unsuspecting sandwich man, and hitting a broken iron fence. He slides in the mud. His jacket is soaked.

Outside the New York Coliseum at Columbus Circle, he spies four different subway entrances. Then a young girl with an umbrella.

"Which is the fastest entrance to get downtown?"

"East Side or West?"

"East!"

"Go across to the Gulf & Western Building!"

"Thanks!"

Guts ducks between two trucks, four cars, and an ice cream wagon, then literally dives over the railing at the G&W subway entrance.

He makes a jittery dash down the slick steps, looks both ways, then runs past the token booth, pulling out fifty cents to throw at the booth attendant on the way to the entry turnstiles. Without stopping, he does two complete double-flips, passing over the turnstiles and landing feet-down near the foot of the stairs to the subway tracks.

"Did I do that?" Guts has surprised himself.

"I sure don't know why, kid. The trains aren't going anywhere."

The blackout! The West Side subway isn't functioning!

Almost breathless, the news he read on the air comes flying at him as fast as the image of the crowded platform at the bottom of the stairs.

Approaching panic. Thoughts of incineration come flying back into his head. No! He won't give up. With G-d's help, he will make it!

Somebody jabs him from the left.

"Huh?"

Part of the crowd is heading back up the stairs.

"Shirley! I'll meet you back home! I'm going to try and catch the bus." A woman pulls her shopping bag out of the crowd.

Guts looks down at the unopened subway car which sits next to the platform. Then the idea. *The only thing keeping that train from running is electricity.*

Guts turns and bounds back up the stairs. His eyes scan the upper level for a private place. Men's room!

Locked. Broken. Guts spins around, glancing from post to post. He heads over to a large beam in the far corner from the stairs. He removes his left shoe, then turns the heel.

Inside are fourteen small metal bars. *The amplifier.*

Concentration.

Thuk!

Thuk!

He's ready.

Nine Minutes to
Possible Implosion

Down the stairs, through the crowd, to the rear of the train.

Heads turn and stare.

Where is that man going?

HE JUMPS DOWN ON THE TRACK.

A crowd gathers at far end of the platform.

What is that man doing?

GUTS PUTS HIS BACK TO THE CROWD.

There are three rails for the subway car. Two guide rails and a track that provides electricity.

What's going on down there?

GUTS CONCENTRATES. CONCENTRATES. CONCENTRATES. THE STRAIN. THE BUILDING FLOW. HE CAN *FEEL* THE SYNAPTIC ENERGY RISE AND EBB, RISE AND EBB, AN ELECTRICAL TIDE. Ahh! The amplifiers vibrate. The flow is peaking.

Acrobatically jumping backwards on the platform of the rear car, Guts positions himself on an angle to the third rail. Then a headstand. Delicately, he moves around until his chest faces the track. Slowly, carefully, locking his feet and arms into position,

Guts, forms an arc with his back bent inward and his chest thrust convexly toward the third rail.

Then he lets loose! The electricity flows! The train begins to move!

What is going on over there?

BENEATH HIS OPEN JACKET, GUTS' CHEST TURNS A SWEAT-SILKEN RED. HE STRAINS HARDER! HARDER!

The crowd rushes into the train. They don't *worry* about the man at the end of the train. They *wonder*.

Guts strains.

The motorman begins to pull the train out of the station.

He does.

The cars begin to roll past the platform, steadily, perhaps a bit slower than usual. Tired commuters, stranded and unable to fit in the already-crowded cars, await the next train. Then, building like a slow crescendo on the faces of the rest of the crowd, comes the reaction to Guts, the cosmic greaser!

As the train passes, jaws drop, eyes pop, necks slip forward, and short gasps reverberate off the station walls. The crowd sees a man with a firm, red, sweating chest, hanging upside-down between the door and the floor of a rusting subway car. In the middle of his chest are fourteen small, neatly aligned bars.

The man appears to be in a state of intense concentration. The train is almost out of the station. The rear car begins to pass into the tunnel. At the very tip of the platform, a five foot blonde stretches out to get a closer look at the human dynamo. He gazes sideways, nods, and smiles.

"What's cookin', good lookin'?"

The car passes into the dark of the tunnel.

Six Minutes to Possible Implosion

Guts begins to tire.

The Rockefeller station stop.

The train resumes. What if there is another train ahead? Will he be able to move it with the amplifier? Unlikely. He hopes for the best. It happens.

Forty-second Street. The train pulls into the stop without incident. As the last car is about to pull up to the platform, Guts relaxes the flow. The train stops. Semi-safe under the cover of darkness.

Baffled passengers watch from the rear window.

Guts flips down from the headstand. With his back to the crowd he removes the amplifier and replaces it in his shoe. No risks in the rain. He wipes his jacket dry and drops down to the track.

Through the edge of the tunnel, Guts views the crowded platform ahead. He cuts through two tunnels, pulls himself onto the uptown platform and runs!

Up the stairs into the—

SUNLIGHT. The rain has stopped: that will make it easier.

He takes off.

Run! Madison

Run! Lexington

Run! Third Avenue

Then up ahead! The United Nations—42nd Street and First Avenue!

Then—

BLACK.

Four Minutes to
Possible Implosion

"Mister! Mister!"

Hazy, hazy.

"Mister, are you all right?"

A balding man in a black hat shakes Guts' shoulder.

"Wha?"

"Mister, you fell down and hit your head. Are you all right?"

"Wh—yes, I think so. Thank you."

He stands up, wobbly.

"You sure?"

"Yes, thank you."

Guts wonders. The third blackout since he arrived.

Could it be the additional drain from the amplifiers?

Could it be—the thought is cut off.

THE RADIOFRENETIC MATERIAL!

How much time is left? IS THERE ANY TIME LEFT?

The running begins again.

First Avenue! The United Nations.

Then the highway! The water!

Guts arrives at the same time as an official limousine.

Without thinking through a plan, he cuts to the right of the Forty-Second Street Pier, jumps up and scales a supporting beam of the FDR Drive. At the top he flips onto the cement embankment and in a follow-up move zips off the protective lining

in his jacket.

Reducing the assembly time to a quarter of what it had been, Guts positions the reconstructed monitor for a direct reading of the bubbling area. The amplifier bars fly out of his hands onto his chest. A reading flows with similar speed.

IT'S THE RADIOFRENETIC MATERIAL.

He reaches into his pants and brings out his sunglasses. With one hand he locks the lenses in concave positions and slips the pair on his face. With the other he begins to dismantle the monitor for reconfiguration as a part of the translator.

The skeleton of the monitor overlaps on the amplifier bars. The sheets of circuitry are laid onto his shoulders. Guts is oblivious to the stalled traffic, the distant siren, the alarmed look on the mayor's security men.

He gropes for translator parts. He gets them. Now for the difficult part. Attach them to his chest and immediately begin an intensive channel.

CLTIK! CLTIK!

He spreads the amplifier bars as he intensifies his concentration.

Strain! Strain!

He doesn't notice the motorcycle cop behind him.

"Excuse me, sir!"

No recognition.

"Sir!"

No recognition. An arm reaches out for Guts' shoulder. Guts reaches up quickly, alters the configuration of bars on his chest and spins around as the motorcycle flies backward in response, pinning its rider to a stalled car.

Guts notices with pain, spins and faces the water. His skin brightens. Streams of water slide down his skin.

The strain is climaxing now. The energy flows through translators, through water, through silt, wood, and garbage.

The radiofrenetic material is enveloped. Pulled to the surface. It keeps rising, a deadly "balloon" tied to a string of energy.

The child is in pain now. His body strains red, bleeds sweat, smiles. He Pushes! Pushes!

Implosion! Blossoming orange-red—small.

Deadly.

Dead.

Mark Gutstein breathes and the machinery falls to the pavement. He moves to help the policeman.

Two men thank their creator.

Epilogue

Roscoe LeJour smiled like a man taking his first step in silk pants without underwear.

"That's our man!"

He held out the morning paper which affirmed what he had already seen on television. Roscoe was proud. Of Mark. Of himself.

He felt proud as he read the headline:

UNIDENTIFIED MAN CAUSES NUCLEAR IMPLOSION. AEC OFFICIALS SAY ACTION MAY HAVE PREVENTED MIDTOWN HOLOCAUST.

He thought about the publicity one phone call could bring. Then he acted out of respect.

He said nothing about it.

Barrie Chase does not rise. She smiles about her morning dream and feels last night's worry. She sleeps.

Light sings through the stained glass windows and colors the wooden benches. Mark Gutstein's shadow blinks the tints as he heads toward the shulcain aruch. His father had told him about the shul in Brooklyn where he had daavined with his father.

Now Mark would pray here as two generations did before him.

The morning warmth bathes the minion.

Shema yisroel adoshem eloheinu adoshem echod.

Afterword

Guts was completed in my family's home in the Flatbush section of Brooklyn. It is fitting that I was able to complete it there before my family departed—not in spirit—for new pastures.

Our home was where I developed a love for comics and fantasy illustration. It is where I discovered Ray Bradbury and Harlan Ellison and it is where my best friend Johnny Wolfe and I discussed our favorite heroes.

House, this story's for you.

rose
TM

Rose In the Sunshine State
by Joann Kobin
Illustrated by Jeff Jones

When these books went into production with the directions of nine heroes clearly defined, I felt an absence of one special sort of story. I felt that the book needed at least one character whose heroics were on a predominately personal scale. Everybody in the book was doing something that could qualify as "hot" newspaper material. I wanted one story to show that intimate heroics were as important as headline adventures.

In addition, I felt it was important to have at least one hero/heroine whose age exceeded fifty years. "Old" characters are rare in heroic fiction. Superman, Batman, Sherlock Holmes, Doc Savage—the closest we get to an "old" hero is Dr. Watson. The Shadow? As they say, "Who knows?"

Enter *Aphra* Magazine, a small literary publication (quarterly with a print run of under 5000) devoted to feminist literature. Volume 5, Number 2 presents a short story by Joann Kobin, entitled "Rose in the Sunshine State." It is a slice from the life of a sixty-eight-year-old Jewish woman in Miami, Florida.

It is a beautifully written story and it presents an unusual possibility: What if the author developed the life of the character further, taking it on it's own level of action in the direction of "heroic adventure."

I posed the question to Joann Kobin. She reacted with the following:

"It would be helpful for me to understand how you see 'Rose' fitting in with the other stories which, as you said on the phone, were quite different."

In answer, Joann, I say that Rose's feelings and actions toward her friend Gerda and the hundreds of old, neglected people of the sunshine state are as much as home in a book of heroics as anything else.

As for the relationship of Rose to the "Weird" part of our title, well, when was the last time you read a pulp adventure starring a sixty-eight-year-old woman?

Jeff Jones, the illustrator for "Rose," is one of the most sensitive, intelligent, and exciting artists in the fantasy field. From his early efforts for Warren Publications, Jeff has grown into a highly popular book jacket painter and graphic storyteller.

As a fine artist, Jeff imbues his work with an unmistakable blend of romanticism, irony, and ethereal beauty.

With regard to his work on "Rose," Jeff writes:

"In this story there seemed very little point in depicting a scene literally from the story. Not only would this not have added anything substantial, it would have detracted from the story by insulting the reader's sensitivity—the story is not really about Florida or Rose or sunshine."

PART I

Rose, wondering if the pains in her chest would get worse, watched a pelican fall into the bay. How carelessly it dropped into the water, a jumbled flutter of wings and feathers and splash, sloppily, not a swoop or a precise dive like the gulls. When it emerged she hoped she would spot a fish hanging out of its pocketlike bill. The bird flapped its wings and lifted itself out of the water: no fish. It flew across the bay to the N.J.A. golf course on the island. No Jews Allowed. Today, as on most days, there was scarcely a sign of human life on the smooth green hills and slopes of the golf course. Perhaps there were no more Gentiles in Miami. The sun was getting lower in the sky.

Am I making my heart hurt? Am I doing it to myself? She reviewed the facts. The doctors could find no irregularity on her cardiogram. The pains continued and were real enough. What hurts hurts, conceded the doctors, and they prescribed heart-condition medicines. All in all, fourteen pills a day, red, pale yellow, and turquoise. The doctors were a team who shared her. Not one of the four could find any explanation for the pain or the occasional attacks of tachycardia that she suffered from: those frightening times when her heartbeat went clear out of control and vibrated her entire body, even shaking the bed. If the body were an orchestra, the drummer had gone wild.

"I am making myself tense. I keep wondering why Gerda didn't call and why I can't reach her. I must stop worrying. I command you, Aorta, relax!" She pictured herself a conductor with a baton: "Rose, ree-lax. Calm down-n-n. . . . "

Her hand flagged the air. The sun picked up the glitter of her almost-three-carat diamond ring, and the sparkle, purple and gold, caught her eye. She looked at her hand as it came to rest on the arm of the lounge chair. Veins showing blue. Pale brown blotches between the knuckles. Nails nicely manicured. A faint

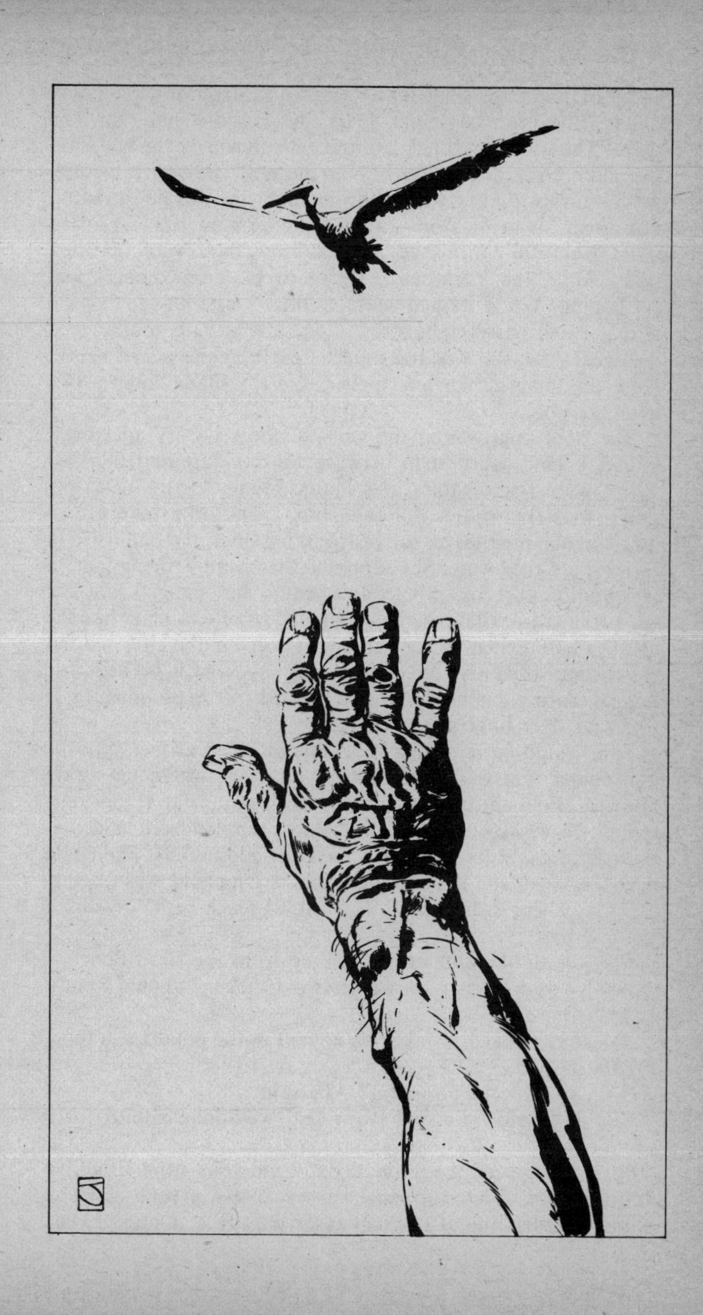

trace of joints growing imperceptibly more prominent. Nice hands. She was sixty-eight years old. Good hands. No pain there. The water sparkled, and the gulls flew over the bay, over the palm trees across the bay at the golf course. A picture-postcard view that no longer thrilled her. She was not a visitor, not down for the season. This was home now: the last apartment, beautifully furnished. The old heavy dark wood furniture was sold in New York before they moved. A new dining-room set bought. Wood stained white, antique white for the tropical climate, and pastel upholstery. Cool. Everything cool.

Already the sun was too much. Carefully she raised herself from the lounge chair and moved into the shade under a tree near the pool.

The pool area was in the back of the six-story apartment house, a landscaped strip between the building and the bay. There were round tables and chairs, lounge chairs all empty now, and luxuriant foliage and trees like overgrown houseplants, their leaves too lustrous and thick and patterned to be real; but they were. She supposed they were. Hoping that no one would appear on a balcony to catch her, she picked a leaf off a tree, a tree that resembled a giant schefflera plant like the one she had tended by her window at home in the city, and felt the smooth thickness of the leaf. She squeezed it between her fingers, harder and harder until it yielded a drop of moisture. It was real. Her fingers felt sticky.

Sam would be returning from the golf club at five. Not the golf course that was across the bay, but one where Jews were allowed. Four-thirty. Soon she would go upstairs and start dinner. Now she sat. Some of the doors that led from balconies to apartments were open. The day was cooling off. She could hear the tenants in the house talking. A telephone was ringing. "Gerda, where is she today? Why can't I reach her? Why didn't she call me?"

She heard Abe and Frieda talking from the third floor.

Abe's voice: "What are we having? Chicken? Should I put it in the oven now?"

"Yeah, go ahead; it takes an hour. Put the potatoes in too," Frieda answered.

"The potatoes! Too early!" Abe said.

"So it would hurt to have a real well-done potato for a change?"

Rose recognized the intonations of old Jews from Brooklyn or the Bronx. That surprised her because everyone acted so refined, with a kind of *goyische* reserve. In fact, in order to buy into the house she and Sam had to be passed on by the elected board members of the house. There was a very proper and genteel coffee klatch with introductions and questions: What kind of work did you used to do? What hotels did you used to stay in when you came down on vacations? Where did you used to live in the city? They had lived on Park Avenue and Sam had been in ladies' sportswear. They passed the test. She was not fat, she wore pastel pantsuits and Gucci shoes, and Sam wore Bermuda shorts and matching knee socks and a pale paisley silk ascot in the neckline of his shirt. She went to the hairdresser's on Friday mornings and met her sister-in-law, Lil, for lunch on Wednesdays. Sam played golf twice a week. The board didn't have to worry about noisy visiting grandchildren: they had only one grandson, who was grown up, sixteen years old. Accepted by the board, they were able to buy the apartment, a privilege for fifty-one thousand dollars, and now only one year later Sam himself was a board member.

A phone in one of the apartments was ringing again. The voice that answered it was unfamiliar to Rose. Mumbled conversation. Quiet. Then the voice, loud, a mixture of annoyance and pride. "That phone hasn't stopped ringing since eight-thirty this morning."

Rose looked at the pool, blue and unrippled, perfectly smooth. The stillness was again punctuated by a phone ringing, but this time from behind a closed door. The phones were ringing, she thought. Her phone also started ringing at eight-thirty in the morning. Has so-and-so made it through another night? The invitations for a bridge game and dinner out were just a cover-up for the Big Question: Are you still alive? It was a network of people checking up on each other. "How did you feel today? Have any pain? When do you see the specialist?" Moe is in Beth Israel with phlebitis. Irma is at Miami General for a GI series. Thank God, Sam was perfect. He watched himself.

But Gerda had seemed well on Thursday. Today was Tuesday. Rose took off her sunglasses and folded them into her eyeglass case. She wanted to go upstairs and try Gerda's number again. On the two days that Sam played golf she and Gerda made casual plans to meet, to go shopping together; lately, they took walks and once three weeks ago they took a bus to the George Victor Campbell Museum, a mansion that had been turned over to the public. It was built on a lagoon and housed a fabulous art collection. Gerda had loved it. Smiling, she'd said, "I remember Venice when I am here, the way the *terrazia* goes right to the water and the stone pier sticks out into the bay with a small boat tied up to it." The museum served drinks on the terrace. They watched the gulls and the pelicans. A pelican had caught a fish. Gerda pointed to it. One thing about Gerda, she had eagle eyes. She saw things that Rose didn't see.

Time had passed so pleasantly that afternoon, and yes, so interestingly, that Rose realized, sitting on the museum terrace, how much she had grown to like Gerda, that heavy foreign woman with her dyed red hair, fashionless dresses, her serious-looking tortoise-shell glasses, too large for her face and too dark in color for Florida.

She had first met Gerda two months before: she had been coming home from shopping on Bayshore Avenue and had boarded the bus that carried the Golden Agers around the small man-made island for only a ten-cent fare. The heat of the day had left her fatigued, with tightness in her chest. The air-conditioning in the bus was scarcely operating. The passengers chatted to each other and mopped their brows. More old people boarded the bus. Then Gerda got on, slowly, awkwardly, with two shopping bags, one a green old-fashioned net bag, the kind Rose hadn't seen for over thirty years, the other a large paper bag with rope handles. She sat down next to Rose and started talking to her as though she were an old friend.

"I've finally taken myself to see the *yom,*" Gerda said. "You know what *yom* means?" Not waiting for Rose to answer, she said, "The sea, the ocean—beautiful." Then, apologizing for her poor English, she asked, "How do you say 'It brings life'?"

"Renewing?" Rose offered.

"Yes, it is renewing. I breathe in deep." She sucked her breath into her cheeks and chest and held it there, then exhaled slowly. "I am young again." She smiled at Rose. "I speak four languages. Yiddish, Hebrew, German and Polish, and someday I hope to speak English well."

Rose smiled reassuringly. "You speak fine."

The bus started to move. The air was humid and close. "Jack," someone said to the bus driver, "what's wrong with the air conditioning?"

Jack drove through the small business section without stopping. "It's working," he said unconvincingly.

"You look very hot." Gerda concentrated on Rose's face. "You are sick?"

Rose shook her head no. The bus was finally in the residential area.

"Cooler outside now than in here." Gerda said. "My apartment is near. We get out and walk a bit."

Surprised at herself, Rose agreed. She felt safe with this woman, almost as though she were a child and this old red-haired woman her mother. Gerda must have been at least in her early seventies.

Jack brought the bus to the curb. "Be careful getting out, girls." They took the steps cautiously.

Outside there was more air, a light breeze. "Girls!" Gerda snorted. "I am no girl. I am an old lady, seventy-three years old. Or do old people grow young down here in the sunshine?"

"They grow older faster," Rose blurted out, the words coming with force from some unacknowledged well of feeling, "from loneliness." She was not sure why she had said that. She hated whining. Now she was sorry.

Gerda was thoughtful. "We are lonely," she said, slowly nodding her head. "That's right." They walked silently for a few minutes. Gerda walked in old-lady shoes, black ones, her feet splayed out to the side. She was heavy on her feet. Her legs were stiff.

The tight feeling in Rose's chest relaxed. Walking was good for her but usually she avoided it. Dr. Fishman had told her to walk at least one mile a day. She had warned Sam, "You better walk your dog," but then when he suggested a walk, she always found reasons to decline.

"I am Gerda Feldman. My apartment is in the pink house on the next block. 'Pink'—is that right?"

"I am Rose Abeles. Yes, pink—or you might say mauve, which is slightly paler than pink."

"Mo-ive," Gerda pronounced. "I never heard that." Gerda practiced new words. At the museum when they saw an old Italian painting of the Madonna, Gerda had plagued her about the name of a certain shade of red in the angel's robe. "Do you mean crimson?" Rose had asked. Gerda shook her head. "Scarlet?" No. "Magenta?" She couldn't think of any others. She tried. "Oh, vermilion?" Once Rose had studied oil painting at the Y. Gerda smiled. "Yes, vermilion. What a beautiful word."

The two women walked along the palm-lined street. "You'll stop a few minutes at my apartment for iced tea and a piece of cake," Gerda said.

Rose refused. What did she want to go inside the woman's dingy, cheap apartment for? But Gerda pressed. "I want to show you," she said, "some things," Rose, against her better judgment, let herself be swayed.

It was getting late. Rose could smell other people's suppers cooking and she left the side of the pool. The lobby, air-conditioned and shadowed after the daylight, had a staged appearance—a bowl of plastic yellow tulips on a long trestle table, a couch that never had been used as far as she knew, and a mirror from which Rose turned her face sharply. Upstairs the apartment, cool and dim, with lemon-colored drapes closed against the afternoon sun, sang out silence, a deep lonely silence, and Rose, aware of the stillness of the apartment, felt suddenly helpless to answer the quietness with a sense of her own vitality, that is, if she had any: she was herself one of those tidy persons who keep their edges neat, don't spill over into places, speak quietly, laugh with their eyes, not with their throats. And now she was tired and worn out, not that she had done anything. Putting her pocketbook on the credenza, she walked to the telephone. She dialed Gerda's number and waited. No answer. She wished Sam would come home.

Switching on the fluorescent lights of the kitchen, Rose opened the refrigerator and took out a small roasting chicken. At the sink she held it under the faucet so that water swooshed through its cavity. She carefully rubbed paprika, salt and garlic on the chicken until it was evenly seasoned orangey-red flecked with black dots. She put it on the roasting pan and slipped it in the oven. Set the dials. The red light went on.

While she peeled potatoes Rose thought about Claire, her daughter, to whom Sam and she had taught "Honesty is the best policy" and lived to see the day they regretted her having learned the lesson so well. Claire had been down to see them for a week in February. "Aren't you bored shitless down here, Mother?" Claire had asked.

"Daddy loves it here."

"But what about you?"

"I miss my job. But how long can you be a volunteer in an old people's home? I was getting older myself than some of the residents I was supposed to be helping."

"But you were head of the whole volunteer program, Mother. You supervised over thirty-five volunteers. What do you do with yourself here?".

"I keep busy." She had tried to explain how she kept busy but it hadn't been easy.

"You ought to volunteer someplace," Claire had said. "You're turning into a golf widow."

"I know I should but it isn't easy starting all over again."

"Oh, come on, Mother!" reprimanded Claire.

"Look, you're good at changes," Rose had told her, having in mind Claire's two husbands and ten jobs. Even college—she had transferred three times. "I'm not." Claire hadn't discovered yet that after a certain age change equaled loss.

Then Rose had met Gerda, found a friend, and life didn't seem as dull and lonely as it had.

Sam was suddenly standing in the kitchen. "Oh, God, you scared me." Rose jumped.

"Did you meet that woman today, honey?" Sam asked.

"You mean Gerda? No. I haven't been able to reach her. She didn't call me last night and today there's no answer."

"She'll call." He kissed his wife's cheek. For a short while they talked about his golf game and which of his friends had treated for lunch. Then Rose turned to the telephone and called Gerda's number. Still no one home.

That night, finding it hard to fall asleep, Rose kept the television on, a late-night talk show, the lights off, and hoped she would doze. Sam was breathing heavily, asleep. The gray light from the TV as it reflected off the blueness of the walls and their blankets had the eerie luminosity of a moonscape. She loved the moon expeditions and felt an affinity for the astronauts, their strange weightless moondance, the silence of their explorations. When there was a scheduled moonshot she would call up Claire and check whether Luke, their grandson, was watching the launch on TV. Neither Claire nor Luke gave a damn if they missed History. "He's out with his friends," Claire had said. "He shouldn't miss this shot; it may be the last one in his lifetime." In response to that, Claire had answered something but she couldn't quite catch it, something about doing things being more important, something about reality.

She glanced sideways at Sam. He looked cadaverous. The TV light flickered over his face. Forty-six years of sleeping next to Sam. His lips sank into his mouth; his remaining four teeth had been extracted last week. Strong Sam had played golf the same afternoon. Strong or not, she felt afraid. What happened to Gerda? Go over to the apartment in the morning. Call the police. The hospitals. The morgue. Last year Sam's younger brother dropped dead in the barbershop. Sam's younger sister, only sixty-six, died a few months later, weighing eighty-four pounds. Subtraction. Everything was subtraction, she thought. First Addition; then Subtraction. The Lord must be a mathematician. He multiplieth thy seed; he divideth waters. He giveth and taketh away. Nowadays He mostly taketh away. Rose concluded.

She tried to fall asleep but thought she heard rain, a downpour blowing up quickly like a summer shower; she got out of bed to look but it was only the palm trees in the wind. They fooled her. In the distance she could see the light of the big hotels. Behind the hotels was the ocean, far away. She went back to bed.

Gerda: Had she mentioned that she had any family? A son who taught microbiology at the University of Hawaii. A niece in Nyack, New York. On TV Johnny Carson was smiling. He had just made a joke. He was proud. The audience applauded. Sam jerked in his sleep. Rose closed her eyes. When she and Gerda had gone to the George Victor Campbell Museum, Gerda had tripped over the root of a banyan tree and had taken a bad fall on the path. Rose helped her to get up. No bones were broken but on the bus ride home Gerda was pale and quiet and kept rubbing her knee where the stocking was ripped. She would not talk about her health. Did she have a disease of the central nervous system? The awkward walk. The sudden loss of balance. Rose fell asleep propped up against the pillows while Johnny Carson introduced new smiling guests on his show.

"Drive me to Gerda's apartment, please, Sam," Rose said at seven in the morning. "I just called. Still no answer. I'll get the superintendent to let me in."

Sam agreed, if Rose would relax and eat breakfast. "She probably went away for a few days, maybe to Disney World."

Rose put coffee in the electric percolator, "You know, Sam, I think Gerda died."

Sam answered, "You're crazy, Rose. Why should she be dead?"

Outside the coolness of their apartment house, the morning was bright, the sun already blazing. Sam remarked on the whiteness of the buildings, the palm trees, the fragrant scent of the air. "Some scene, huh? I bet it's twenty degrees in New York City today."

Never was she less interested in scenery or statistics. Once in a while she became angry with Sam for his rave reviews of Florida. After all, they had lived a lifetime in New York and it hadn't been that bad. "I read in the paper that the royal palm trees have a disease and they're going around inoculating them with an antibiotic," Rose said matter-of-factly.

"Yeah? A regular syringe?" Sam turned on the air conditioning in the car and left the door open for a few minutes. Soon cool air was blowing out of the vent. "I've never been inside Gerda's place," Sam said. "It looks lousy from the outside." They drove up in front of the house. Sam pointed to the air-conditioning units in the windows, motors purring loudly, drops of water making puddles on the sidewalk. "They don't have central air conditioning."

"Inside it's very nice," she said defensively. "You'll be surprised." She was worried that Sam wouldn't sense in the apartment what she had come to value there. For a few moments Rose's concern about Sam's reaction to the apartment eclipsed her dread of finding Gerda a corpse on the floor.

The superintendent in his first-floor apartment hadn't seen Mrs. Feldman for a couple of days. "A nice woman. She keeps an eye on the old folks in the house who don't get around too well. You know, shops for them, bakes them a cake, things like that." He was a short sallow man in his late fifties with a graying crewcut. "Call me Hank," he said as he rummaged in his desk for the passkey. His apartment had the stale, close smell of old cigarette smoke mixed with cooking odors. The desk drawer was a jumble of keys with worn fragments of tags on them, some knotted together. The key was not there. Rose felt nauseated. Throwing up usually preceded her attacks. "Hank, may I use your bathroom?" Rose asked. Hank pointed the way. Inside the bathroom she stared at the toilet and waited, leaning against the sink. She struggled and waited and saw that the toilet that she would have to hang head over was dirty. She waited. Nausea passed. She left the bathroom. Hank had found the key and handed it to Sam. "Thanks, Hank," Sam said, pressing a dollar bill into Hank's hand. Then he turned to Rose. "Did you vomit?"

"No," said Rose, "thank God."

They trooped up to the second floor, Rose taking the steps more slowly than Sam. He unlocked the door. He walked quickly, officially, through the living room and into the bedroom, scanning the floors, the bed. The small bathroom was empty. She was not there.

Relieved, Rose sat down on a hardback chair. Sam opened the refrigerator. He took out the milk and smelled it. "It's still good," he said playing detective.

"Where is she?"

"Relax, Rose." Sam, sitting on the sofa, surveyed the living room. "No so bad. Not like what I expected." There were hanging plants and a Chagall print, a picture of Jerusalem, the winding streets, domed buildings. Nearly all the walls had been covered with cloths and shawls. Above the record player and table were large white linen tablecloths cross-stitched in reds and blues and yellows, bright floral patterns. Over the beige couch was a silk piano shawl with a green fringe, embroidered roses. A faded paisley shawl hung between the two windows, its shades of burnt orange, gray, black blending one into the other.

Beneath the paisley shawl was a cabinet with glass doors, photographs on its top. A picture of a heavy-set woman with black hair pulled tightly back and deep brown eyes dressed in a nurse's uniform in front of a small hospital. "Is that Gerda?" Sam asked.

"She was a nurse in Haifa when she first came to Israel after the war."

Sam picked up another photograph: a young American-looking couple.

"That's Gerda's niece from Nyack." Rose knew the story of each photograph.

"Nice-looking girl," Sam said.

Rose remembered the record of Jewish songs that Gerda used to play sometimes when she visited. "Listen to this Theodore Bikel album, Sam," she said. The music filled the apartment: the solo voice, the simple piano accompaniment. We should buy that record, Rose thought, But then recalled that they had sold their stereo before the moved South.

Sam opened the glass door of the cabinet and took out a large silver wine cup, ornate and gleaming. It was the Prophet's Elijah's cup used at the Passover seder. He held the cup to the light, rotated it slowly, turned it over, let his fingers play over the silver scrollwork. Rose watched him. He was, she saw, drawn into Gerda's world, perhaps back into his own childhood. "I'll make some Sanka," she said gently.

"Some nice stuff she has here," Sam said.

In the kitchen Rose checked the breadbox and found a half loaf of sponge cake topped with melted brown sugar and almonds. "Taste this cake," she ordered Sam, setting plates on the table. "Gerda bakes beautifully."

Sam was holding up two brass candlesticks. "I bet these are a hundred and fifty years old."

"They were a wedding gift from Gerda's mother-in-law from Minsk," Rose said. They had talked about their families, their in-laws, their children: Gerda had one son; she, on daughter. She was suddenly very comfortable.

Rose remembered telling Gerda about Claire, her twice-divorced thirty-eight-year-old hippie daughter who lived in a vast, skimpily furnished apartment on Central Park West with her sixteen-year-old son, and took in boarders. One of the boarders was a man with long black curly hair and a red beard. Who knew what went on? "She had a great job," Rose explained to Gerda. "For once she had a decent income and Sam and I could relax. Then the next thing, she quits it and starts working, for hardly any money at all, for the Women's Liberation. She gives lectures and says she's setting up a business as a consultant for women who need advice on career management." She's the one who needs advice on career management!" Gerda had laughed. "Then Sam and I went to talk to her, and do you know what, Gerda, this thirty-eight-year-old liberated woman and mother had a dirty neck. Her neck was filthy. She hadn't washed it in two months." Gerda howled, slapping her thigh.

Rose sipped her coffee. The dirty neck didn't seem so terrible now. The rest of their talk came back to her: the strain of visits when Claire came down to see them. "She's so critical. Her father worked all his life. Now he's retired and he loves it here. He loves the weather, the golf. He can take walks without being mugged. And she calls this place an 'ecological nightmare.' She notices the orange peels and garbage floating in the bay. She talks about the big hotels and the raw sewerage in the ocean. Her father shows her new condominiums, newly developed areas, and she says. 'It's too bad.' "

Rose saw Sam turning over an abalone shell in his hand. Gerda had a seashell collection arranged on a small table. The sunlight made the shell's rainbow center glow. Sam was suntanned. He looked healthy. It was the right move, Rose thought. He loved it in Florida.

Gerda had taken Claire's part. She wanted to meet Claire. She had understood Claire's reactions. Gerda's face came into focus; the dark, intelligent eyes and tortoiseshell glasses, the pale and smooth skin, the lips still full, the incongruous red hair, streaked with gray and black. "I understand what Claire says," Gerda had said. "Some days I see the garbage too. When the wind is hot and humid it doesn't smell right. Like in Venice when it is the sirocco. The bad winds and heaviness in the air. The canals smell. Something stinking."

Gerda's agreeing with Claire had made her feel protective of Sam. "It's better here than in New York" she told Gerda. "Sam deserves this."

Apparently not hearing that, Gerda continued. "The day I met you on the little bus I had come from the *yom*. It was beautiful, shining. I felt happy, but then I saw the garbage on the beach brought in by the waves. Phew!" Gerda shuddered. Phew.

Sam saw Rose shudder. "What are you thinking, honey?" he asked.

She didn't want to explain. "The Sanka must be cold by now, but at least taste this cake." Sam put the abalone shell back amidst Gerda's collection.

"Tumbala, tumbala, tumbalalayka. Tumbala, tumbala, tumbalalayka." Sam hummed. The record turned itself off. They sat at the table, Sam eating his cake. The drone of the air-conditioning unit was more audible without the music; every so often it made a clanking sound as though it were clearing its throat.

"Central air conditioning makes a big difference," Sam observed. Then he saw the tension on Rose's face. "When we get home I'll call the police."

Rose thanked him. She washed, dried and put away the dishes, checked to see that everything was in its place. She replaced the silver Passover wine cup in the cabinet. They left the apartment, forgetting to return the passkey to Hank.

The day was still cloudless. Hanging on to Sam's arm, it appeared to Rose that she was being pulled along. The perfect weather irritated her: the sun would shine in spite of all tragedy, in the face of death and destruction. The heat made her angry. She thought of the bad smells Claire and Gerda had talked about and sniffed the air. Everything was deceptive. The air smelled fresh and clear. With certainty she knew that Gerda was dead. But how could she vanish so completely? That wasn't fair.

The car was hot. There was no cooling it off on the short ride home. Beads of perspiration formed on her forehead and above her lip. She had trouble getting air and couldn't wait to rest on her bed in her own cool room.

Keeping her head turned to the wall, she refused to watch Sam talking on the telephone and wished that he had used the phone in the kitchen, not the one in the bedroom. Closing her eyes did not alleviate the constriction of her throat. "Oh, God, Oh, God," she wanted to wail, but didn't. Sam called two hospitals. They had no patient by the name of Gerda Feldman. The police station made him hold the line. "What's happening?" Rose asked Sam.

"They're checking their records," Sam answered.

"What's taking them so long!" No, they had no record of anyone by the name of Gerda Feldman.

"Officer," Sam said, "check your records for Sunday and

Monday. If there was an accident it probably happened on either of those days." The officer found nothing. He promised to check more thoroughly, "investigate," and call back. Sam gave him their phone number.

"I wish I could think of the name of Gerda's niece, the one in Nyack," Rose said. "But I can't remember what Gerda told me her name was." Her hands felt icy cold and her mind was a blank.

"Don't concentrate on it and maybe it'll come to you," Sam suggested. He turned on the TV, a morning quiz show.

"I'm trying to remember what I thought of when Gerda told me her niece's name. I thought of something. I know! I thought of delicatessen coldcuts!"

"Coldcuts!" Sam exclaimed. "You mean salami, bologna, pastrami?"

"Yes," Rose said, "keep going."

"Corned beef, liverwurst, ham."

"Liverwurst! That's it!"

"You're kidding!"

"Braunschweiger. Carol and Bernie Braunschweiger in Nyack. Gerda talked about Carol and Bernie."

"Coldcuts," muttered Sam, shaking his head. He offered to call Nyack information and get the number.

What should she say to Carol? Rose wondered. Maybe—I'm a friend of your Aunt Gerda's here in Florida. I haven't been able to reach her for a couple of days. Have you heard from her?" Tensely Rose recited several possibilities.

Getting up from her bed, she walked around to where the phone was on a night table next to Sam's bed. She dialed directly. The phone was ringing. A woman's voice answered. "Is this Carol?" Rose asked. It was. Then Rose launched into her introduction: "I am a friend of your Aunt Gerda's . . . " But before she could finish, Carol said, "How sweet of you to call. I didn't know whether Aunt Gerda had any friends in Florida. We held the services yesterday, a very simple funeral and interment." Carol went on and on, sweetly, kindly, about the family who attended, the son who couldn't get a flight in from Honolulu on time to make the funeral, the snow flurries at the cemetery.

"Oh-h-h," Rose moaned. She had no questions, no words.

"So nice of you to call us," Carol said. "I'll have to fly down and take care of Aunt Gerda's apartment and things. I'll do that in ten days. What is your name and number so that I can get in touch with you when I come down?"

Rose turned to stone. Funeral and interment. She wanted her friend Gerda, not the niece from Nyack. "What happened to my friend?" she wanted to ask. How did she die? But Rose couldn't talk.

"Give me your name and telephone number so we can meet. I can't tell you how much I appreciate your condolences. We'll miss Aunt Gerda."

Rose felt anger tightening in her like a spring. Like hell they'll miss their Aunt Gerda. She spoke into the phone. "My name is Helena Rubinstein," she told the niece, "and my number is 762-4165."

"Helena Rubinstein?" Carol asked. "The cosmetic lady?"

"That's right," Rose said. "Be sure to call when you come down." And she put the receiver down on the phone.

Sam stared at her. "Why did you give her a phony name and number? Are you crazy?" But Rose had already leaned her head back against Sam's pillow and closed her eyes; she didn't hear him, not a word.

She saw Gerda and herself in Gerda's apartment, watched them as one would watch home movies: the embroidered cloths on the wall, the silver candlesticks, the photographs, the shell collection; Gerda in her dark-framed glasses was sipping a cup of Sanka; music sounded over the whine of the air conditioner. She saw them sitting on the terrace of the museum. A pelican was flying overhead, then it swooped down. With her eyes still closed, blueness surrounding her, cobalt and lapis-lazuli, she was at crater's edge, floating, falling. Opening her eyes, she stopped herself. The bird hit the water with a thud. "Did you see that?" Rose said, turning to her friend. But Gerda was not there.

PART II

Lately, Rose had been using the Buick more often, insisting that Sam be dropped off at the golf club and then picked up later at a prearranged time. She had driven her sister-in-law, Lil, to lunch at a lovely restaurant on Key Biscayne, escorted Lil's grandchildren to the Seaquarium, and about a week ago had taken Mrs. Orenstein's sister-in-law, Rita, to the optometrist as a favor. The trip to the optometrist had been an emergency situation. Rita had flown down from Baltimore to visit her brother, Sanford Orenstein, in the hospital.

One day during her stay, Rita was out on a balcony talking to Nellie Orenstein at a table by the pool five stories below, when

her glasses slid off the bridge of her nose and dropped onto the concrete, practically at Rose's feet. Rose, who had been resting in a lounge chair overlooking the bay, heard the sister-in-law exclaim that without her glasses she was good for nothing. Disquieted by the broken glass around her and the sister-in-law's shrill despair about the difficulty in replacing it, Rose responded by volunteering to drive Rita to her own optometrist in Fort Lauderdale.

As it turned out, Rita remained as shattered as her glasses, talked incessantly, and made Rose nervous. Rita was like a chicken without a head. The optometrist kept them waiting and Rose ended up getting to the golf course an hour and a half late, by which time Sam was sure that she had had an accident or an attack. So much for do-goodism. But all in all, Rose had enjoyed driving the car, regaining confidence behind the wheel.

Therefore, it wasn't surprising when she received word of a visit (a postcard of Montezuma's floor-length feathered headress) from her daughter Clare, en route from Mexico to New York, that Rose told Sam that she would call for Claire at the airport by herself.

"I'll drive you," Sam had said. Bills, bank statements and bank books were spread out on the dining room table. Rose was opening the mail and Sam, his mind on money, was paying bills.

"No, don't bother. You don't need to break your date with Eddie Baum." She had a sudden and strong desire to meet Claire alone without Sam.

"What the hell is she doing in Mexico in November anyway? I didn't even know she was going."

"It must have been a spur-of-the-moment thing."

Sam made a grimace. "Where does she get the money for things like that? From that boarder who lives with them?" Sam was balancing their bank statement. "And who takes care of Luke?" Their grandson's name, its New Testament origins, always stuck in their throats, and Sam in particular usually called him "the boy." Puzzled, Sam looked past Rose to the window view of the tops of palm trees and asked whether Claire had a job. How Claire got her money bothered him.

"I don't know," Rose replied weakly. Although she tried to keep up with Claire's life, it wasn't always easy. "But no matter, Luke is a fine boy."

"Yeah, he's growing up nicely," Sam admitted, "even with the mish-mosh. I hope he stays that way."

On the day that Claire was due to arrive, Rose drove Sam to

Eddie's house and then proceeded to the airport. She passed the classy residential neighborhood with its white and mauve stucco apartment house, its well-cared for tropical plantings, and its Spanish-style private homes with backyard pools that seemed perpetually unused. Beyond there, the landscape grew desolate: flat and treeless; careless. The stores, set far back from the road, were ugly with their ample parking areas, a feature that turned every shopping plaza into a used car lot. The Super-King food marts and the patio furniture stores, Toyworld, dry-cleaners and cut-rate drugs. She drove by the good bakery where she and Sam used to shop for company dessert—a chocolate marble cake or a small cheese cake, with its dry, cratered moon-like surface. The last time they were there the salesgirl had treated them so gruffly, ("She was rotten," Sam had said outside the shop so condescendingly—"Did you get a number—you've gotta have a number or I can't wait on you".), that she swore to Sam that she would never buy there again, and he had backed her up one hundred percent. For a while, until Mrs. Orenstein told her about the Pastry House, Rose did her own baking and found it satisfying. Gerda had been a superb baker.

Inside the air-conditioned Buick, driving with surprisingly little effort, Rose imagined introducing Claire to Gerda and having ice tea and cake together at Gerda's apartment. Although Gerda had been dead for six months, Rose sometimes found herself thinking about her as though she were still living. Maybe because there had never been a real goodbye, a proper goodbye. Claire would inspect everything in Gerda's apartment, would run her fingers over the embroidery, admire the antique paisleys, turn over the sea shells in her hand. The picture was so vivid that Rose could actually see the abalone shell in Claire's hand, the shell and Claire's rings shifting color as she turned the shell over and around in the light of the window. When Claire was a child it had been impossible to take her into a gift shop. Once she broke a Wedgewood cigarette urn which they had to pay for. Not that Claire was destructive; it was more that she had to touch and get involved and be active and energetic. Rose could hear Gerda asking Claire to explain "career management" and how it came about in such a country as this that women needed liberating. Once she and Gerda had discussed women's rights, and Gerda talked about the meaning of the Passover seder: that it symbolized freedom which could never be wholly won because each generation saw a new form of slavery and fought new battles against oppression. The meaning of freedom was itself always changing. An interesting idea, Rose had thought.

In her mind she heard Gerda and Claire discussing these issues—Claire with her usual energy, Gerda with an ability to get straight to the heart of the matter. Rose felt excluded. Not that her friend and her daughter wanted to omit her from the conversation, but more that she couldn't form words fast enough: Rose was a tennis player, her racket poised but unable to hit. She ended up watching the volley. Then sadly she gave up the game and studied the shades of the embroidered roses on the silk piano shawl.

Turning up the fan of the car's air-conditioner, Rose felt a wave of cold air blowing on her chest. Out of the blue she remembered her mother, who had died some thirty years ago, and the slight chill edge that her mother had always shown to her. These days she found herself redressing old grievances. What in God's name did she ever do that her mother should hold against her? Nothing, she decided. She had been a remarkably untroublesome child. Then why did her mother have that edge? Was it because her mother was a widow who worked hard as a milliner? Worried about supporting her three children? Her mother trimmed hats at home. There had been a large table in the back room covered with hat trimmings, an assortment of ribbons, bows, gauzy veils, artificial lilacs and cornflowers, tiny clusters of wooden fruit, small fuzzy feathers, and, best of all, miniature pale blue birds. Her brothers and she had had few toys. How she wanted to play with those trimmings!—but it was her mother's work and she could only look.

The sky was clouded over, the day not so hot. Rose was able to endure the heat. She walked briskly from the parking lot to the Pan American waiting room, eager to see Claire. Tempering her enthusiasm, Rose reminded herself that these reunions and visits were never easy. Her own hopes now were that she would not ask of Claire what she knew Claire could not give.

The passengers of Flight 61 Y from Mexico City filed down the corridor: Mexican men with neat mustaches in blue and gray suits, several well-dressed couples, women in pantsuits, wild-haired young men in sunglasses made from mirrors, a tall, slim black man with a soft leather shoulderbag the color of butterscotch, a woman with long dark gray-streaked hair wearing jeans and a fiery orange backpack. My God that was Claire! Rose looked again. Claire wore a Mexican peasant blouse over jeans, a large pack on her back, and shuffled in red clogs. Why wasn't she wearing appropriate traveling clothes—a suit, a dress and jacket, an attractive slack outfit? The pack must have been heavy because Claire swayed forward. "Mother, mother," Claire called.

The women hugged, cheeks brushing, and Rose, touching Claire's shoulder blade and the small of her back, was happy to hold her daughter. Rose led Claire to the baggage claim desk, but Claire stopped her. "I want you to meet a friend, Mother." Claire turned to locate the tall black man and led Rose over to him. Always the thing that was hardest to accept, Rose thought defeatedly. Is she having an affair with this black man, black as the ace of spades, and does she want him to stay at our apartment? Going too far, Rose thought. Going too far. He cannot stay with us.

"This is a friend of mine, Mom—Richard Jones. I met Richard in Mexico." Rose extended her hand and smiled. His finger nails were very white; his hand warm and dry. "Richard has family here and we're going back to New York City on the same flight."

Relieved, Rose tried to make conversation. "You met at Acapulco?"

Claire replied before Richard could open his mouth. "At a campground about seventy-five miles north of there. I bought a tent, a real beauty Mother, and camped for less than eighty cents a night at a beach on the Pacific that was Paradise—cloudless skies, banana trees, fresh fish off the boats . . ."

While Claire talked, Rose inspected Richard Jones, who seemed amused by Claire's idyllic description of Mexico. He was at least six-foot-seven-inches and thin with a close-cropped Afro and a long face and a pointy beard like something out of a film about an evil king. His eyes were bloodshot. Maybe he was a basketball player, or a drug smuggler. Claire jotted down Richard's relative's name so that she could call him about arrangements for the flight home. Rose was surprised he had family. Maybe it wasn't an affair. Richard smiled formally and took off, moving loosely and proud, holding his head high like an African prince. Rose saw him amidst a semicircle of conical thatched huts in a jungle clearing. Zebras and giraffes. A boiling sun. Tribal rites.

Claire took her mother's arm. "Dad's not here? You drove to the airport by yourself? That's great." She guided her mother to the exit. "My baggage is on my back so we don't have to wait." They walked between rows of parked cars. "He's a nice man," Claire said, aware that her mother was still wondering about Richard. "He taught me how to snorkel . . . you should have seen the fish. Mother you would have loved them. . . ."

"What does he do?"

"Richard? He's in black studies at uptown Hunter College."

When they reached the car, Rose was tired from walking and she suggested that Claire drive. Settled next to Claire in the front seat, ashamed of having gotten bogged down in Richard's background, she wondered about the point of all her questions. In truth she would probably like hearing about the colors and patterns of the tropical fish more than about Richard Jones or whoever else Claire was going with. Why did she keep grilling Claire? She leaned her head back against the seat and invented fish, irridescent blues and greens, bright yellows with dots and stripes, some long and sinewy, some almost round and two-dimensional, glowing silver, and others like underwater butterflies, their fins and tails rippling and transparent. During the rest of the drive home Rose and Claire talked easily. They stopped to pick up Sam at the golf course.

The silence, the dim lemony softness of the apartment, cast a momentary unease on the three of them, a confusion of time, or history, a sense of important people missing (Luke, the chubby toddler proud of new red sneakers, his handsome father, Alan) or a suspicion that perhaps it was, in fact, thirty years ago and Claire was their little girl. ("Time to practice the piano," "Set the table for dinner, please Claire," "Get your knapsack out of the living room.") For the first time Rose perceived the vulnerability of Claire's position with them: her oneness, their coupleness.

It was suppertime, and Claire, enthusiastic about Mexican cooking, made guacamole, a smooth piquant spread, with an almost overripe avocado she found in the refrigerator behind the cottage cheese. Rose watched Claire mince onions minutely, keeping the onion as far away from her eyes as she could. Claire's hands, dark from the sun, were ringless; two years ago there had been stones and twisted silver and Indian turquoise on every finger. Expressive hands. And competent. Claire had studied Japanese flower-arranging, pottery, gourmet cooking, yoga, and ballet, and had worked as an administrator in the housing relocating department. She had been a cabbie, a route-mapper for the department of sanitation, (a job she had gotten because she knew the City so well after having been a cab-driver), and a model for art classes at Cooper Union. That was half the list.

They had the guacamole on saltines with gin and tonics while the steaks were broiling under Sam's watchful eye. Rose shuttled china and silverware from the kitchen to the dining room. "You know, Claire," Sam said goodnaturedly, "your independent outlook is all to be admired, but how can you expect to keep getting jobs if you quit after such a short time?" The steak sizzled and popped.

While Claire gulped her gin and tonic, Rose, wanting to stop Sam, told Claire that the guacamole was delicious, just the right amount of chili powder, not too hot. For Sam, money talk was love talk. Rose had just figured that out herself and wondered if Claire understood. The question of job security had hung tensely and divisively in the air during so many dinners; it was enough. But if Claire were upset by her father's lecture, her face did not show it. Her expression was neither defensive nor hurt. Perhaps she did understand her father.

Sam squeezed by them, proudly carrying the sirloin on a wooden cutting board. With time on his hands he had recently taken to both shopping and cooking. "You know, Claire," he said, setting the board on the table, "up to a point it's good to change jobs. The 'big if' is whether you do better."

He was right. Rose wanted to agree with Sam, he was right about that, but Claire spoke first. "It hasn't always been easy to keep going—no less do better, Dad."

Sam hated to hear that. If Claire had bad times, he, as her father, did not want to talk about them. (Moreover, what could he say that he hadn't already said at the time when Claire was getting divorced from Alan?)

Instinctively protecting Sam from pain, Rose asked Claire to explain to Dad now nicely her business was going and about NYU's offer to have her give a ten day in-service training session on "how to choose a job" for women graduates. Slicing the meat, Sam was silent, unable to respond to Claire's reference to things not always being easy, almost as though she had told a dirty joke. A trickle of blood from the steak spilled over the edge of the cutting board. Sam didn't notice it, and Claire ran for the sponge and soaked it up. "Let's eat first and talk later," Claire said, resistant to her mother's prodding. Then, by surprise, on her way to her seat, she kissed each of her parents on the cheek, and patted her father on the back, commenting on how perfectly done the steak was.

Claire seemed different. Just as everything, according to her daughter, was "so mellow" in Mexico, now Claire seemed "mellow," less on edge, less tense, not so touchy and argumentative. They ate silently for a few minutes, then Rose jumped up from her seat. "You know, honey," she addressed Sam, "I wonder if Sanford Orenstein is out of the hospital yet."

She peered out of the sliding glass door, opened it, and stepped out on the small balcony to catch a glimpse of who was sitting around the pool. In the past few months she had begun to keep an eye out on the tenants in the house. Not that she knew their every move, but she had a general sense of who was away traveling, who had gone North to visit children and who was ill. Looking down from the balcony was becoming a habit for both of them. Dinnertime now, the pool area was deserted. Rose saw the sun setting behind the hill of the golf course across the bay. The water was dappled with yellow-gray light. Pelicans, dipping in and out of the bay, were fishing. The concrete around the pool was creamy white and the pool itself was as smooth and peaceful as the reflecting pool of a mosque. Sanford must be out of the hospital by now.

"Mother looks different, has better color . . . ," Rose overheard Claire say as she returned to the table.

"She's been driving a lot, getting out, doing things for people", Sam explained. "She likes it down here now."

"You know, Ma," Claire said, turning to her mother, "you're depriving some social service agency of your talents."

"Some talents!" Rose said drily. "Speaking of talents, there's a concert at the George Victor Campbell Museum tomorrow afternoon." An invitation to an afternoon concert had come in the mail about a week ago and Rose had marked it down on her calendar. She hadn't been to the museum since Gerda had died. She hadn't felt like traipsing out there alone, putting on an act that she was enjoying herself, sitting alone on the terrace watching the clouds sail by. Rose suddenly had an idea and turned to Claire. "Do you think Richard Jones would like to join us?"

"Who's Richard Jones?" Sam asked. Claire told him about the black man she had met in Mexico. "He'd be the only Negro in the place," Sam said. "How would that make him feel?"

"More to the point, Dad, how would you feel?"

Rose addressed them both. "They thronged to see Sammy Davis, Jr. at the Colonnades."

"Mother!" Claire said sharply.

The next afternoon, dressed in maroon double knits, white shoes, and a soft white cotton shirt, Sam let Rose drive to the concert. Since Rose knew the way, Sam devoted his energy to giving a running commentary on the sights. The building boom may have died down in New York City but it hadn't lost any steam here. It had been rumored, Sam explained, that an Arab oil company was going to invest a fortune in a new resort on the beach. "The closest thing to investing in Israel." Sam chuckled at the irony.

"Is there really any beach frontage left?" Claire asked dubiously. They sat in the front seat, Claire in the middle. "And is there really an ocean behind those buildings—or is it a stage set?"

"They'll tear down the old dumps. They're firetraps, those old hotels." Sam had a reverance for the new.

Rose heard Sam tell Claire that many years ago those decrepit hotels had been the finest in Florida. The cool day reminded Rose of late September in New York, her old neighborhood on Second Avenue, the vitality and life of the city—the libraries, the movie houses, the food stores. Fall brown school shoes in the shop windows and autumn leaves in metal pails outside of florist shops. Baskets of green and orange gourds. When she was a child living on Second Avenue her aunt and uncle owned a delicatessen two blocks from her own house. Whenever she ran in to see them, her uncle used to slice a thin piece of corned beef for her, passing it over the counter on the blade of a big knife. Her Aunt Flora, a mousy person who was always chopping cabbages for cole slaw, gave her pistachio nuts from a lopsided glass jar.

The traffic moved slowly; frequent stops for red lights. A narrow canal with elegant yachts ran alongside the thoroughfare. Stranded now in a protracted vacation, Rose found herself trying to pretend it was natural to live a life at a resort. Very natural. Fun. The light changed. Only last week she had received an invitation to a party at the Farbers' in West Palm Beach, a costume party with an Oriental theme. "I'll go as a geisha girl," she told Sam. "Rose Graubard Abeles, daughter of Morris and Sophie, the milliners of Second Avenue, niece of the kosher delicatessen owners, cousin of Izzy Stein, the stickball king of 54th Street who died in the flu epidemic, now the most sought-after geisha girl in the Sunshine State," Sam, inspecting the invitation, had the idea of going as Mao Tse-tung—that would make those reactionary Farbers raise their eyebrows. Of all the people they knew, Jonah Farber was the only person about whom Sam had a bad word. It had to do with lucrative government contracts for Navy pea jackets during the war. "Jonah cleaned up," Sam once said, implying that there had been plenty of dirty business. Sam had absolutely no taste for dirty business.

The neighborhood changed again from fancy condominiums to small run-down hotels with names like Palm Courts, Ocean View, Seaside Gardens, the Colony Arms, and delapidated apartments with signs outside, "Rooms and Kitchenettes," "Off-Season Rates." The paint on many buildings was not fresh, and dripping water and time had stained great abstract patterns in coppery-brown on the once white stucco. Some of the hotels had porches crowded with old people sitting in green rockers. "It's a shame," Claire said, "they moved down here to look out on the ocean; now in this neighborhood there's not even a place for them to get near the water."

"They scarcely survive on Social Security," Rose said, "and without Medicare they wouldn't even be alive. Their children forget about them, their grandchildren don't even know what they look like and the state resents the burden." The force of feeling in her statement surprised her, and she pulled back from the conversation.

Pointing in front of Claire toward Rose's window, Sam said, "There's a fine piece of ocean-front real estate for sale. It would make a lovely little park if the city bought it."

"The city would never buy it," Claire said flatly. "The price is probably so high that it'll go for an office building or a shopping center or something like that. It's probably owned by one of Richard's Nixon's friends. This country is sick. Next year I'd like to go to Cuba."

"Well, Miami is crowded with Cubans who came here," Sam said reproachfully, turning his head away from Claire, "because they didn't think Cuba was so hot. And they're doing well here."

"Sam," Rose said, "that's a wonderful idea about the park. It would be an oasis in this section."

With only ten minutes till the scheduled time of the concert, they walked directly from the parking lot to the museum terrace. Sam, reading the program notes as he walked, informed them that one of the museum's rooms, reconstructed from materials brought over from a Florentine palace, contained an enormous tapestry that had once hung in Queen Elizabeth's drawing room.

"This place reminds me of Venice," Claire said as they sat down at a small umbrellaed table. She dangled her Mexican string bag over the back of the chair. The tables and chairs had been left on the terrace for the concert, arranged closely around a wooden platform set up for the musicians. Behind the platform was the bay flashing in the sunlight, the sky, the seagulls, the pelicans, and the city, faintly visible, rising on the shore in the distance.

"That's what Gerda said. That this terrace reminded her of Venice. I forgot you were in Venice."

"In 1967 with Dave."

"You've certainly seen the world even without a lot of money."

"I'm lucky, Mother, I'm from the privileged class; no matter how far down I go I pop up like a plastic Bozo." Claire turned around and searched the terrace. "I wonder if Richard will show up."

A waiter appeared and took their order for drinks. Rose fished into her handbag and located her mother-of-pearl pill-box, a gift from Luke on her sixty-fifth birthday. She set out a round red pill (a multiple vitamin) and a turquoise and white capsule (for the heart) on the metal table, in anticipation of the iced Sanka the waiter would bring. She felt uneasy. There was the memory of the exposed banyan tree root over which Gerda had tripped while walking on the terrace path. She had bruised her knee and torn her stockings here. Now Rose sat on the spot where Gerda had rested, very pale, after the accident. Rose shuddered. She thought of the sagging old women in baggy housedresses and unsteady men with canes on the porches of the shabby hotels. Age had gotten them nowhere, so what was it all about? The drinks arrived and she swallowed her pills half-heartedly (what good did they do?) while the pianist in white jacket struck notes so that the flautist could tune up.

"Did you tell your friend that the concert begins at three?" Sam asked. "It'll be a shame if he has to walk through this crowd in the middle."

"It will be," Claire said. "I didn't picture the crowd being so WASP-y. Richard will cut quite a figure here."

"Claire, is he an angry person, Richard? Angry at injustices?" The question seemed to pop out of the blue.

Claire was confused by her mother's question and before she could reply, the musicians began to play. The movement began with the piano and flute together, then the cello. Rose inhaled deeply and leaned back. Seagulls, as if they were drawn to the music, circled over the terrace, soared out over the bay, and returned. Passages of music were carried off by the breeze. At the table next to theirs, a corpulent, red-faced man in a blue seersucker suit dozed and snored lightly and two women sat with identical white patent leather bags in their laps. Rose gazed at Claire, thinking how beautiful she could be if only she wore her hair pulled back from her face.

During the momentary pause at the end of the first movement, Richard Jones, who must have been wating at the back of the terrace, approached their table with long strides. He nodded imperceptibly to Claire and took a seat. Startled, Sam turned to see Richard, accidentally knocking over his glass. It rolled towards the table's edge and was miraculously saved, like a fly ball, by Richard's long arm and fast reflexes. Sam gave Richard a grateful glance. Claire sipped her own drink with relief and a waiter moved in silently to remove Sam's glass.

The second movement resumed with the cellist playing a somber melody, the flute and piano joining in soon after it began. The pianist's page-turner, a blonde girl in sneakers, wore a beatific smile and hovered over the piano like an angel. The cellist's long knobby legs awkwardly framed the cello. Heads at tables around them, Rose observed, were turning to stare at Richard. He wore a purple and crimson embroidered pill box hat, a violet robe that came down to his calves, complicated sandals and the over-the-shoulder bag which he had sported at the airport. Was that traditional African dress? He no sooner looked like an ordinary Negro than the Emperor Jones. They must think he's a visiting dignitary from Ghana or Dahomey, or a United Nations delegate. Everything about him was elegant—but still his height and thinness, his pointed beard, his seriousness gave him a quality of austerity. If Gerda had been here she would have soaked up the splendor of Richard's appearance. "A sight to see," she would have sighed. "A wonderful sight to see." Not bound by any brand of provincialism, Gerda had a taste for the strange and exotic.

The sadness of the flute and cello caught Rose's attention and she experienced a shadow as if a cloud had passed over the sun, dulling the sparkle of the water, and darkening the gulls. Soon only the pianist was left playing. The music quieted to a few soft-fading notes, a flame about to gutter and die, then vanish completely. All was stillness and shadow. In that moment the seagulls appeared ominous, transformed into buzzards that were circling dead flesh, carrion. They circled and circled. Rose's heart froze. She raised her hand, her fingers spread apart like an open fan over her chest. She closed her eyes. When Death comes there is no time for goodbyes.

Then, after that instant of suspension, that brief eclipse, the musicians started up again, cheerful and energetic, smiling at the audience as if they had perpetrated a brilliant musical joke.

Rose breathed, opening her eyes. The cloud sailed past the sun. "I am breathing, I am alive," she whispered to herself, pressing her hand against her chest, feeling her heartbeat and the warmth of her body.

"Excuse me, did you say something to me?" Richard leaned toward Rose. Embarrassed, she shook her head, avoiding his eyes. Yet somehow she was touched that this black man had noticed her gestures and mutterings. She became more comfortable and looked at Richard's face. His eyes were kind.

While the trio played, Rose daydreamed about the lot for sale which they had passed on their way to the museum; it would make a perfect small park. It would provide a destination for short walks for the old people in the neighborhood. There could be comfortable benches and tables with green and white striped umbrellas and chairs, all looking out to the ocean, to the "yom."

On the way home she would make Sam stop the car at the lot so that she could jot down the name and telephone number of the realtors. That way she could investigate who owned the property and propose that they donate the lot to the city. Surely there must be a way to get a big tax write-off. Mayor Lindsay had gotten small parks in New York City, "vest-pocket parks" they were called, with fountains, trees, one even had a waterfall. What a shame it would be if a large building went up on that lot. After all, why did people move down here? For a view of big buildings they would stay in New York.

A few hours later, Richard, who Rose had invited for dinner on the spur of the moment, talked about his trip to Dakar, the capital of the Western Republic of Senegal. He described the Memory Men or "Griots" who sing oral histories of their tribe's past. Sam, intrigued with "geography" (as he called it), was eating up every word of Richard's account.

When it came to being sociable, Rose thought, Sam did better with strangers than with his own wife and daughter. Of course Richard *was* very interesting. She wondered whether he was born in West Africa or in the U.S.

Clearing up after the meal, She and Claire maneuvered separately in the kitchen. Claire strained to hear Richard tell about his pilgrimage to Goree, an island off Dakar from where slaves had been shipped to America. He drew a picture of the cramped, grim dungeons and the sickness and confusion of the imprisoned Africans. Rose wasn't listening. On the way home from the museum she had written down the name and address of the realtors who were handling the vacant ocean-front property, and now she was planning her next move. A letter or phone call? Should she approach the problem politically? Go to the city council and try to get some councilmen involved in the project? Or would it be better to appeal directly to the owners for the donation of the land for a park. Perhaps she could form a committee of the elderly residents of that neighborhood who could state their needs to the owners or the city council. She thought about starting a purchase fund, but that seemed painfully tedious: there were enough fund-raising dinners, drives, raffles, telethons, appeals, luncheons, bazaars.

Although Rose was not listening to Richard's words, she did hear his resonant, confident voice (a magenta voice) and told Claire what an interesting person Richard seemed to be. "He speaks so knowledgeably."

"He could at least offer to help with the dishes," Claire grumbled.

Rose defended him. "He's talking so nicely to Daddy, let him be."

Claire looked at her mother's face. "You seem awfully abstracted. What are you thinking about?"

"About the ocean lot," Rose answered hesitantly. "It shouldn't be developed commerically. It should be used for a park or plaza."

The project seemed like a gargantuan and fruitless undertaking to Claire, who urged her mother to return to her past specialty as an organizer of volunteers. "Think what you could do down here with a corps of volunteers. I bet there's a tremendous need for homemaker services or arranging transportation for the elderly to clinics and medical services." When the subject approached Claire's field—careers, creating jobs, providing needed services and getting paid for them—she was all energy, powerfully persuasive.

The conversation between the men in the living room had run down like a spinning top which was about to topple on its side and stop, and Sam, who was certainly playing his part as a host with vigor, suggested a game of scrabble. As he took out the scrabble set from the credenza, he offered Drambuie to Richard, who accepted.

Rose declined an invitation to play and went into her bedroom. The idea of driving old people to clinics didn't thrill her. Whereas ten years ago illness was no threat (she frequently took the aged residents of the home where she worked to the hospital for special treatments or physical therapy) now it seemed frightening, too much responsibility. Her own body was undependable. If she had anything to say about it, she preferred to keep illness at arm's length. Why court it? It comes looking for you. What if she had one of her attacks while she was taking some poor soul to see the doctor? Was that fair? It would be like the blind leading the blind.

No, it was the idea of an oasis that excited her. A clean, peaceful park in the middle of the bustle, perhaps with some sculpture to please the eye or with a boardwalk where people could walk and take in the salt air—like at Coney Island. The ocean was renewing. It felt good to watch it, to see the waves break, to watch the tides change. She took out a pad of paper from her desk and started to compose a letter:

Dear Mr.———,

Scottsman and Salvadori informed me that you were the owner of the property on Keys Avenue and 32nd St. An outstanding contribution to the future of our city would be a small neighborhood park or plaza that would provide a place for the elderly of that neighborhood to . . .

Rose didn't notice that Sam had come into their bedroom until the TV set began to blare. "I won the game by sixty-four points," he announced. "I beat a college professor. What do you think of that?"

"Good, Rose said, and in a lower voice asked Sam what Claire and Richard were doing now. "Just talking," Sam said indifferently. He undressed, pulled down the covers of his bed, and stood his pillows up against the headboard so that they formed a backrest.

With her pencil Rose drew an arrow from her first sentence to the period of the second sentence. The letter sounded smoother if she reversed the order of the sentences. Maybe all she could hope for was that the owner of the property would sell at a low price. A new idea occurred to her. She had read in a newspaper about a federal program that helped towns purchase sites for conservation and parks. Something to check into. Exhilarated, she stopped herself. Maybe Claire was right. She should do what she knew how to do: be a candystripe girl at a local hospital. But why shouldn't she try for the park! Actually she had always been a good organizer. She knew how to apply for federal grants and a few years ago she had actually been responsible for getting a volunteer project funded with government funds from both state and city. The program on the TV changed to a hillbilly singer playing the guitar, Sam dozed off. He had forgotten to take out his dentures and with his teeth in, he looked young.

Wondering if there was a listing in the telephone book for a department of parks or a department of conservation, Rose tiptoed out of the bedroom. The living room was dark, the drapes pulled across the sliding glass door, blocking out the lights from the pool area. Neither Claire nor Richard Jones was there. The apartment was silent except for the TV. Richard might be in Claire's room. Were they sleeping together here in this apartment? She could knock on Claire's door under the pretense of saying goodnight and find out. She decided against that. Richard might have left without saying goodbye to them. He seemed like a gentleman.

She took down the telephone number for the department of parks on the same scrap paper on which Scottsman and Salvadori's number was written and returned to the bedroom where she snapped off the TV. Restless, she paced out to the living room again, this time pulling back the drapes in order to get a view of the pool. A breeze had blown up, ruffling the pool's surface with undersized waves. She imagined the ocean tonight, rough with whitecaps, and the air, salty and damp with sea spray. Perhaps there was a full moon. The design for the park should include plans for lighting at night so that people could stay outside on an evening like this one to stroll or sit on benches, take in the breeze or listen to the surf. There were certainly a lot of angles to consider. She walked back into the bedroom; she had to finish the letter she had started. She thought ahead. In the morning she had two phones calls to make before she drove Claire to the airport.

Afterword

The story originated from a one-liner that reverberated in my head and ended on paper. Sally, a good friend who had just returned from visiting her Aunt Erna in Florida, told me the following: "The phone doesn't stop ringing from early in the morning; they call to check up on each other." Suddenly the characters appeared along with the plot: what happens when nobody answers the phone.

Byron Preiss read the first part of "Rose" in *Aphra* and asked me to write part two. I had to feel my way through what Gerda's death meant to Rose, how it converged with other parts of herself and her experience to shape her future.

The story touches on the terrors of dying and living in a culture of garish and jarring discontinuities, and of course that means my own fears of "Hotcakesland"—to use Thomas McGuane's word.

In spite of all fears, I need to love. I love Gerda because she stands firmly rooted in the possibilities of the present, with one foot in the past; one in the future. And Rose—I love her because she can still feel, wonder, be angry, get depressed, appreciate—because she still craves connectedness with important things.

Minstrel of Lankhmar

Minstrel of Lankhmar
A discussion with Fritz Leiber

The word *privilege* remains with me.

What a *privilege* it was to spend an hour or so with a writer so talented, so respected, and so enjoyed by his fellow professionals and readers of science fiction and fantasy.

In planning this book, I wanted very much to give younger readers an idea of what the old pulps were so that they would better understand the intention of this new publication. I thought there were three ways to best accomplish this: with a story that related to the old pulp heroes, with an historical introduction, and *with a non-fiction piece by one of the original pulp authors.*

Fritz Leiber is one of the original pulp authors to make a successful and lasting transition from the old pulps to the modern fantasy field. He is the creator and chronicler of Fafhrd and the Grey Mouser, a duo of sword-and-sorcery heroes whose new adventures* have continued over a period longer than any other pulp star, bar none. He is an award-winning novelust and short story writer. His book, *Conjure Wife,* stands as a classic of American literature, as effective in these days of women's liberation as it was at the time of its release in 1940. His *Dangerous Vision* "Gonna Roll Them Bones," a science fantasy told in American folklore form, received the Hugo and Nebula awards for best novelette of 1967.

What better choice than Fritz to discuss the old pulps?

I met Fritz on a cool day in San Francisco. He is a tall, white-haired man with a deep, rich voice. He is full in both movement and stature.

Fritz speaks as he writes: clearly, cogently, and entertainingly, with intelligence and wit.

This conversation will give you a few introductory and personal insights into the world of pulp magazines as perceived by one of its most acclaimed writers. Fritz Leiber's actual work in the pulp field focused more on the supernatural/weird pulps than it did on the heroic pulps such as *The Shadow* or *Doc Savage*. Nonetheless, you will find most of his statements pertinent to the content of this book.

For those of you unacquainted with the original pulps, there are a few short footnotes on some of the names Fritz uses in this conversation.

*Written by the original author in prose form.

WH: The first thing that came to mind when I thought about discussing the old pulps with you was your connection to them as a child. *Weird Tales*[1] came out in 1923; that means you were about thirteen years old.

FL: That's right.

WH: You immediately took a liking to it?

FL: No I never—to tell you the truth, I never read *Weird Tales* regularly. I would pick up an issue from time to time and I would read it, but I didn't see one out of five. I read the first issue of *Amazing Stories* when it came out, you know, the first all-science fiction magazine, in 1927; I read that steadily for three or four years; and to tell the truth, the only other pulp I recall reading was *Short Story Magazine*. If you remember, that was sort of a diversified pulp. Their speciality was simply that they were all short stories. They were all about three to four thousand words long, detective mystery stories, very little science fiction, historical adventure, you know. Just a mish-mosh of types. I read that occasionally, but I really wasn't a heavy reader of the pulps.

WH: Any early memories of trips down to the newsstand? Were you drawn to the pulps?

FL: Not tremendously, no. As I say, I was taken with *Short Story* and *Weird Tales*—when I was young, you know, around fourteen or fifteen, I was kind of ambivalent about it. I liked some of the stories; others I simply found too scary. Well, that's the truth. When I first ran into Lovecraft[2] it was in *Amazing Story*. He sold one story, "The Color Out of Space," to *Amaz-*

ing back around 1926, and I remember reading that and finding it a very depressing story at the time, a very frightening and kind of gloomy story, it struck me as. It wasn't until three or four years later that I became interested, really interested in stories of that sort and considered, eventually, writing them myself.

WH: It's so rare when a reader of a magazine becomes a writer of it. That was the situation with you and *Weird Tales*.

FL: Well, I had ambitions to become a writer, and when I first started writing the only thing that gave me sufficient kick to actually create a story was the idea of something happening that contravened the laws of science, the generalizations of science, the idea of something from the unknown coming in and upsetting things.

WH: You wouldn't call yourself anti-science.

FL: No, no, I wouldn't call myself anti-science. That was more the basis of the supernatural horror story, the sort of thing that Poe and Lovecraft and others wrote, a story in which something frightening happens. Something along the lines of the genuine appearance of a spirit of the dead or creatures from another dimension or the power of witchcraft being demonstrated.

WH: Like in *Conjure Wife*.

FL: Yeah, that had that premise, and—no, the feeling was that we were—we really were skeptical, we were a skeptical and scientific generation, and so the idea of playing around just in an artistic way with the possibility of things happening that went against science, why, this was attractive, but—the result was, generally speaking, a story of terror, of fear.

WH: You got a kick out of raising those emotions, I imagine?

FL: Yeah, oh sure. I think that's the point with stories of that sort—that the basic desire of the listener is to be scared, to experience fear in such a way that it's not serious, but that he gets a pleasant shiver out of it. The difference amounts to this: The fears of that sort give you gooseflesh, but say the prospect of being cut up by a homicidal maniac with a butcher knife, this wouldn't produce gooseflesh, it would make you feel sick and desperate, and you'd have this desire to just strike out blindly or escape. I don't think the fear of being put in pain or of being killed is the same as the fear derived from a Poe or Lovecraft story. That's a different sort of terror altogether. It certainly doesn't raise goosebumps.

WH: So, your way of putting together a story of fear is to

remove the reader from the immediate aura of fear that may actually be surrounding him.

FL: That's true enough, yes, but at the time the stories I was trying to write were the stories that people like Poe have written and writers like Algernon Blackwood and Arthur Mackin in England and some others of that ilk have done. It was a rather traditional sort of horror story.

WH: Were you influenced much by other American pulp writers?

FL: I admired a lot of them. I certainly was much taken with Lovecraft, and he had some effect on me, all right. Definitely But not so much on my style as in a special way. I didn't really want to imitate his kind of writing. I've never fooled around with writing stories about the Chthulu Mythos, but—

WH: Did you meet Lovecraft?

FL: No, I corresponded with him about the last eight months of his life. He kept up an active correspondence with a number of people during the last year of his life, as he had in the past. It was rather amazing, you know, really. I mean, he was going to die in eight months and he undoubtedly was suffering from the ailments he died of, and yet he was perfectly happy to plunge into a huge correspondence with a newcomer like me, you know, and I wrote him long letters in return and this kept up for about six months.

WH: Almost to the time he died.

FL: Yes. The last two or three months he had to go to the hospital once and he wrote shorter letters, but he was still going up until almost the end. I admired the man, several things about him. His literary integrity; he felt if you were going to write about something, you ought to research it carefully and write it carefully and try to make a good job of it; and on the other hand, in the realm of the supernatural and so on, he was a complete skeptic.

I wrote him enthusiastically about Charles Thorpe, who was a collector of a lot of, you might say, *anti-science* material, mostly newspaper clippings about strange things that science couldn't explain and didn't want to hear about—the typical, you know, flying saucer and poltergeist stories, but especially when there is a lack of really exciting news in a more ordinary field, he debunked that greatly. He said that sort of stuff was an interesting source for the writers of weird stories.

WH: When your work first came out in *Weird Tales* and *Unknown*—

FL: In *Unknown* first, then *Weird Tales*.

WH: How did you feel about it? Pride?

FL: Oh sure, sure I was proud. There were only a few places publishing fantasy at that time. *Unknown* lasted only about four years. It was killed by the paper shortage during WW II. *Weird Tales*, *Unknown*, *Astounding Stories*, sure I was proud to be in those magazines because they were the only places in which you could publish fantasy.

WH: Who did you feel was reading them at the time? You said that you were not that interested in them as a teenager.

FL: I imagined that people like myself were reading them just the same, sure.

WH: When you were writing for the pulps did you have feelings about where those magazines were going? Did you feel there was any future in them? Did you expect to graduate to what you're doing now?

FL: I didn't know. By and large I didn't think of them as having a future because at the time it was only rarely that material that was first printed in the pulps were reprinted elsewhere. There were some collections done in England of the stories out of *Weird Tales*, but very few publishers, you know, hardcover publishers, were interested in fantasy—or science fiction for that matter. There would be an occasional novel that you could call science fiction. More often than not, it would be British to start with, you know people like H.G. Wells, Aldous Huxley's *Brave New World*, and the American publishers weren't interested.

It was around the end of World War II that the first anthologies of science fiction were published by paperback publishers. I think there was Wolheim's[3] *Short Novels of Science Fiction*. That was a big step in its day. A few other collections like that started things going, and then it wasn't until a couple of years after the little science fiction presses, Fantasy House, Arkham House, Prime Press, and Gnome Press, that the big name publishers saw a market, and went into it themselves.

WH: Do you miss the old pulps?

FL: No.

WH: You don't miss them at all?

FL: No, I really don't. I mean, the material that was good and of lasting interest in the pulps, that sort of stuff you can sell both to hardcover and paperback publishers.

WH: Ballantine is releasing the "best" of the old *Planet* pulp stories in paperback form.

FL: Well, the science fiction pulps were always a little bit different from the others. It was just once or twice that, say, when Edmond Hamilton was doing the *Captain Future* [4] stories, that they began to approach the hero pulps, I would say.

WH: Do you see much future for the remaining science fiction pulps such as *Galaxy*, *Fantastic* and *Amazing*? Do you expect them to be around ten years from now?

FL: I expect two or three of them will be around still. It's natural—I mean, that's mostly just a problem in sales. I mean, a paperback doesn't date, doesn't go out of date like a magazine that has a month and a year on it, so it's just more logical to produce paperback collections and anthologies of originals than to publish pulps. The chances are better saleswise.

WH: Before we move off the subject of pulp history, I thought you might be able to share some of your observations of the view most people held of the pulps during the time you were reading and writing them.

FL: I'm not terribly into this, but the pulps were surely looked on as fiction for juveniles, for kids and for young people, especially with the adventure stories. Some of the people who were interested in fantasy, would buy *Weird Tales* but be embarrassed by the covers that looked too lurid or had those sort of featureless, generalized nudes on them, you know, and there were people who would buy *Weird Tales* and tear off the cover as soon as possible.

WH: Just like the people who Kurtzman[5] would parody in cartoons about early *Mad* readers.

FL: The dime novel was a sensational form of literature for adventurous adolescents, mostly male to start with, I would say; and it was looked on that way. Right now you have the academic people and so on kind of beginning to get terribly interested in science fiction, but God knows they were contemptuous of it for a long enough time before then.

WH: Seems to be the same for all forms of popular fiction.

FL: Yeah, true enough.

WH: To get on to your heroes, Fafhrd and the Grey Mouser[6]. They were created in your college days, weren't they?

FL: A friend of mine named Harry Fisher and I invented them in our correspondence. We wrote each other long letters and began introducing bits of fiction. We had no serious idea of writing stories at that time. We were just entertaining each other, and we would invent characters for serious or humorous or satirical purposes and then write fragments about them. It's easy to write the opening to a story as long as you don't have to finish the story.

So my friend Harry Fisher and I built up the characters of Fafhrd and the Grey Mouser in that way, and later, when *Unknown* came along, I decided to write a story about them and submit it for publication. It was a story of about 12,000 words entitled, "Two Sought Adventure." Wonder of wonders, the magazine bought it. In fact, John Campbell, the editor, was rather skeptical. I remember he had me sign a notarized statement that they were really my characters and I hadn't plagarized them from some obscure source he didn't know about.

But that was how I came to write the Fafhrd and Grey Mouser stories. To some extent, they had anti-heroic elements right from the start. I mean, the idea was to have supermen who weren't all that great, you know, supermen who drank and who might lose out, who always won partly by good fortune as well as by being muscular and intelligent and so on.

WH: When you started them, it was purely for entertainment reasons?

FL: Yeah.

WH: They've been around for about thirty-five years now. Have you changed your attitudes at all toward the purposes of your stories.

FL: No. All stories are for entertainment, including the plays of Shakespeare and all the rest of them. I just don't care for stories that are getting preachy and are trying to do something new to the reader to improve him or something of that sort. No.

WH: I think that's where a lot of the television heroes and the like have attempted to expand the scope of heroic fiction.

FL: Yeah. Well, I can understand it. It is a natural development, just like when the comics began to reform and have doctors and judges and good lawyers for their heroes. It's a natural development and it's a good development, because it increases the scope of the field of fiction and mind, so I'm all for that. I mean, I think that's justifiable just on the grounds that it's a new kind of hero, so why not?

WH: Do you see a future for heroes?

FL: Yes.

WH: Do you think they will be becoming less and less necessary in a society like this?

FL: No, heroes in reality are a pretty rare breed.

WH: How would you define "hero"?

FL: Somebody who happens to have the motivation to do something that really needs to be done yet involves difficulties and dangers. I would say it amounts to something like that.

I think it is important that a hero live by whatever code he follows. Once you push materialistic philosophy so far that the hero is always motivated by self-interest, I think you begin to lose something. I feel that at different levels he will have a code and that this is important.

WH: I notice that we keep saying "he" and "hero." In putting together these questions, it occurred to me that there were rarely any "she" pulp heroes. This is especially interesting in light of the fact that there were many comic book heroines in a period not that much later than the pulps.

FL: Yes.

WH: There's no good reason for this.

FL: No, there isn't, and it's being modified now, I think.

WH: There still are very few female heroes in adventure fiction.

FL: I think I have more stories that are told from the female viewpoint than male, certainly in science fiction. In fact, on the whole I think I've always been quite a bit of a feminist. In novels like *The Big Time* and *Conjure Wife* and quite a few others, *The Wanderer*—

WH: *Conjure Wife* (a novel that slightly whimsically postulates that all women are witches) really flows nicely.

FL: Well, that was the sort of thing you could get away with in *Unknown*, which was a very open type of magazine on the whole. For example, John Campbell would point out to me when he bought a Fafhrd and Grey Mouser story, "Well, this is really a story that's more the *Weird Tales* type, but I think it's so good I want to buy it." Oddly, at the time *Weird Tales* was kind of down on sword-and-sorcery. I don't know. They published the Conan stories with great enthusiasm and apparently a lot of reader response, but after Howard's death they grew progressively away from sword-and-sorcery. The editor, Farnsworth Wright, had bought the Conan stories. When he died the editors in New York were rather dubious about sword-and-sorcery and in the last seven or eight years of the magazine they published hardly anything in that line. They did publish Bradbury. I think he was the principal author of the late *Weird Tales* that was really good, Bradbury and to a lesser degree Robert Bloch and Manly Wade Wellman and August Derleth. They weren't bound by any rules of their own—which partially shows how open *Unknown* was to different sorts of material.

WH: The old pulps, including *Weird Tales* with its bizarre examples, had a lot of violence. One thing that we're attempting to do in *Weird Heroes* is to deemphasize violence. The strategy of so many pulp characters was to hit first and talk later.

FL: Yeah.

WH: Of course, it's nothing new to change the emphasis of a genre, but it is remarkable that this has been done so infrequently in the history of published heroic fiction.

FL: I would like to qualify that. Take sword-and-sorcery for instance. You can start with the Tolkien books[7]. Certainly the Ring books don't overemphasize violence.

WH: True.

FL: And what about Moorcock,[8] all his Elric stories and so forth. In writing the stories of Fafhrd and the Grey Mouser I never felt that violence was the natural solution. Sure, people got involved in fights. It was the kind of age where there was dueling going on and such. That's one reason for going back to those times—so you can have a certain amount of fighting and violent expression, but in thinking of the Fafhrd and Mouser stories I've written the solutions are rarely produced by violence, by simply killing off the villain and that solves the problem. The villains frequently, almost always, survives in my stories. They don't get killed off and the final solution is apt to be a sort of draw, and the main achievement of the hero is that he gets away. He doesn't get killed. He survives, but without victory.

WH: Well, look at television today—just turning it during a night's worth of programming—there is so much brutality and murder in the course of three hour's drama. Fortunately, not the comedy yet, but even in the news there's a hype to the violence. Then in the paperback field, there are those out-and-out bloody BUST-THE-MAFIA covers and violent mentality crimebusters. The relative number of violent heroic fiction continuities in any number of media are still insanely high.

FL: A problem like that gets fairly complicated. I'd say in the first place that the idea that I think is childish and misleading is that there are villains—that there are good guys and villains—and you can solve problems by killing off the villains. This seems to me a juvenile approach to life; not necessarily juvenile, but just stupid, because old people are as apt as young people to think that it's a good idea. I mean, "juvenile" is really a bad word because it assumes that kids just somehow naturally think of things in terms of good guys, bad guys and solving problems by getting rid of the bad guys, and I don't think this is typical child psychology to start with. I don't think kids necessarily reason that way. They find that for games, sure, you have to have two sides—

WH: Cowboys and Indians.

FL: Cowboys and Indians and something like that, but they are as apt to have the Indians win as not, at least in the many versions that I can recall playing.

And so I think that the idea of solving a problem of getting rid of the bad guys so that the good guys can take over and everything will be great is, well, life doesn't work out this way.

On the other hand, I think that operating in one's imagination in a world where you can do physical things like fight and so on that you can't do in real life, this can be real, a healthy emotional release.

It's like the question of guns. We live in a culture, in an age, where guns are becoming more and more of a hazard, because our culture really doesn't accept them or condone them and certainly the whole idea—the ideas of democracy and socialism—the good ideas to my mind—are in the direction of nonviolent solutions to problems, and so although they are fun things, as parts of games and parts of the world of imagination, they don't work in reality. I mean, I can see a culture gradually working toward legislating them out of existence, but on the other hand, I don't see the same thing applying so much to fiction, because after all, with fiction we use the imagination and the first rule there is to explore any possibility, and this includes both the violent and the nonviolent possibilities. Once you start to make rules for the imagination, then I tend to draw the line. I don't believe in it. On the other hand, I certainly believe in encouraging, in fiction as elsewhere, encouraging imagination itself, which is the exploration of all solutions and not just one kind. Some kinds of fiction seem just trapped in the idea of violent solutions to everything and this rubs me the wrong way. What you are doing sounds to me like increasing the range of imagination. That's what it makes possible for the writer, and all that's good.

WH: Beautifully put. I consider it so important to move beyond the basic hero vs. villain confrontation in which violence plays a resolving role. There *has* to be more. There *is* more.

In putting together this book, I was very conscious of the authors' freedom to write what he or she wants to write, but at the same time I felt strongly about the need to reach higher, past the old violent heroic molds to something new. What that "something" is can be witnessed in many of the stories in the book. Ted White's "Phoenix" uses the mind as a playground for fantastic adventure. Steve Englehart's "Viva" finds strength in things natural. She doesn't kill the "villain"; she saves him.

The pulps merit respect for their ability to evoke atmosphere, excitement, and a feeling of epic adventure. *Weird Heroes* aspires to entertain the reader, but it does so with a conscious effort to innovate. The result, hopefully, will be new heroes with a strong respect for human life.

The pulp heroes held this respect too, but it was often more selective. A character earned respect if he was "good" in the eyes of the hero. Pulp heroes were not predominantly unsympathetic to human foibles, but they often acted as judge and jury.

WH: If you had to eulogize the pulps, what would you say?

FL: Eulogize them?

WH: As you knew them during the thirties and forties.

FL: I knew them mostly as the only place where science fiction stories were published, or where stories of supernatural horror or fantasy could be found. It's very hard to place them anywhere else. The number of people who contribute to *Weird Tales* is rather amazing, people like Tennessee Williams and Val Lewton, who eventually became producer of a film called *The Cat People*.

WH: Do you have any thoughts on the future of heroic fiction?

FL: Oh, I think it'll be around.

WH: As long as there are heroes?

FL: Yeah.

WH: As long as there are people.

FL: Well, it seems to be a remarkably hardy sort of fiction. It keeps coming back. There's something terribly attractive about simplifying life and going back to more primitive living conditions. We had a big dose of it just now in the sort of anti-technology feeling in the idea of getting back to nature, going out on the land, raising your own food and so on. That's romantic, but it's interesting, and in its way very good. I think that the desire to operate on a simpler level is pretty characteristic of the way the mind works, the way the imagination works.

With the same vitality of thought that characterized Fritz' discussion, we concluded our talk.

Now as I sit here writing this, I am comforted in the knowledge that I will never have to wait to meet a giant of modern literature. I have already met him.

(Transcript edited and revised for publication).

Those of you unfamiliar with Fritz' work, can search out paperback editions of *Conjure Wife* (Penguin), *The Second Book of Fritz Leiber* (DAW), *The Best of Fritz Leiber* (Ballantine), and the Fafhrd/Grey Mouser adventure series *Swords Against Death*, *The Swords of Lankhmar*, *Swords in the Mist*, etc. (Ace).

Footnotes:

1. Weird Tales*: a pulp magazine, based in Chicago. It specialized in tales of monsters, ghosts, fiends, and Conan, the Barbarian. The stories it published included those by some of the highest regarded authors in the genre (Poe, Howard, Bloch).*

2. H.P. Lovecraft, a writer of supernatural horror stories. He is regarded as one of the best in the supernatural horror field. Many of his stories centered around death and decay. "Pickman's Model," the story of a painter of horrible subjects, was adapted for television and appeared as a segment of "Night Gallery," starring Bradford Dillman.

3. Donald A. Wollheim; noted anthologist of science fiction books. He is presently publisher of DAW science fiction.

4. Captain Future, a science fiction pulp hero whose magazine ran from 1940 to 1951. Almost all of the Captain Future novels were written by Edmond Hamilton. He was a super-scientist hero, with a Doc Savage-like host of associates.

5. Harvey Kurtzman, editor of Mad *Magazine in its original comic book form.*

6. Fafhrd and the Grey Mouser, Fritz Leiber's pair of adventurer heroes whose escapades take place with light-hearted flourish in the land known as Newhon, of which the most corrupt city is Lankhmar.

7. Tolkien, author of the famous Ring trilogy, a set of fantasy novels of epic proportion, each carefully developed and populated with an extensive cast of characters and environments.

8. Michael Moorcock, a British science fuction and fantasy writer. His hero, Elric, is known for a series of unusual and fantastic "sword-and-sorcery" adventures.

GREATHEART
SILVER
TM

Great Heart Silver in Showdown at Shootout
by Philip José Farmer
Illustrated by Tom Sutton

When I called Phil Farmer to ask him to develop a new pulp hero for this book, I called on one of the most acclaimed writers in the science fiction field, a winner of Hugo and Nebula awards, a pulp historian extraordinaire, a popular author of "biographies" of Doc Savage and Tarzan, a screenplay treatment writer for the second Doc Savage movie, a literary gamesplayer, and the chronicler of the incredible *Riverboat* trilogy.

I was also calling on a nice man. Phil accepted the offer and he was the first author in the book to complete it. He is a professional of the highest caliber.

The last story in a book is often something special. A final send-off for a hopefully exciting literary experience. Greatheart Silver is no exception. He represents an heroic legacy from one of the pulps' foremost historians.

Throughout the reading of this book, you may have wondered about the whereabouts of the old pulp heroes. "Whatever happened to the Shadow? The Black Bat? Operator 5? They must be about eighty years old by now."

You won't find the Shadow, Doc Savage or Wu Fang in this book, but you will find Phwombly, Captain Nothing, Doc Ravage, and Won Fang. Those, and a host of other characters, are a mixture of Phil's childhood memories and his own brand of heroic insanity.

I won't describe the story you are about to read except to say that it is a funny and epic adventure. Greatheart himself is a low-key, friendly hero. You'll like him.

When Phil completed this story, subtitled "Showdown at Shootout," he told me that subsequent adventures would be a bit more '*serious.*' Those of you who become Greatheart fans after this story are in for a treat with volume II, as Phil gets a chance to make good on his pledge in "The Return of Greatheart Silver." Frankly, I wouldn't be the least bit bothered by any major violations.

Tom Sutton, who contributes five full-page plates for this story, is one of the best humorous graphic storytellers to come along since Kurtzman and Elder. In addition, his tight, dramatic line style has embellished the work of such popular artists as Gil Kane and John Buscema. His ability to do both dramatic and humorous subjects made him a prime choice for

"Greatheart." Phil Farmer is delighted with the results. By the time you read this, he may have already purchased the originals.

GREATHEART SILVER
in
SHOWDOWN AT SHOOTOUT
or
The Grand Finale

With a cast of hundreds! Heroes and villains enough to satisfy all! The Battle of the Century! Popcorn and beer sold between the acts! Gentlemen, please remove your hats.

Author's Foreword

All Golden Ages end.

The great heroes and great villains of the pulp-magazine era would be old men, old indeed, if they were still living. But it's sad to think of them dying with their boots off, their careers uncompleted, decaying into senility, blind, deaf, noses running, salivating, dirtying their sheets, babbling of green fields. So it is only fitting that this tale have them and their days as they lived—in the glory of their youth.

This adventure contains a certain amount of levity, but any parodying is done with love. I hope all will pardon me. But, to be safe, I apologize beforehand to the following: Secret Agent Number One, The Avenger, The Black Bat, Captain Satan, Captain Zero, The Crimson Mask, Dan Fowler, Doc Harker, Doc Savage and his aides; Monk and Ham, Doctor Death, Doctor Yen Sin, Don Diavolo, G-8, Herr Doktor Krueger, The Green Ghost, the Green Lama, the Lone Ranger, Tonto, Nick Carter, the Moon Man, the Octopus, Operator #5, Pete Rice, the Phantom Detective, G-77, the Scorpion, Secret Agent X, the Shadow, the Silver Buck, the Spider, the Whisperer, and Wu Fang.

James Bond, Doctor No, Fu Manchu, and Sir Nayland Smith are not pulp characters. But they have all the characteristics of the heroes and villains who appeared on less expensive paper.

My apologies to them, too, along with my love.

GREATHEART

1.

The Mad Fokker struck again.

2.

Greatheart Silver had no idea that he'd soon be meeting the Mad Fokker. He knew about him, of course. The world have been hearing for six months about him and the gang that had been terrorizing the Southwest and California. Banks and loan offices were robbed, plutocrats kidnapped, dirigibles pirated, oil storage tanks drained, research institutes deprived of radioactive materials, army arsenals looted, and extortion practiced on a grand scale.

The Blimp Gang, as it was called, had some members who seemed to be scientists gone wrong. The cotton growers of the Southwest had parted with six million dollars because of the so-called Brain Trust of the Blimp Gang. The trust had developed a mutant, an insecticide-proof boll weevil which would be loosed unless six million dollars were chuted into a wild area in the Superstition Mountains. Government scientists had tested the boll weevils the gang had provided as proof of its boast. Sure enough. The weevils thrived on the most potent of poisons. The scientists advised that the money be paid. A day later, the scientists had red faces. And most of them had no jobs. Though immune to insecticides, the mutations died after their first meal of boll. Otherwise, they were perfect.

The world, excepting the cotton growers, laughed. "Blimp" Kernel, head of the gang, undoubtedly laughed. His most famous aide, the Mad Fokker, must have laughed, too. But then he was always laughing. His high-pitched cachinnations terrified his victims as he robbed them, and they floated down to the pursuing police as he flew off in his tiny three-winged airplane.

The Fokker *was* mad. Everybody agreed on that. Who but a crazy man would land on a city street (after clearing it with a few bursts from his machine guns), run into a bank, rob it, and fly away at rooftop level? Who else would shoot up state police patrol cars and helicopters just for sport?

Another great coup was the London Bridge Extortion Plot. The Mad Fokker put a note in a paper sack of horse manure, then dropped it on the head of Phoenix chief of police. The note was cleaned and then read. It stated that the historical monument over Lake Havasu would be bombed unless two million dollars was paid. The authorities told the Blimp Gang to go to hell. Not a cent would be paid. Anti-aircraft guns and radar equipment were installed at London Bridge. Air National Guard planes were alerted to fly at a moment's notice. A regiment of National Guard, armed with heat-detecting missiles, was added. Come ahead, the authorities said.

Two weeks passed; nothing happened. The third week, during a rainstorm, the Mad Fokker attacked. He came in just above the lake surface, thus evading radar detection. Just before he reached the bridge, he zoomed up and over it, dropped a package, and fled, zigzagging, a few inches from the water. The package opened up like a great white flower and burned, doing little damage. But the heat-detecting missiles, launched to catch the triplane, headed instead for the heap of thermit on the bridge. Moths to the flame. London Bridge flew apart, up, and then down.

The following day the Mad Fokker dropped another note in a paper sack, weighted with cattle manure this time, splattering the governor as he walked down the steps of the capitol building.

"NEXT TIME, PAY UP. NO BULL."

3.

Greatheart Silver was thinking of this and laughing to himself. He was standing in the bridge of the AZ-8, midway through the second dogwatch. Before him Steersman Chesters sat in a chair in front of a control console. The steersman was smoking a cigarette and monitoring gauges, dials, and instruments though he was not actually steering the great zeppelin. This was usually done by a computer, which also operated just about everything on board. Beyond the control console was the curving window of the bridge. This was not in a control gondola which hung below the fore, as in the old-type dirigibles. It was set within the hull, below the nose.

Ahead and below was the Arizona night. In a short time the lights of the Phoenix area would be seen. The zeppelin was already in its downward path toward the hangar. The air was clear and relatively still. The roar of the starboard and port jets was muted here; the loudest sound was the steersman humming to himself. Radar had reported that there was a storm forty miles to the north, but the airship would be in its hangar before the storm reached the Valley of the Sun.

The dirigible of the Acme Zeppelin Company bored through the night, carrying passengers and freight in no hurry to arrive at their destination. The atomic pile in its lead casing squatted within the center of the ship, silently issuing heat which would be converted to electrical light and power.

Mr. Greatheart Silver, first mate of the AZ-8, was content, perhaps even happy. He had wanted to be a gasbagger ever since he had taken an overseas trip in one. He'd been ten at the time, and now he was thirty. In a few years, he would be eligible to pin on a captain's bars.

It hadn't been easy. His parents had died when he was seventeen, and he had had to get a football scholarship to put himself through college. On graduating, he had turned down offers to play professional football and had entered the officers' academy of the Acme Zeppelin Company at Freidrichshafen, West Germany. At the end of three years he had gotten his third mate's papers. Now, six years later, he was one step—a long one, true—from captain.

At the moment, he was thinking of home. This was a small and expensive apartment in the Great Hohokam Tower. His fiancée, Ms. Regina Graves, with whom he shared the apartment, was probably feeding his birds right now. Then she would fix dinner for him, and they'd go to bed early. He had to rise at six A.M. (civilian time) to get to the AZ-8 at seven, an hour before take-off for the Pasadena port.

He visioned with pleasure his fiancée, a tall lovely blonde, bustling around the apartment. She might even dust off the big oil portrait of his great-great-great-great-great-great grandfather. This had been done by John Singleton Copley in 1772 and was, aside from its sentimental value, worth two hundred thousand dollars on the market. It showed a big old man with a large head, broad face, and white wig, clad in the velvets and lace of the period. The face was lined but merry and did not look at all like a buccaneer's. Yet the family tradition was that he had been a pirate who had escaped from a vessel taking him to England for trial and an inevitable hanging. He'd shown up in New York with a bagful of guineas (doubtless stolen), and in a short time had become rich. The source of his wealth was reputed to be smuggling. He had added to it by marrying a young widow of an affluent Hudson River patroon. During the Revolution, he had become very wealthy through smuggling, which was at that time approved by the American authorities.

Along the wall were a dozen other paintings and blowups of photographs. One was of Thomas Jefferson, an even more distinguished ancestor of Greatheart. His descent from him had been through Sally Hemings, the quadroom mistress of Jefferson and half-sister of Jefferson's deceased wife.

Next to the president was Greatheart's great-great-great-grandfather, the Sioux warrior, Crazy Horse.

Near it was a photograph of another ancestor in whom he took pride. This was his grandfather, a famous gunfighter of the Old West. The picture, taken when he was in his thirties, showed a handsome man with black hair distinguished by a tip of gray, like a tiny horn, just above each temple.

Greatheart was satisfied that he had let none of his forebears down. He might not be a pirate who'd terrorized the Spanish Main or a president of the highest distinction or the greatest tactician of the Sioux nation or a saddle tramp with the fastest draw in the Old West, but he had done all right. He was close to attaining his own goals, and his profession had a certain glamor to it.

Greatheart turned around, and his contentment gushed out of him like water from a ballast sack. By the entrance stood a semi-transparent figure.

It was a middle-aged man with a red-and-white striped jersey, crimson velvet pantaloons, one huge silver-buckled shoe, and brown hair, bound in a pig-tail. He was leaning on a crutch to compensate for a missing left leg. A large green parrot sat on his shoulder and screamed silent obscenities.

The figure jerked a thumb at the entrance, drew a finger across its throat, and faded away.

Greatheart had seen such apparitions before. He was always startled. Sometimes, it was John Silver. Other times, it was his Indian grandmother or Crazy Horse or his grandfather, Silverhorns Silver, or Sally Hemings. He didn't know why Thomas Jefferson never appeared. At first, when he'd thought that the figures were ghosts, he'd supposed that the president was too busy, wherever he was, to make an appearance. He'd transmitted his warnings via Sally, who was used to doing all the menial labor anyway.

Later, he'd figured out that they could not be ghosts. For one thing, his grandmother was still living. They were actually symbols projected by his unconscious mind. He had some kind of psychic sense which told him when a situation was going to change for the worse. His conscious mind didn't detect the danger, but his unconscious did, and it used the figures of his ancestors to alert him.

He whirled around just in time to see a light on the console begin flashing red and to hear a buzzing issue from beside the light.

"The skyhook!" he said to Chesters. "Why's it being let down?"

"I don't know, sir," Chesters said. "There's a UO on the screen, too." He indicated with a nod the blip that had appeared.

"Put it on DIST," Silver said. He strode to the console, flicked a switch, and said, "Skyhook room! What's going on?"

There was no answer. Chesters said, "It's a small airplane, sir. It must have come from beyond that mountain there. It's climbing toward us."

"Magnify," Silver said. On another screen the blip became a small single-seater aircraft with three sets of wings.

"The Mad Fokker!" Chesters said.

Silver did not say so, but he knew why old John Silver had appeared, why the skyhook room had not answered, why the hook was being lowered. The piracy of the AZ-10 and AZ-15 had started like this: Passengers who were members of the Blimp Gang had seized key points, the skyhook was let down, the Fokker's plane was secured, the crew was tied up, and the passengers' money and valuables were taken, along with the most desirable cargo. The AZ-10 had been landed first, but the AZ-15 was unloaded while aloft.

Three men, masked and holding automatic pistols, entered the bridge.

Two minutes later, Chesters and Silver were bound to chairs, taped so tightly they looked like mummies. Their mouths and eyes were also covered, but they had the use of their ears. Silver forced himself to repress the rage that sent the blood thumping through his head and drowned out all sound but that of his frustration. The voices of the pirates were those of old men and, yes, one sounded just like the recording of "Blimp" Kernel.

Knowing this helped nothing. There had been no doubt about the identity of the gang.

Suddenly, a maniacal laugh burst in his ear. Then he cried

out as the tape was ripped from his eyes. Before him stood a man of middle height, masked, wearing the helmet and goggles and uniform of a World War I AEF flying officer. His hands were gnarled, blotched with liver spots, and bulging with huge blue veins. Behind the goggles were thick spectacles, and behind them were two large watery gray eyes.

"Zo, *schweinhund*!" the man yelled in a brittle voice. "Traitor! You work for the Huns; you fly your *gotverdamt Luftschiff* over the U.S. of A., hah!"

His right hand slapped Silver across the cheek. Tears of rage trickled down Silver's high cheekbones, but he did not reply. The officers of the other zeppelins had been slapped and insulted by the madman, and the more they talked back the more they had been struck.

"I spent my youth serving my country as no one else served, and what did I get for it? Suppression of my identity, no public notice, private neglect, and then the bastards were so secretive about my record they lost it! They said I couldn't even get their measly pension! And I was put into an insane asylum! I, who had saved my country, the world, from its greatest perils time after time! Locked up with the crazies! *Ach*, the shame of it all!"

Silver let him rave, and finally Kernel spoke to the Mad Fokker in a soft voice, the words of which Silver could not hear. He strode out, and Kernel replaced the tapes on Silver.

He could not see what was happening, but the events were reconstructed later. As with the AZ-10, it was landed behind a mountain. Pima Control had detected the triplane and the AZ-8's change of course and notified the authorities. Helicopters had left the state police HQ and Luke Airfield, but by the time they arrived, the gang had dispersed. The zeppelin was drifting, its computer turned off, the passengers locked up, its crew tied up. At an elevation of one thousand feet, the Mad Fokker had disengaged his plane and flown into the storm sweeping southward. A few minutes later, the storm struck the airship. It also hit the choppers, which in any event could not have put men aboard the zeppelin.

The gas cells of the dirigible, punctured by the pirates, lost their helium rapidly. The AZ-8, at an altitude of five hundred feet, smashed into the side of a mountain.

Silver heard a rending of framework as the great rings and girders crumpled. And then he lost consciousness.

4.

The Acme investigators, the CIA, the FBI, the police, the reporters came and went. The pain stayed. After a while, the agony in the stump of his left leg eased off into something tolerable. But the agony of knowing that he was forever crippled would not go away. It haunted him even in his dreams: he was sitting on a sidewalk and holding out a hat for passersby to drop coins in while around the corner young women were laughing at him.

Regina, lovely and blonde as always, visited him three times. She cried a lot, but it was evident that the tears were caused by the prospect of marrying a one-legged man.

"Why did this have to happen to me?"

"I feel for you," he said. "So I release you. We're through, *kaput*. You only loved my body, Regina. To you I was just a handsome face and a pair of great legs and the rest I won't mention. Anyway, I was beginning to see how shallow you were. I didn't want to admit it to myself, but I would have eventually. So, get out and don't come back!"

He was lying. He hadn't seen at all that her psyche was as thin as the skin on a dirigible. He'd been too much in love.

"I'll go because I think it's best for you," she said, blinking, the tears rapidly drying up, her makeup running. She looked like a sexy Raggedy Ann with about as much sawdust inside her but none of the compassion.

"Anyway, you have good medical insurance," she said, "and the company will give you a good pension. You won't have to work for a living."

"And I'm still a human being, even if not a whole one," he said. "And I have a brain. That's more than you ever had or will have."

"Up yours," Regina said and stormed out.

Greatheart wasn't depressed. Instead of becoming melancholic, he became angry. This, his doctor said, was a healthy reaction. Depression was anger turned on oneself. It was far better to project it at others, especially if they deserved it, as Regina did.

Greatheart said, "You're a good doctor, Doc."

When Silver found out that the good doctor was now dating Regina, he didn't change his mind about his qualifications as a physician. But he did think the doctor was a rotten human being.

"Love knows no ethics," Doctor Rongwon said. "Eros

shoots his arrows where he will, and we defenseless mortals have no shields."

"You should have been a lawyer, Doc," Greatheart said. "A shyster instead of a quack."

"Always kidding," Rongwon said. "A good sign. And here's good news. Next week we start fitting you for your prosthetic leg."

"The better to kick you with," Greatheart said. The doctor, laughing, exited. Greatheart threw his ashtray and broke a picture. The nurse said that was a healthy reaction, too. "What about some healthy stimuli?" Greatheart said. The nurse, middle-aged but handsome, said, "You want me to play Jocasta to your Oedipus?"

"Everybody's too educated nowadays," Greatheart said. "No, I'm not looking for a mother image or incest. I just want some loving. Maybe I want to prove I'm still a man, too. Does that turn you off?"

"Ever since my husband died two years ago," she said, "I've been propositioned by nothing but old creeps. And I've turned every one down. I don't think you're a creep, and I could stand a little loving myself."

"It won't be a little," Greatheart said.

"I'll see you about half-past midnight," she said. "The night supervisor is my buddy and very *simpático*. We won't be disturbed. But you might have to fight her off later. She has eyes for you."

"The more the merrier," Greatheart said, and the nurse exited laughing.

His happiness didn't last long. Just after breakfast the following day, two police detectives entered his room. They didn't take long to get to the point of their visit.

"Your apartment was ripped off last night."

The burglary had been detected when the manager noticed that the door to Silver's apartment was partly open. He had reported this to the police, along with the information that the Copley painting was missing, the photographs and the furniture had been slashed, and the birds had been released out the windows.

Greatheart groaned and said, "You better question Ms. Regina Graves."

Regina, however, had a perfect alibi, if her friend wasn't lying. Greatheart thought he was, but there was no way of proving it.

The final blow was the discovery that the insurance on the

Copley had lapsed the day before its theft. He'd left it up to Regina to make the payment, and she had not done it. On purpose, no doubt.

"What else can happen?" he said to himself.

He found out after lunch, when the president of the American branch of Acme visited him. Mr. Micawber exuded joviality, but the small eyes above the big nose were disconnected from the hearty speech and the florid gestures of good fellowship. Mr. Micawber was the son of the founder of Acme, an Australian immigrant who had started business in a small way. Roadrunner traps were his speciality, but these never seemed to work, and he had gone bankrupt in a short time. Then he had gotten a loan (from a Mafia loanshark, it was rumored), and gone into other lines. When he died, he had left millions to his only heir. Mr. Micawber owned many industries and businesses, but the Acme Zeppelin Company was his pride, the nearest thing to his heart, aside from his daughter. It was he who insisted that the symbol of Acme be a stylized roadrunner. This was probably to illustrate the humble beginnings of his fortune. Every one of his zeppelins bore on its upper and lower vertical stabilizers a huge roadrunner.

Mr. Micawber—who never just walked—swept into the room. With him were his omnipresent bodyguards and his beautiful titian-haired secretary.

"Don't rise, my boy," Mr. Micawber said. "We don't stand on ceremony."

Greatheart thought his words were ill-chosen, but a mere employee did not reproach the great Micawber.

"How are you, son?"

Silver opened his mouth to reply, but Mr. Micawber swept on. "Terrible thing, terrible thing! Ninety million dollars lost when the AZ-8 crashed! Fortunately, we have insurance, and anyway there's no use crying over spilt milk."

Greatheart couldn't restrain himself. He said, "I wouldn't say that a hundred people killed and fifty badly injured are exactly in the category of spilt milk."

"They were insured," Mr. Micawber said. "One has to take the historical perspective on such things, not to mention the financial and fiscal. All flesh is doomed to become grass, or its equivalent, and in the economy of nature, in its statistical function, what's the difference if one dies now or later?

"Anyway, my boy, I'm not here to discuss philosophy—a time and place for everything and this isn't the time or the place. Now, we've been reading the reports of the piracy, and what I'd like to know, son, is if the reports are true?"

"You have my statement," Greatheart said. "I told the truth. What is this, anyway? What are you getting at?"

"It's this, my boy. When you became an officer of Acme Zeppelin, when you took the oath at Friedrichshafen, you swore to defend your honor, the honor of the company, and to hold its interests close to you heart. Closer, we might add, than your own."

"I don't remember saying that," Greatheart said. "And I memorized the oath; I can recite it to you letter-perfect now."

"In effect, we mean!" Micawber cried. "In effect, my boy! The point is that we have been considering the foul piracy of the AZ-8 and what might have been done to thwart it. There is some excuse for the AZ-10 being taken so easily, though not much, we assure you! There was no excuse for the AZ-15's ripoff, since, once warned, twice armed! Or is it forearmed? Anyway, the captain of the AZ-15 was discharged . . ."

"I thought he retired," Greatheart said.

"That was for public consumption, my boy. PR, you know, the backbone of the business. No, son, he was discharged, but even so he was given his pension. The company has a heart, believe us. Besides, he would have sued if he hadn't gotten it.

"But your case is different. You were the officer in charge when this regrettable business occurred, and so . . ."

"The captain is responsible, whether he's in the bridge or not."

"Don't interrupt, son. The captain is dead, as you well know, and so you as captain ex tempore assume the responsibility. And a captain who permits his charge to be so easily pirated is no captain of mine, son."

"I can't believe this," Greatheart said. "The captain died after the ship was taken. I was never in any sense the senior officer. Besides, what could I do?"

"You could have screened out the thugs posing as passengers and crew members. And if that failed, as it did, you could have resisted. Now, we are making no accusations . . . do you have that?" he said to the secretary, who was writing on her tablet. She nodded, and Mr. Micawber said, ". . . no accusations. But there was undoubtedly complicity . . ."

"Get out, you phony bastard!" Greatheart shouted.

"A good officer never loses his temper," Micawber said loftily. "In any event, you are no longer an employee of Acme Zeppelin. For one thing, and this should suffice, the loss of your leg disqualifies you as an airship officer. You know the rules.

As for a desk job, we think not, son. Trust is everything—trust and loyalty—and while we make no official accusations, or, indeed, unofficial, trust is in doubt and loyalty seems to have been lacking. Besides, you have just insulted me, and that is reason enough for your instant dismissal."

"You're branding me a crook without the slightest evidence!" Greatheart said. "You're crazy! And a crook, too!"

"You lack good judgment, as well as a leg," Micawber said. "No one talks to Bendt Micawber like that, son. So, I bid you adieu. But don't worry about your hospital bills or your prosthetic leg. The company honors its obligations."

Micawber swept out; his employees walked out.

5.

"You haven't got a leg to stand on," the lawyer said. "Oops, sorry!"

"Then old B.M. is going to get away with this?"

"We'd have to take it all the way to the Supreme Court," Seymour Sheester said. "And I doubt that it'd rule that Acme would have to hire you back. You do have a definite physical disability which might interfere with your ability to operate the ship and safeguard your passengers. As for Micawber's accusations, you have no witnesses of your own to that. The old man is crazy, and he thinks everybody's a crook because he's one. But he functions one hundred percent; he's crazy like a coyote. No, you don't have a case. What's worse, you can't get on another airship line as an operations officer. They have the same rule about disabilities. Besides, though there's no way to prove it, they will honor Micawber's blackball. Good business, you know."

"And all because I didn't commit suicide by resisting that gang," Greatheart said. "I hate that bunch of crooks, and I hate Regina. But I hate Micawber even more."

"Hate buys no cookies," Sheester said cheerfully. He stood up, held out his hand, and said, "Sorry I can't do anything for you. What do you intend to do, by the way?"

"Well, I can't play football," Greatheart said. He shook Sheester's hand and then walked to the window. He stared out of it at a landscape as bleak as his future. Rocks and cactus and rattlesnakes.

After a while, he turned, slowly because it was only a week after his leg had been fitted to the stump, and began walking slowly back and forth. At the tenth circuit, he stopped. A man was looking into his room. The man came in holding a bird cage and a slip of paper. The cage held two huge ravens.

"Put it on the table," Greatheart said, and he reached out for the receipt.

"You don't seem surprised," the attendant said.

Greatheart laughed and said, "No. My grandmother wrote me that she was sending them. She's too old to come see me. She's a hundred and one years old."

The attendant said, "She lives on an Indian reservation?"

"Grandma is a full-blooded Sioux. I used to stay with her during the summer vacations when I was a kid. It was great fun. I played with the reservation kids, and they taught me to speak Sioux. Grandma taught me bird language."

Seeing the attendant's brows go up, Greatheart said, "Grandma was a sorceress, or anyway she claimed to be. She had a way with birds, and she said I had her gift. Her house was full of birds, and birds were always hanging around the place."

He grinned and said, "No wonder she was called White Spot."

"You'll have to keep them in the cage," the attendant said. "If you wasn't in the rehabilitation ward, you wouldn't be allowed to have them at all."

Greatheart uttered some croaks, and the ravens, looking alert, croaked back.

"What'd they say?" the attendant said, grinning.

"Quote. To hell with the rules. Unquote."

The attendant said, "I gotta go now."

Greatheart opened the cage, and the big glossy black birds flew onto his shoulder and pecked softly at his ear.

"Let's see," he said quietly, " what'll I call you? We don't want to use your true names, buddies. No one's going to get your number. How about Huggin and Muggin? After the two ravens that sat on the great god Odin's shoulders?"

The birds croaked at him, and he said, "You like them, heh? O.K. Back into your cage. We'll obey the rules until I get this leg working, and then we're getting out, and we're going to make some rules of our own."

They croaked twice and flew back into the cage. Greatheart did not bother to close its door.

6.

A month later, Greatheart Silver sat in the office of the manager of the Phoenix branch of Acme Security-Southwest. "Welcome aboard," Mr. Spood said. "Here's a toast to your career." He and Silver lifted their glasses of fine Kentucky bourbon and poured the amber down the hatches. Mr. Spood was always toasting something or other. Perhaps this explained the lack of security in his own office. It had been easy for Silver to let himself in, bypassing the electronic alarm circuits, and to reprogram the data and communications computer. When Mr. Spood's secretary had typed out an inquiry for validation of Silver's references the next day, she had received full confirmation. The central clearing computer in New York had replied—or seemed to—that Greatheart Silver's references were in order and that Mr. Micawber himself had taken the trouble to O.K. them.

"Tough luck about the leg and all that," Mr. Spood had said. "But evidently old B.M. thinks highly of you. And what he thinks highly of, I approve most heartily. If I didn't, I'd lose my job, haw, haw!"

Now he was saying, "Ordinarily we wouldn't hire a handicapped person, but then what the hell, you aren't really handicapped, are you? I saw what you can do with that electromechanical marvel of a leg. And those birds! Man, you're going to be a gem! Who'd ever think of private-eyeing with trained birds? Nobody'd suspect that a raven was taking pictures of them and transmitting their conversation? Right?"

"Right," Silver said.

"I'm putting you under the charge of Fenwick Phwombly. He's an old guy, older than he says he is. That dyed hair and those contact lenses don't fool me. But he's an excellent operative, though you may find him to be a little eccentric. Anyway, here's a toast to him and you and Acme Security-Southwest, sometimes referred to by employees in less happy moments as AS-S, haw, haw!"

"Here's to justice," Greatheart said.

7.

Silver trained with Phwombly for two months before he was given the grade of Junior A-man. By then, Silver, who learned fast, had mastered more than the rudiments of investigation. Experience taught him much, but listening to old Phwombly was worth ten years of practice.

Phwombly was very tall and somewhat stooped, which was to be expected of a man who had to be in his late eighties. He was half deaf but too proud to wear a hearing aid. His makeup almost concealed the wrinkles, and his huge curved nose had no broken veins, except in certain lights. His eyes behind their thick trifocal contact lenses burned as if he were only twenty

RYE

years old. He was spry, too, except sometimes in the morning when his arthritis was "acting up." And sometimes, when he forgot himself, his natural voice issued from his throat. This was dry and brittle, but when it slipped by him, he would say, "Time to wet the whistle," and he'd pull a flask, a relic of the 1920s, out of his coat pocket.

If the flask happened to be empty, Greatheart remedied the lack. The hollow spaces in his leg were handy for carrying booze and salami sandwiches. They were handy for other things, too. But first things first.

"Greatheart, heh?" Phwombly said on being introduced. "An Indian name, no doubt, since your grandma is Sioux?"

"That's what everybody thinks," Silver said. "Truth is, it's of British origin, and it was given to me by my father. He was a great reader, and his favorite book was John Bunyan's *Pilgrim's Progress*. He named me after a character in it, Mr. Greatheart. He was the one who helped the wife and children of Christian after he'd deserted them."

"Yeah?" Phwombly said. "I missed John, though I read about his brother Paul when I was a kid. I didn't have much time for reading after 1914. Been pretty busy since. You might not believe it, son, but I was a big shot, especially in the thirties and forties. Wealthy, too. I had a private gold mine in Central America. My Indian bloodbrothers supplied me with gold so I could carry on my battle with the evil that lurks in the hearts of men. I operated outside the law because that was the only way to get things done, to ensure that true justice triumphed. I was a quick-change artist, too, the best. Oh, Doc Ravage and the Arachnid and the Phantom Dick and the Punisher were good, but compared to me they were bumblers. I musta done away with a thousand or so crooks, high and low, though I was more humane than the Arachnid. He musta slain his thousands. In fact, between me and Doc and those others, I'm surprised that there were any criminals left in New York City. But no matter how many went to jail or died, their number increased daily. It was like there was a crook factory operating day and night."

"Social conditions breed them," Greatheart said.

"Social conditions, hell!" the old man said. "Didn't you ever read Sartre? That's one guy I read a few years ago when I was on relief and didn't have anything else to do. Every man is responsible for his own fate, his own destiny, his own character. Social conditions are just an excuse to screw somebody. How do you account for so many rich men being crooks if social conditions make crooks?"

"Psychological conditions?"
"Then there isn't any free will. But I know, from my own experience, that every man has free will. I battled, and I lost. My Indians decided to rip me off, and they kept the gold for themselves. I was broke, and I was too old to get a job doing the only other thing I was good at. I was a great flier, you know, and the best damn spy—I don't care what they say about Agent 8-•—in World War I. I served the Czar in the first two years of the war, and he gave me a family heirloom, a ring worth thousands."
"Where is it?" Silver said.
"I had to hock it! When the funds from it ran out, I took odd jobs here and there. Then I went on welfare, me, that did more for my country, for the world, than any ten men you can name."
"How'd you get *this* job?"
"I told the manager I'd turn him in as a drunk if he didn't hire me. So, here I am, back in the harness again. Though in a small way. There's a McDonald's. Turn in, time for chow. Me, eating at a hamburger joint, me, who once dined at the most expensive restaurants in Manhattan! Me, who belonged to the ultra-exclusive Radium Club!"
"Listen," Greatheart said, "You surely can't be . . .?"
Phwombly burst loose with a mocking maniacal laugh that chilled Greatheart's skin.
"Yes, I'm the only one who knows the evil that men have in their hearts!"
Greatheart was stunned with awe.

8.

At 15:40 of a Thursday, Phwombly burst into Silver's office. "Forget about your reports! We've just gotten an assignment! It's what I've been expecting and what I've been longing for! Tomorrow and tomorrow and tomorrow craps on this petty pace . . . but no more, Silver! The day I've been waiting for is almost at hand!"
The old fellow was shaking, though Silver didn't know if it was from excitement or incipient palsy. Or both.
"Where and what is it?" he said calmly.
"It's the town of Shootout, and the Blimp Gang may be planning to rob it. And there will be others there, many others!"
Greatheart didn't press him for details. Phwombly was always reluctant to give out more than minimum information. He claimed that subordinates shouldn't know more than a piece

of the plan. Then, if they fell into the hands of the enemy, they couldn't give the enemy much. Greatheart agreed that this was, in certain situations, a good policy. But it had puzzled him how it applied to divorce cases and skip tracings that had been their only jobs so far.

He and Phwombly got their equipment together, loaded it into a motorhome, and drove out of Phoenix to the southeast. Shootout, he knew—everybody knew—was the scene of the famous Kayo Corral Gunfight. Marshall Watts Upp and his brothers, Doc Hyloday, and Basher Missters had shot it out with the infamous Clinton Brothers. The town was in the midst of its annual celebration of this event.

The motorhome was equipped with air-conditioning, a small laboratory, a smaller lavatory, bunks, a shortwave radio, TV, a kitchen, a bar, and a radar set. Silver drove while Phwombly sat at the bar and muttered of past glories. Then he broke into curses when Huggins decided to use his shoulder instead of the papers Silver had laid out for the ravens. "If you don't housebreak those .*!+& birds, I'll let them have it with both my .45's!"

"Don't swear around them," Silver said. "They've picked up enough bad habits already."

Phwombly went back to muttering while Silver tried to figure out what might be happening at their destination.

The bank at Buzzard Gulch, a tiny cowtown near Shootout, had been robbed that morning by the Blimp Gang. Since the bank was under the protection of Acme, Silver had expected to be sent there to investigate. Instead, he and Phwombly were going to Shootout. Maybe the boss believed that the bank there, also an Acme client, was the next target. He and Phwombly would try to lock the barn door before the horse was stolen.

But the old man seemed to have some inside information. He acted, almost, and maybe indeed, as if he were going to a long-awaited rendezvous. Oh, well, he'd just wait and see what happened.

Meanwhile, his idea of getting into the Acme superorganization and exposing Micawber's crookedness didn't seem such a good one now. In his desire for vengeance he had overlooked the fact that it might take years to work up to a spot where he could get the goods on old B.M. Actually, he might never have the opportunity.

However, he did want to catch the men who were responsible for the deaths of those on the AZ-8 and the loss of his leg. He was now even hotter to get them than to face Micawber. And now it looked as if he would be given the chance.

He did have one item of information which had slipped out of Phwombly. One night they'd been following a woman in a divorce case. The woman, Mrs. Spood, in fact, had gone into a tavern. Silver and Phwombly had taken a table close to her and to preserve appearances had had to drink a lot. Phwombly, after seven double bourbons, had started talking to himself. It was then that Silver learned the identity of the Mad Fokker. Phwombly, in his dialog with himself, had stated that the criminal had to be the man known only by the code name of 8-•. This man, once the foremost aviator and spy of the Great War—after Phwombly, of course—had done great deeds. He'd shot down more enemy planes than Richthofen and his whole Flying Circus, 1238, to be exact, but he was given no official credit because of his espionage activities. Besides, it was well known that 8-• was insane, though usually quite competent, and that had to be kept a secret from the folks at home.

And so, when the Armistice came, 8-• was carted off to an asylum and locked up. He'd been seeing so many monsters, supposedly created by the great German genius, Herr Doktor Krogers, his mortal enemy, that he could no longer be ignored. His delusions had always operated in favor of the Allies, true. When he shot a bunch of German planes, which he thought were flying leopard-men or radio-controlled vampire bats, he was hurting nobody but the enemy. Now, though, it was peacetime and he couldn't be allowed loose. He'd be mothballed until the next war to save democracy.

The next war came, but the existence of 8-• was forgotten. The new generation of generals and paper-shufflers knew nothing of him. Besides, he was too old.

"That's the way they treat vintage heroes," Phwombly had muttered, the tip of his huge nose almost in his bourbon. "I don't blame old 8-• at all for escaping from his padded cell and taking to crime. What? Spend all his life in a puzzle factory? After what he did for his country? And what's he supposed to do after he gets out? Go on welfare, like I did? Yes, that's him all right. There's only one other man who could fly a plane like he does, and he's sitting at this table. So it must be him. Carry on, old fighter! Too bad I have to track you down and put you away again! But that's life! Duty calls! The minions of evil must pay through the nose, or whatever, for what they've done. But why? Ah, yes, but why?"

Either the booze, or the philosophy, or both, had gotten to him. He slumped over, and Silver had had to carry him out before the management called the cops. Mrs. Spood had run away with her lover to Mexico the next day.

9.

Shootout was a small village of about five hundred permanent population, most of whom existed on the tourist trade. Its business section was two blocks of buildings constructed to look as they had in 1881, when the famous gunfight had taken place. The city hall and the Canary Cage Theater were the only original buildings left. The Boot Hill cemetery (one dollar per customer at the entrance) was outside the town. It contained a number of wooden crosses bearing amusing commemorations of the sudden demise of citizens during its heyday: HUNG BY MISTAKE. MURDERED BY THE UPP GANG (put up by supporters of the villainous Clinton boys). HERE LIES SOAPY SUE, SHE GAVE HER LAST FAVORS TO DEATH. DEALT FROM THE BOTTOM OF THE DECK AND NOW HE'S IN THE BOTTOM. DON'T LAUGH, STRANGER, AS I AM SO SHALL YOU BE. STRUCK IT RICH BUT WAS KICKED BY A MULE.

Actually, most of the Hill's inhabitants had died of dysentery, syphilis, or liver cirrhosis, but these were not glamorous enough to be noted. And, in fact, most of the graves were empty. The bodies had been moved to another location for sanitary reasons. What the tourists didn't know wouldn't hurt them.

Shootout this October night was a lively place, crowded with visitors, many dressed in Western costume, the streets decorated with flags and pennants and posters. Greatheart drove through the narrow pedestrian-packed street slowly to the other end of town and parked on the side of the road. Phwombly had phoned for reservations at various motels but had been informed that there wasn't a room available. If they had not had the motorhome, they would have been obliged to find quarters in Buzzard Gulch, seven miles away.

They washed up and then had a few drinks. Presently, they heard a car pull up by them, a door slam, and a voice call. Phwombly admitted a tall white-haired gray-eyed old man wearing thick spectacles. He was dressed as an old-time Western lawman. This was just what he was.

"Pete Ruse, sheriff of Buzzard Gulch," he said, extending a vein-ridged hand. After accepting a drink, he told them all he knew about the holdup in his hometown.

"I was taking my noon nap when they struck," he said. "I'm

getting up there, you know, and now some people are saying I'm too old for my job. Hell, it coulda happened to anyone. Anyway, I heard the commotion and ran out in my longjohns. By then the Mad Fokker had taken off with the money, and his confederates—ain't any of you from the South, are you?—was ten miles away. They was riding motorcycles. I radioed to the state police, but the Mad Fokker chased them down a gulch with his machineguns. The other Blimpers abandoned their choppers, they was stolen, anyway, and took off in the blimp. By the time the police copters got there, the blimp was gone. Probably deflated it, put it in a truck, and drove off to their HQ. That Mad Fokker, he's really something! He landed in a street that ain't wide enough for two Packards side by side, turned the plane to face the bank, let loose a couple of bursts, incidentally taking off the manager's toupee, ran in, took the money from his confederates—no offense if you're Southrons—and ran out. Slick as a baboon's hind end."

"We think the gang is planning to rob the bank here during the festivities," Greatheart said.

Ruse's eyes lit up, though not very brightly. "Yeah? We'll see about that! Pete Ruse always gets his man. I'm planning on retiring soon, and I don't intend to let those .*/+!ing .as!*/! spoil my record! Whatta you say we go into town now and look things over?"

They rode back in Ruse's 1946 Cadillac, a collector's item which Ruse meant to sell to finance his retirement. Ruse parked by a fire plug. They got out, leaving the ravens sitting in the back seat on a newspaper, and started to enter a Chinese restaurant. Ruse stopped suddenly to stare at two old men on horses riding by. The one in front was a white man with long white hair. He wore a black mask and white neo-Western clothes. His horse was a beatup nag that must have been beautiful when young. Behind him rode an old Indian, a red band around his forehead.

"Hell, that *can't* be!" Ruse said. "Not the Long Ranger and Pronto! They wouldn't dare. They know I'm liable to be here! Naw! They must be tourists!"

Phwombly peered across the street, but the two riders weren't the object of his scrutiny. "That garbage truck!" he said, clutching Silver's arm. "Parked by the Hell For Leather Saloon!"

"What about it?" Silver said.

"Scorpio!" Phwombly said. "That S.O.B. uses garbage trucks in his operations! His headquarters was beneath an incinerator plant when he operated in New York!"

Phwombly rubbed his hands with delight—or he was restoring the circulation—and said, "Yeah, my theory's working out! They're all together now! Too old to do their foul deeds by themselves; too old to get respect from the young punks any more! So they're putting their old white heads together!"

Silver was beginning to see what Phwombly had in mind, but he didn't believe it. Was the poor old fellow a victim of senility?

He pulled his partner into the Ga See Chow Restaurant. Pete Ruse followed them in. It was a large place, but it was jammed. The lights were dim, and the air was curtained and stinking with the fumes of tobacco, Acapulco Golds, and Tia Juana Merdas. Though it held at least a hundred customers, it was strangely quiet. Everybody seemed to be whispering, and even the clatter of silverware on plates was absent. The proprietor, an aged Chinese (and pigtailed!) told a waiter to bring out a table for them. This required that all the other tables be moved closer together. The customers got up and shoved their tables nearer to their neighbors, though their expressions revealed that they didn't like doing so. For a while, the place sounded as if a landslide was coming down on them. Then silence returned.

"I don't like this place," Silver said. "It makes me nervous."

"Are you kidding?" Phwombly said. "This is where everybody's hung out!"

Silver shook his head but didn't say anything. The old man was too proud of his knowledge of up-to-date slang.

They sat down, the backs of their chairs against those of the people behind them. The two Acme agents ordered chop suey, bird's nest soup, thousand year old eggs, and rice wine. Pete Ruse ordered a steak and beans. Phwombly stared at the ancient Chinese who was taking their orders. When the old man, who seemed hard of hearing, bent over near Phwombly, Phwombly sniffed loudly. After the waiter had left, he whispered to Silver, "Smell his breath? That's Doctor Sen Sen or my name isn't . . ."

He put his hand over his mouth to hush himself. Ruse said, "Who's Sen Sen?"

"One of the most dastardly villains that ever infected the fair face of earth, the athlete's foot of mankind," Phwombly said. "But did you pipe the proprietor? Notice the tall forehead and the green eyes behind those thick glasses? If that isn't the archfiend, Doctor Fyu-men Chew, I'll eat my hat."

"It might turn out to be better food than this stuff," Ruse said disgustedly as their orders were placed before them.

GA SEE CHOW

Phwombly shushed him, and Ruse was silent until the waiter left. "Whatever these guys are, they're rotten cooks."

Phwombly cupped his right ear and said, "Crooks?"

"COOKS!" Ruse bellowed, and everybody in the restaurant leaped up, their hands under their jackets. They glared around and then, somewhat sheepishly, sat down. Phwombly got up and strode to the big counter on which the food was placed for the waiters. He peered into the kitchen for a minute and returned, looking somewhat groggy.

"The opium smoke's so thick in there you could get constipation just breathing it," he said.

He sat down, shaking his head. "It wasn't easy to see them through that cloud. But there they were. Doctor Terminal, Won Fang, and Doctor Negative, archfiends all, masters of men's minds, cooking in a chop suey joint! Enough to make you cry, and I haven't cried since I was five years old. Well, there *was* the time when my radio show was cancelled . . . never mind that.

"Anyway, one of them looked me in the eye, and I saw a gleam that bodes nobody good. And the one I thought was Won Fang, well, a big purple spider slipped out of his pocket while he was frying hamburgers. Won Fang used to breed mutated snakes and lizards and spiders, you know. Poisonous all. I'll bet that spider was left over from an old job."

He sat down, saying, "Don't touch the food until I check it out," he reached into his coat and pulled out a set of vials. While Phwombly mixed their contents in a water glass, which he'd emptied on the floor, Silver looked around the restaurant. Phwombly wasn't the only one testing the food.

Phwombly sat back with a sigh and said, "It's O.K. I didn't think they'd try to poison us anyway. Even *they* couldn't get away with that in a place like this. Besides, it'd attract attention from the local fuzz and maybe ruin their operation."

Ruse took a bite of the steak and said, "What the hell?" and spit the piece out onto his plate.

"Oh, yeah," Phwombly said. "The chemicals ruin the food. We'll have to order again."

"I can't afford to pay twice!" Ruse said. "You don't know how little I get paid! And what with inflation . . ."

"We'll put it on our expense account," Silver said. "Have another drink."

They waited a long time for the second order, because almost everybody had sent the first dinner back. Meanwhile, Silver listened in on the conversations at the tables. He pressed a button in his prosthetic leg, and a tiny antenna slid out of the irradiated plastic. It missed the minute hole he'd left in his trouser leg for its admission and tore a hole in it. He cursed—the pants were from an expensive Beverly Hills shop—and then he put a tiny speaker in his ear. This was attached to a slim wire which ran under his clothes to an attachment on his leg. It was disguised as a hearing aid, but he doubted it was fooling anyone. Almost everyone had hearing aids in their ears; the place could have been mistaken for a convention of deaf people. He leaned over and whispered to Phwombly that he should talk very softly.

"WHAT?" Phwombly said.

Silver wrote a note and handed it to him. Phwombly, after reading it, growled, "I already knew that. You think I'm wet behind the ears?"

It was necessary to point the antenna directly at the table to be eavesdropped, so Silver had to go through some strange contortions. But nobody acted as if they even knew of Silver's existence.

Phwombly reached out and put his hand on Silver's wrist. Silver was annoyed by his nervous tapping, and besides he didn't want people to get the wrong idea about their relationship. Just as he started to speak harshly to the old man, he caught on. Phwombly was tapping out a message in code. He wanted Silver to use Morse to tell him what he was hearing.

The other customers must have observed him. All of a sudden, almost everybody stopped talking, and wrists and palms were being fingered staccato. Pete Ruse, looking around, said, "Say, what kind of a place is this?"

Silver cursed again and pointed the antenna at one of the only two tables at which men were still talking. The diners there were dressed in gray flannel suits, white shirts, and black ties. It wasn't hard to figure out that they were FBI agents. Silver reported their talk and Phwombly tapped back, "Yes. And the three old geezers with the young punks are Dan Fooler, the greatest G-man of them all, Valiant Kilgore, second-greatest, and G-Double-7, third greatest. They must have come out of retirement for this. Kilgore, by the way, is Won Fang's archnemesis.

"Word's got around that all the big evil ones are here, all members of the Blimp Gang. Nobody told me about this, but then they know that I don't have to be told to know. It's the gathering of the clans, boy, the big roundup, the last stand, the grand finale!"

Silver swiveled to zero the antenna in on a group of dark heavy-set men eating spaghetti and drinking wine at a table in the corner. They were talking, but the language, though it sounded like Italian, was almost unintelligible.

Phwombly came to his rescue. "They must be speaking a dialect, Chicago Sicilian. The big guy who's drinking Alka-Seltzers is Joe 'Sour' Lemono. He's the head of WAX, Western Auxiliary Board. That's the West Coast branch of the Mafia, which many claim doesn't exist, but I know, I know. I also know why they're here. The Blimp Gang has had the effrontery to muscle in on their territory, and WAX is here to rub them out. The grapevine says the dons, East Coast dons, are unhappy with Lemono, and if he doesn't come through, it's *finito* for him. In fact, those thugs at the two tables by his are from EBB, the Eastern Business Board. They're here to rub him out if he doesn't come through."

Phwombly rubbed his hands and said, "It's the big shape-up, all right."

He stopped and then noted excitedly, "Hey, that bunch in the opposite corner!"

"Use the Morse," Silver said.

Phwombly ignored him, saying, "Those guys must be the CIA. See the gent with the white moustache? That has to be Secret Agent Ecks. No man has ever known his true face. Unfortunately, he's getting forgetful, and he can't recall it either. I say, 'What's the difference?' He never used it anyway."

"How'd you recognize him if he always has a new face?" Silver tapped.

"It's because every time I see him he has changed his features."

While Silver was trying to figure this out, three men entered the restaurant. One was almost seven feet tall. Though he must have been in his late seventies, he had a physique which wouldn't have disgraced Tarzan. Behind him came two men in wheelchairs. They were trying to get through the door at the same time but were wedged together. They were hollering insults and striking each other on the head with canes. The blows, despite their feebleness, were bringing blood. One old man was a thin fellow with the sharp foxlike features seen in cartoons of big-shot shysters. The other was incredibly hairy, massively muscled, and had a face that looked like a reconstruction of the Java Apeman.

The giant stood watching them, a look of long suffering on his handsome face.

"Doc Ravage!" Phwombly transmitted. "And his two aides, "Porkchop" and "Chimp," everybody calls them. Last I heard, they were in a nursing home. But Doc's brought them out for the battle of the century! I told you this is the big one!"

He quivered with delight.

The two very senior citizens suddenly quit caning each other. Their gnarled hands dived under the blankets over their legs. The blankets must have concealed some controls. Loud explosions deafened the diners, fire and smoke shot out of the rear of the chairs, frightening everybody, and the two vehicles surged forward. But the rockets propelling them only wedged them more tightly. In addition, they tilted forward and cast their occupants sprawling before the feet of the giant. He stepped forward, his face showing extreme irritability, and kicked one of the chairs. It flew out into the street, knocking down an old lady. He returned, picked up the two raving oldsters by their coat collars, one in each hand, and replaced them in the chairs. These were somewhat crumpled, and he had to straighten the wheel of one with his bare hands. Muscles like piano wires bunched like coiling pythons under his bronzed skin and tore his shirt along the arms, around the chest, and on the back.

He went out to the sidewalk, helped the old lady up, wrote her a check—which she threw in his face—and returned to the restaurant. "You two punchdrunks make any more trouble," he said loudly, "and I'll ship you back to your knitting, cheating at cards, and feeling up great-grandmas! *I'm fed up*!"

The oldsters grinned shamefacedly and wheeled their chairs behind him as he walked majestically toward the proprietor. But Chimp banged Porkchop once over the head with his cane while a table was being brought in. Doc turned around at the thud of wood on bone, looked at Porkchop, who had slumped down unconscious, and said, "What's wrong now?"

"He's getting old," Chimp said gleefully. "He's always falling asleep. Why, only the other day, he had this nurse backed up into a corner, what a peach, couldn't have been a day over sixty, and he started sawing wood while he was ripping off her dress. I had to finish it for him, haw, haw!"

"It's all in the head," Doc said, "which, from what I hear, is where you spend most of your time anyway. Shape up, Chimp, or be shipped back!"

The manager wiped the blood off the two, and Chimp revived Porkchop by throwing beer in his face. Porkchop straightened up, muttering, "Your Honor, this woman lies when she says I promised to marry her," saw Chimp's grin, and said, "Wait'll I get you!"

At that moment a scuffle broke out between a man with a heavy Russian accent and a man with a heavy English accent. Apparently, the fight had come about because of the closeness of the tables. Due to this, the Russian had mistakenly transmitted his message to the Englishman at the next table instead of to his own Russian partner. Whatever it was he'd communicated, he'd angered the Englishman. The latter was a tall gray-haired man with a deeply lined face and bloodshot eyes behind bifocals. The waiters hauled the two away from each other, and after some low-voiced exchange, the two bowed to each other and returned to their seats.

"Why," Phwombly said, "I do believe that's Jim Binde! Secret Agent 00-something or other, I forget. What's he doing here? Wait a minute! I know! One of those cooks must be Doctor Negative! He was supposed to have been asphyxiated when Jim dropped that load of guano on him. But I know he got out and escaped the atomic blast afterward, too! So, young Binde came here to chalk up the final score with his old enemy. And that explains why the Russians are here. That gray-haired guy he grappled is an agent from the terrorist organization. Used to be called SMERDE but now it's ISPANAZHNYENIYE. They're here to end an old feud, too. And that explains why the CIA and the FBI are here. They're keeping an eye on the foreign agents."

"What about that bunch of Chinese at that table in the corner?" Silver said.

"I should have known. They must be agents from the Hwing Ding, a Chinese terrorist group. They're here to pop off the archfiends Fyu-men Chew, Won Fang, Sen Sen, Negative, and maybe Terminal. All these S.O.B.'s gave China plenty of trouble, you know. And Ecks and Fooler are watching them, too, you can bet. Oh, boy, oh, boy!"

The waiter started to serve them, and they quit communicating. When he'd left, Phwombly brought out his vials again. Pete Ruse, whose stomach was rumbling, said, "You dummy! You'll have to order again!"

Phwombly glared at him and said, "I forgot I'd been served the first time. So much going on, you know."

"Let's get out of here," Ruse said. He shoved his chair back and stood up. "You ain't going to learn anything more. These guys are on to what's going on. There's a good steak house down the street. The smell of Chinese food makes me sick, anyway."

As they went out onto the street, two men entered the restaurant. One was a middle-sized white-haired man with thick spectacles. Behind them were two gray eyes that looked as cold as wintertime windowglass after a heavy frost. The man behind him was goateed and in the costume of a Kentucky colonel. A patent medicine bottle stuck out of a pocket of his coat.

Phwombly chuckled and said, "Dick Bendsome, the Punisher himself. And Doc Barker."

"For a minute, I thought Barker was Colonel Sanders," Silver said.

"He's put on some weight," Phwombly said.

"For Chrissakes, let's eat," Pete Ruse said. "If I don't eat regular, I get irregular."

10.

After dinner the three drove back to the motorhome, which they then drove back into town. After Silver parked it by another fire plug, they settled down to observe the passersby. The windows in the rear and on the sides could be polarized with a push of a button, permitting them to see without being seen. The first thing they observed was a cop ticketing the motorhome for illegal parking.

"Don't worry," Pete Ruse said. "I can fix it."

Phwombly said, "There goes the garbage truck. Hey, if that isn't Scorpio himself driving it, I'm a dingbat! Look, his arm's dangling out the window, and his big ring's showing. I can see the scorpion on it from here. He used to wear a ring with an octopus on it, you know, and he called himself the Kraken. Then he lost the ring, or it was stolen, and he couldn't find another with an octopus on it so he bought one with a scorpion on it and changed his name.

"And, hey, there goes Dick Windworthy, the Arachnid. He's got on a good disguise, but he forgot to tell his helper, old Ram-Chandu, not to wear his turban. And he's also carrying his violin—takes it with him wherever he goes now. A dead giveaway. I heard he was so hard up he was putting on dark glasses and playing his violin on street corners while Ram-Chandu passed the cup around. Things sure aren't what they used to be."

Silver noted down the names and brief descriptions while the old man rambled on and on about the good old days. Once, Pete Ruse broke in with a discovery of his own.

"Cut me for a steer if that ain't Dude Onley, the Copper Kid! So he's here for the showdown, too! Look at him, a rambling wreck of a man who was as good as any mysterious avenger to ever roam the West righting wrongs. In his heyday he was called the Silver Simoleon. He'd put a silver dollar at the feet of a crook, and if he knew what was good for him he left the country."

Pete shook his head.

"Now he's called the Copper Kid. He went broke and he can't afford anything but pennies."

At the end of two hours, Silver had a long list of twenty positive identifications and a score of possibilities. There was George Luck, the Green Sheet, who'd been spotted because of a piece of green cloth sticking out of his pocket. There was Jed O'Hill, the Green Llama, once well known for his terrorization of evildoers and his bad spelling. After having spent some time in Tibet mastering the mystical techniques of the lamas, he returned to the States to use them on criminals. He always wore a long scarf which he used as a bullwhip, and he occasionally swallowed some radioactive salts which charged his body with several hundred thousand volts. Any crook who laid hands on him was electrocuted without due process of law. Once, he escaped from a dangerous cave by putting a light bulb in his mouth and illuminating his path.

There was Gary Adieu, Captain Lucifer, The Red Masquer, Donald Diabolo, the magician known as the Vermilion Mage, and Esteban Hatcher, the Luna Head. The latter was identified by the hatbox he was carrying. Phwombly said this contained Luna Head's robe and fishbowl-shaped metal helmet which concealed his features. Phwombly also tagged Richman Curtwell Van Debt, titled the Phantom Dick, and James "Bearcat" Guerdon, known as the Gargler.

"Hold on!" Phwombly said. "Can it be? Yes, it is! Another Englishman! Sir Daines Neighland Smythe, the foe of Doctor Fyu-men Chew! He's made up to look like a cowboy, but I'd know him every time. He always looks like Sherlock Holmes in disguise."

Silver decided he wouldn't ask how he knew that.

"And there's Secret Agent Operator No. 4 + 1," Phwombly said. "Note the ring with the skull cut on it? It contains a vial of poison gas. He also wears a rapier in his belt."

"Spotted 8-• or Blimp Kernel yet?" Silver said.

"I've never seen Kernel, not under that name, anyway. He must be one of the great ones, though, otherwise the other great ones wouldn't work for him. And I might not recognize 8-•. He's almost as good at disguises as I am. But I wonder where

Herr Doktor Krogers, 8-•'s great enemy, is? Surely he wouldn't stay away. Oh, oh! There goes Tony Winn, the Black Night Owl. Notice the dark glasses and white cane? He used to be blind but he secretly got a doctor to transplant a dead man's eyes, and now he just pretends to be blind. But *I know*! Say, what time is it?"

Phwombly had hocked his watch before he got hired by Acme and had never gotten around to redeeming it.

"Twenty minutes after midnight."

"No wonder I haven't seen Dirk Alone, Captain Nothing," Phwombly said. "He becomes invisible from midnight until dawn. It's a great help in combating crime, and it wouldn't hurt a bank robber, either," he added. Silver thought he detected an envious tone. "But it's a handicap, too. He obtained his power of invisibility accidentally, during an experiment with radioactivity. He has no control over it, and he's gotten into some embarassing situations because of that. He's been jailed three times for getting caught in the ladies' room. But he escaped every time."

They decided to drive back to their out-of-town parking space and call it a night. Ruse accepted their invitation to sleep in the motorhome. After an hour of trying to get to sleep, Silver went out to Ruse's car and lay down in its back seat. The snoring of the two old men and the complaints of the birds were too much for him.

11.

Late in the morning, after shaving and showering, all, including the birds, ate Wheaties, toast and hardboiled eggs. Phwombly and Ruse followed these with Geritol, vitamin pills, testosterone, and Ex-lax, and after a while everybody was ready to venture into town again. While Silver drove, his partner cleaned his two .45 automatics and Pete Ruse checked out his trusty six-shooter. This was routine, but Silver became alarmed when Phwombly brought out a box of other armament. His eyes bulged as he saw in the rear view mirror the hand grenades, smoke bombs, M-15 automatic rifles, a 60-mm bazooka, a blowgun with poison darts, wire nooses, throwing knives, machetes, a carton of plastic explosive, tomahawks, bear traps, and an 81-mm mortar. From another box Phwombly brought out the ammunition.

"What is this, World War III?" Silver yelled back.

"It's for the good of the world," Phwombly growled.

"My God, what are we into?" Silver said. "What about all

those innocent bystanders?"

"No one is innocent," Phwombly said, sighting an M-15.

"Come on!" Silver said. "If you can identify these crooks, tell the FBI. They'll arrest them, and that'll be it."

"For what?" Phwombly said. "They'd be sprung in an hour. You don't think any of those great brains have left any evidence behind them, do you? Or witnesses, either. And us few old timers aren't going to squeal. We're going to have the big showdown, finish it ourselves. We've always operated outside the law—most of us, anyway—and that's how we'll do it."

"That's the way I want it," Pete Ruse said, twirling the barrel of his revolver. "I ain't going to die in a drooling ward."

"But all those men, women, and children!" Silver said. "Think of them, the kids! How you going to get them out of the way?"

"The town'll clear out as soon as the shooting starts," Phwombly said. "We have to consider the good of all against the evil that might be done to a few. Somebody always gets hurt; it can't be helped. But it's justifiable."

Silver didn't reply because he could see the uselessness of argument. But he determined that as soon as the motorhome was parked, he would go straight to the sheriff of Shootout. But the sheriff would have to call in the state police and the National Guard to handle this situation. And meanwhile . . . maybe he could get to Dan Fooler, Val Kilgore, and G-Double-7, the FBI men. No, that wouldn't do any good. They were retired, here in an unofficial capacity, and doubtless as determined as the others to ignore legal restraints.

"All right," Silver said, though it wasn't all right. "Are you planning to initiate this or will you wait until the Blimp Gang robs the bank? *If* they do, that is. Maybe they're scared off."

"Not them!" Phwombly said, snorting. "The way I see it, they'll make their try about two or three in the morning,when the streets are cleared. There are two days left for the celebration, so it'll be tonight or the next night. We better get some sack time today, because we're going to be up all night."

"You'll be in jail, if I have anything to do with it," Silver muttered. He stopped the motorhome by the same fire plug. The sheriff's office was only a block away. He'd go to it as soon as he thought of an excuse to get away from his partner. Looking out the windshield, he saw the giant figure of Doc Ravage making his way through the crowd. Behind him, bellowing insults at each other, came Chimp and Porkchop in their

FIRST
NATIONAL

wheelchairs. Their heads were heavily bandaged, and Chimp must have suffered a recent blow in the nose, since it was taped over. Porkchop was wearing dark glasses, so the chances were that he had a black eye or two.

Silver stepped out and looked into the deep blue Arizona sky. "Oh, no," he said, and he turned to Phwombly, who was just stepping out of the vehicle.

"You're the only one who knows?" he said.

"That's right," Phwombly said, looking furtively around.

"If you knew that, why didn't you tell me?" Silver said. He pointed up at the three-winged airplane which was diving straight down, seemingly directly at them.

Phwombly said something but Silver couldn't hear him. The front of the bank blew out in a cloud of smoke and a pillar of noise.

12.

While Silver stared, stunned, Phwombly dived back into the motorhome. He emerged a few seconds later, wearing a broad-brimmed slouch hat and a long black cloak. In each hand was a huge .45 automatic. The midmorning sun, caught on his contact lenses, made his eyes blaze.

"Bring the arms and the ammo!" he screamed.

"How could I carry all that stuff?" Silver said. Pete Ruse jumped out of the door then, and he fell flat on his face. Cursing, he got up unsteadily on all fours and began feeling for his glasses, which had dropped off. Phwombly, stepping back to avoid the machine fire from the strafing Mad Fokker, put one heel on the spectacles. The glasses were broken, and so was Ruse's heart.

Silver hauled the protesting Ruse into the vehicle and got behind the wheel. He had to get the motorhome away. If the Fokker's bullets hit the ammunition in the box, goodbye, Silver, goodbye half the town.

But the crowd, screaming, shouting, was running by and before him. The only way he could move was to run over a dozen people. One thing he'd say for them; they were certainly cooperating with the Fokker in his desire to clear the street.

Doc Ravage was loping along toward the Canary Cage Theater. Behind him sped his two aides. Each held in a hand a tiny submachine pistol while the other hand steered the chair.

Doc Ravage was loping along toward the Canary Cage Theater. Behind him sped his two aides. Each held in a hand a tiny submachine pistol while the other hand steered the chair.

Evidently, the chairs were powered with electric motors; they had previously used their hands to propel them to conceal this fact.

They weren't going fast enough. The triplane, turning at the end of the street, had come back for another strafing run. Machinegun bullets, digging chunks out of the pavement, headed in a line for the wheelchairs.

Chimp, looking back, saw the inevitable. He shouted something at his partner. Flame shot out of the jet exhausts, and the chairs leaped ahead. Silver estimated they were doing fifty miles an hour when they veered off to the left, went out of control, bounced off the sidewalk, and soared through the big plateglass window on the front of the Chinese restaurant.

Doc Ravage looked out from the doorway in which he had taken refuge, saw what had happened, and came running. At the same time, Doc Barker, looking like a Colonel Sanders in pursuit of a chicken thief, ran after him. The bottle was out of his pocket, and it was evident that it held something more potent than snake oil. It had a soaked rag stuck in its neck, and Barker held a cigarette lighter in the other hand. Just as Doc dived through the window to rescue his aides, Barker lit the rag. He threw it after Doc, and suddenly flame and smoke issued from the window. Yells broke out then, and men poured out. Among them were three old Chinese, Doc Ravage, and his two helpers. The wheelchairs were bent but still serviceable, and the jets were flaming. They shot out through the doorway, passed the runners, hit the sidewalk on the opposite side, bounced and went through the plateglass window of a millinery shop. The explosion that followed littered the sidewalk with the EBB Gang and the wheelchair jockeys. Dozens of hats were still sailing like little flying saucers through the air.

By then the crowd had disappeared into buildings or the sidestreets. Silver wheeled the motorhome around as Pete Ruse tried to step out. Pete hit the pavement and rolled over and over until he hit the sidewalk. There he lay, stunned, but still clutching his six-shooter.

Silver completed his half-circle and accelerated down the street. Holes appeared in the windshield, and bullets screamed by him. Straight ahead, moving toward him on a collision course, was the garbage truck of Scorpio. A dozen men stood on its fenders and in the dump, all firing at him.

Silver desperately zigzagged the motorhome, which did not respond with the speed of a passenger car. A tire exploded, and the bumping and the force pulling the steering wheel to one side told him he had better abandon ship. He dived out just as the truck rammed into it. The men on the fenders and in the dump were hurled out onto the pavement, and none of them got up.

A white-haired old man crawled out from behind the wheel of the truck. His face, not much to begin with, had not been improved by its contact with the windshield. Then Silver saw the hideousness did not originate from his features. He wore a mask formed to represent the head of a scorpion. The mask had probably saved his face from being cut, though it had not kept him from being knocked half-conscious.

Silver, crouching, ran to him. The shadow of the triplane passed over him. The plane had almost hit the truck, making Silver wonder if it had been coming in for a landing but its pilot had been frustrated by the collision of the vehicles. Never mind. He had time to put Scorpio out of commission before the triplane could turn again.

Machineguns chattering and grenades exploding distracted him for a moment. He looked down the street and saw that the windows and doorways on both sides of the street bristled with flame-spurting rifles and machineguns. Something dark sailed up into the air, descended, and landed before the front of the Canary Cage Theater.

"Not another mortar!" Silver groaned and then was knocked flat by the explosion. The front of the theater collapsed in a black cloud.

Scorpio muttered something. Silver said, "What?" The old man rolled over, exposing a huge hypodermic syringe. Its needle was stuck in his left hip.

According to Phwombly, Scorpio used this to inject drugs into his victims. The drugs turned them into mindless monsters who murdered and mutilated at his command. Evidently, he'd meant to stick the needle into Silver. But on falling out he'd been, if not hoist by his own petard, needled with his own syringe.

"Get out of town," Silver said in Scorpio's ear. "And keep going until I tell you to stop. And don't obey anyone else's command."

"I obey," the old man said weakly. He struggled to his hands and knees and began crawling. Silver never did know how far he got. The triplane came back, the double line of bullets headed toward the motorhome. Silver ran as fast as he could with his mechanical leg, not very fast, and dived through an open window. He hit the floor just as the ammunition in the motorhome went off. The house shook, and the noise deafened him. Half-stunned, he rose and staggered to the doorway. The door had been blown off. So that was what had struck him, he thought dully. The smoke was clearing outside, and he could see the garbage truck across the street, lying on its side in front of the Hell for Leather Saloon. There was no evidence that there had ever been a motorhome, which was to be expected.

He also saw the triplane bouncing along on the street. The Mad Fokker had certainly cleared everything for a landing. Too well. Its wheels dropped into the big hole made by the explosion, and the fuselage, deprived of wheels, slid down the street. Its propeller bent and then fell off, and the three sets of wings were torn off, and the fuselage disintegrated. And there was the pilot, still holding on to the control stick, sliding along on his rear, smoke curling from the edges of the heels of his shoes and the bottoms of his pants.

Inertia being what it is, he finally stopped. His motionlessness did not last long. Impelled and propelled by the flames leaping from his pants, he leaped up and ran toward a horse trough and dived into it.

At that moment, the blimp appeared above the street.

13.

Silver was too numbed to feel alarmed. But he did have a slight sense of joy when he saw his two ravens circling below the blimp. He had thought they had perished in the explosion. Evidently, they'd had enough sense to get out of the motorhome sometime during the fight. He wished he was with them.

The pilot rolled out of the trough and lay on the ground. His face was still concealed by goggles and a handkerchief. Then he got shakily to his feet and turned, exposing a big hole in his pants and a somewhat blackened posterior. Two men ran out from a nearby doorway, shouting, "Got you, Mad Fokker!" One was Secret Service Agent Operative No. 4+1. The other, in a scarlet mask, undoubtedly was the Red Masquer. The pilot staggered away down the street. No. 4+1 stopped and grabbed his huge belt buckle. Silver watched, fascinated. Phwombly had said that he carried a sword in his belt, though he hadn't explained how he could wrap a sword around his middle. But there it came, sliding out of the sheath of the belt. There went his pants, too, dropping down to his ankles. The sword had cut through the belt and the belt straps. No. 4+1's coordination wasn't what it used to be.

Two more men came out of a shattered store front. One was the man Phwombly had pointed out as the Punisher. The other was Captain Lucifer. The Punisher held a peculiar weapon, a combination gun and knife. It held one .25 caliber bullet, which the Punisher never fired to kill. Instead, he always creased his enemy's head in the middle of the scalp, stunning him. So much for good intentions. Whether it was because of impaired eyesight or shakiness due to age, his aim was somewhat lower than he had intended. The bullet skimmed the flesh of the exposed posterior. The Mad Fokker, stung out of his lethargy, increased his speed. Bullets fired at him, seemingly from both factions, accelerated him even more. He disappeared into the bank.

The Punisher and Captain Lucifer, both breathing so hard that Silver could hear their wheezes across the street, ran back for shelter. No. 4+1, holding his pants up with one hand, was a step behind them.

At that moment the Arachnid ran out of a drugstore. He had somehow found time to put on a disguise, but Silver recognized him from the ring he wore, a ring bearing a scarlet spider in alto relief. His face was made up to look like that of the Wicked Witch of the West after Dorothy's house dropped on it. It was supposed to scare his enemies, but Silver imagined that they were of sterner stuff than the run-of-the-mill crook. Besides, it wouldn't have looked out of place on the Bowery or North Clark Street in Chicago.

The Arachnid shouted, "Stop, Captain Lucifer!"

Lucifer turned pale and on his heel at the same time.

The Arachnid shouted, "I've been looking for you for forty-two years, you bum! I'm the one who thought of the idea of stamping a spider image on the foreheads of crooks I assisted to a bad end! But you took up the idea without giving me the slightest credit! You stamped your devil on crooks' foreheads! No more! You've had it, Captain Copycat!"

The two men grappled each other. No 4+1 quit running, let his pants drop again, and opened the cover on top of his ring. From its hollow interior he took a tiny round glass, a green marble glowing in the sun, and he threw it after the Mad Fokker.

Halfway toward its target, it broke, undoubtedly struck by one of the many bullets flying around. A green cloud billowed out. It expanded to a diameter of about twenty feet, drifting back toward No. 4+1 and the two combatants. It dissipated rapidly, but it evidently was quick-acting. The three oldsters were as still and as green as cucumbers.

By then the blimp was directly above the bank. It halted

there, turned against the wind, its single propeller spinning just enough to keep it stationary. A little car containing one man was being lowered at the end of a cable, the other end of which went through an opening in the bottom of the gondola. Men were shooting from the gondola; their target seemed to be the Ga See Chow. Of course, they had no way of knowing that part of their own gang was trapped in the restaurant.

Doc Ravage stepped out of the shadow of the rear portion of the Canary Cage Theater, which was somehow still standing. Coolly ignoring the bullets and curses hurled at him, he raised the little submachine pistol and pointed it at the blimp's bag. Evidently he meant to punch it full of holes and bring it down on top of the bank. But nothing came out of its muzzle. Either it was out of ammunition or it had jammed. Whatever the cause, Doc Ravage threw it away from him and went back into the Canary Cage Theater.

Meanwhile, Phwombly had appeared on top of a building half a block down from the theater. Ordinarily, he'd have been hidden from view by the false front of the building, but this had been blown off along with much of the rest of the structure. Phwombly had somehow managed to haul a mortar, no doubt captured from the enemy, to the top of the roof. Now he cranked its wide muzzle up, and then he was dropping the shell into it. Smoke and a loud noise came from it, and Silver glimpsed the missile as it went up in its sharp arc. The recoil of the mortar, however, must have been just enough to add the final straw to the weakened structure. The roof fell in, Phwombly with it, and the walls followed. Silver reached for his hat to remove it and place it over his heart. But he had lost it somewhere along the line.

The shell blew up behind the bank. The blimp bobbed from the impact of the shock waves and then settled again. The cable car passed out of Silver's sight, but a moment later it came into view again. The blimp was going to let down another man, the first having gotten out on the roof.

Doc reappeared, this time with a huge spear he must have gotten from the theater stockroom. He raised it above his shoulder, ran out into the street as bullets zinged by, and cast the missile. It soared up and up, a pretty good throw for a young man, let alone a septuagenarian, but it wasn't good enough. It dropped before it came within six feet of the gasbag. However, it wasn't entirely off the mark. It hurtled toward the man in the cable car, and he, believing that it was going to hit him, jumped. Since he had a twenty-foot fall, he was probably no longer interested in the battle.

Doc ran back into the building, agony on his face, and holding himself just above his right hip. It looked to Silver as if he had badly strained himself. Was he out of it, too?

His eyes widened. Phwombly, covered with plaster dust, was crawling out from the wreckage. The old fellow was certainly tough. But if he didn't find shelter, he'd be mincemeat very quickly. Bullets tore up wood and bricks around him.

Silver's hair stood up on end. A groan had come from the back of the building. Cautiously, he went through the door and looked around the room. A man sat huddled against the wall under a table. Silver looked under it and said, "Captain Nothing, I presume? What're you doing here?"

"Waiting for midnight," Dirk Alone said. "I'll be invisible then. And invincible, too."

"Forget it," Silver said. "This'll be long over before then."

He looked up, and he gasped. An old Indian woman stood in the corner.

"Grandma!"

"What?" Captain Nothing said. His hand went toward his coat pocket.

White Spots was shaking her head and pointing at the man under the table. Then she drew her finger across her throat and disappeared.

Silver bent down swiftly and seized the old man's hand, which had just come out of his coat pocket. He twisted it, it opened as Captain Nothing cried out with pain, and a tiny lizard with a scarlet cock's comb and a pale green skin covered by pustules fell on the floor. But it turned, fast as the tip of a cracking whip, and sank two rattlesnakish fangs into the hand of its owner. Captain Nothing screamed once, slowly turned purple veined with gold, and slumped over.

Silver picked up a chair by its legs and brought the edge of its back down against the lizard's back. The pustules shot up inch-high needle sprays of a foul smelling liquid. The stuff burned the floor where it fell and sent up a choking smoke. Silver backed away, waited until the lizard quit twitching and the air was cleared, and returned to examine the old man. The texture of his skin looked so peculiar that Greatheart tested it with his fingernails. Presently, he pulled off the plastic skin of the face.

"Doctor Won Fang!"

During the melee, the old Chinese had become isolated from the others. He'd quickly made himself up to look like Captain Nothing, no doubt hoping to fool, and so kill, any of his enemy who took refuge here. But he had never run up against a man with an unconscious that operated like a movie projector.

Silver explored the room and quickly found another body behind a pile of boxes. Old Valiant Kilgore, ex-federal agent, chief foe of Won Fang. The two had had the final confrontation here. Judging from the absence of any wounds except some scratches on his face, Kilgore had died of a heart attack. Then old Won Fang, exhausted, had crawled away.

Silver returned to the front of the building. The men in the gondola were still shooting, but firing elsewhere had ceased. Maybe, he thought, the others had run out of ammunition.

Silver stuck his head out of the door and whistled three times. The ravens quit circling and headed straight toward him. After they'd settled on his shoulders, and he had soothed them, he took a pen and a piece of paper from his pocket. He wrote a note on it, put it in Huggin's bill, and croaked softly at the bird. Huggin didn't want to carry out his mission, but Silver assured him that there wasn't any danger. Huggin squawked indignantly at that. Silver added, well, there wasn't *much* danger. Huggin flew away across the street at an angle and dropped through the opening in the front of the Ga See Chow. Immediately, an aged Chinese dashed screaming out of the restaurant. He screamed all the way across the street as he headed for the bank.

Silver stared in astonishment. He'd sent a note demanding immediate surrender. The town was surrounded by police and National Guardsmen, it stated, and those holed up in the restaurant didn't have a chance. But if they surrendered now, they might get some leniency. As for those in the blimp, they didn't have a prayer either. Air National Guard jets were just over the mountain. Within a few minutes, they'd be shooting the blimp out of the sky.

He'd signed the note with the governor's name. He hoped they'd be too rattled to wonder why the governor would transmit a message by such unconventional means.

But he'd forgotten about Doctor Negative's psychotic fear of birds. Ever since he'd been buried in that pile of guano, he couldn't stand even the sight of a robin. And so the appearance of Huggin had panicked him. It had also set off a chain reaction that was going to result in just the opposite of what Silver had planned.

Jim Binde, on seeing his archenemy dash out, had run after him. He carried only a knife, which meant that he, like most of the combatants, was out of ammunition.

Behind came a dozen Chinese and a moment later, from

another building, the Russian contingent. The Hwing Ding were after Won Fang, or maybe their old foe, Secret Agent Binde. Or both.

The Russians were also after somebody. It might be the Hwing Ding, which they hated, or Binde, whom they didn't like either, or Won Fang, who'd given them a hard time during the post-Revolution years. Probably they were after all three.

And here came the rest of all those who could run, walk, or crawl. The FBI, the CIA, Sour Lemono and what was left of WAX, and the surviving great old ones. They were out of bombs and bullets, but they had their knives and special weapons and their hands and feet.

In the middle of the street, before the half-shattered bank, they met and mixed in the melee of the millennium.

14.

Doctor Negative was the first to go. In fact, he had left before the final conflict. His heart had given out as he reached the pile of debris before the bank.

Jim Binde did not get long to congratulate himself. He was only sixty-two but looked eighty because of his incessant boozing and smoking. A few seconds after Negative dropped, alcohol and nicotine dropped their guillotine on Binde. He clutched his chest and collapsed beside his enemy.

The Copper Kid succumbed next, pennies spilling from his opened hand.

"Too many years of anticipation of revenge," Silver muttered to himself. "Too much excitement for hearts that had been stimulated by too much adrenalin for too long."

The old men were dropping like stocks in a Wall Street panic.

There went Doc Barker, making his last pitch. Sir Daines Neighland Smythe and Doctor Fyu-men Chew lay with their arms around each other. This was appropriate, Silver thought. During their sixty years of feuding, they'd had innumerable opportunities to kill each other but had always ignored them. Deep down, they were lovers.

Nor would Doctor Sen Sen offend anyone with his breath ever again. It was a question, however, whether it had been a ruptured heart or a broken head that had killed him off. He'd charged Luna Head, who had bent over as he countercharged. Sen Sen's head had rammed into the big opaque metal fishbowl concealing his enemy's features. There had been a loud hollow ringing sound, and both had fallen on their backs, feet to feet. Luna Head didn't look as if he was going to get up either.

Not all the old ones had fallen. The Black Night Owl, wearing dark glasses, was striking his opponents with a white cane in one hand and a tin cup in the other. Donald Diavolo, clad in a scarlet costume, was lashing out with a bullwhip held in his right hand. With his left he was distracting antagonists with magical tricks: an endless scarf, an American flag, a bowl full of goldfish, bouquets of flowers, a rabbit, a flock of pigeons, all from his sleeve.

And there was the Gargler, dressed entirely in battleship gray, masked, striking with the butt of an empty automatic. But there also was Doctor Terminal slipping behind him, a stone axe in hand. Terminal had spent his life trying to destroy civilization, to send people back to the Old Stone Age. He was not a villain but an idealist who thought that technology had ruined man's spirituality with its materialism. All his murders, individual or mass, had been for man's good, though even he had to admit that he had been able to perform his greatest deeds only because of modern science.

Now Terminal smote the Gargler in the back of his head, though not very hard, since his arms were feeble. The Gargler opened his mouth, and the specially-made plates inside his mouth shot out. These were equipment to change the shape of his lower face when he was in disguise. As a side effect, the plates had made him talk in a weird gargling manner. Now he was down on his hands and knees, groping around among a seaweed-dance of legs for the plates. Doctor Terminal was raising the axe to bring it down on the Gargler's buttocks.

Silver's attention at that moment was attracted by two men on horses that galloped out between two burning buildings down the street. Evidently the Long Ranger and his sidekick, Pronto, had been biding their time, waiting until a critical moment. Each had two revolvers; each was firing them wildly as their stallions raced toward the battle. Silver ducked as a bullet screamed by him. It struck something metallic behind him, ricocheted again, and dropped at his feet. He looked at it, saw it was made of lead, and felt a little sad. The days when the Long Ranger was rich enough to use silver bullets were no more.

Pete Ruse came out of his stupor then. He got to his feet, staggered to the middle of the street, faced the oncoming riders, and shouted, "Halt in the name of the law of Cochise County, Long Ranger!"

The masked man on the white horse shouted back, "For Pete's sakes, I'm on the side of the Good!"

"You're an outlaw!" Ruse screamed back, and he emptied

his six-shooter at the masked rider. The Long Ranger had used up all his bullets; Pronto couldn't fire because he'd dropped his gun. It made no difference. Lawman and outlaw had missed with every shot.

Just as the Long Ranger ran out of bullets, his horse stepped in a hole created by a bomb. The Ranger flew up, out, and over while the horse stayed behind. Pronto's horse piled into the other horse, and Pronto followed his senior partner. He landed on the masked rider, who had landed on Pete Ruse.

The horses got, up, but the three men did not move.

At least, this is one time when the Indian comes out on top, Silver thought.

And here came the Green Llama, the long scarf he used for a whip in his hand. He radiated a bright blue light, since he'd just swallowed the glowing blue contents of a bottle. Now he was charged with several hundred thousands of volts. Just let the enemy lay hands on him!

He advanced gingerly around the edge of the closely packed crowd on his thick nonconducting shoes. He was looking for someone to lash with his scarf, which was also, of course, made of nonconducting material.

A man Phwombly had pointed out as the archfoe of Scorpio shambled out of the crowd. He was Geoffrey Justkid, once known to the police and the underworld under two identities. Sometimes he was compassionate Doctor Headbone, a man who liked to distribute dimes to slum dwellers and turn in wicked welfare workers. Sometimes he was the deadly Headbone Slayer, demiser of criminals. Now he was squinting around, obviously in desperate need of his glasses. He crouched, trying to see between the milling feet of the battlers. Then he shrugged, stood up, and charged head down toward the crowd.

Unfortunately, the Green Llama walked into his path. Probably the Headbone Slayer did not recognize him as a friend. He leaped at him, though not very high or far, and bore him into the crowd.

There was a loud crackle, some smoke from the Llama, the Slayer, and a few near them. And the entire mob fell as one man.

There was a silence except for the crackling of flames. The wind brought to Silver the acrid odor of smoke and the not-so-sweet odor of vengeance requited.

Was anybody left? Was he the sole survivor?

No. There still were the men in the bank and the blimp. And here came two figures from the shell of a general store.

GENERAL ST

Phwombly and Doc Ravage. They were holding each other up, wincing at every step, but headed determinedly for the bank. But what could a pair of injured ancients do now? Were they really going into the bank to clean out a dozen armed men?

They were.

As the two disappeared into the building, Silver shouted at them. Then he was running after them. Then he was flat on his face. It took him a minute to find out that his marvelous electromechanical leg had chosen that moment to malfunction. The servomechanisms responding to the neutral currents flowing through flesh and wires to metal and plastic had failed. And his trainers at the hospitals had not taught him to walk with an inactivated limb.

He managed to get to one foot, and he hopped to the bank. The interior was bright and empty. Wreckage filled the lobby. A couple of old men, bearing no evidence of outward injury, lay behind a mound of plaster and wood. Heart failure, probably. He put his head cautiously through the door to the back of the room. The vault door was at the opposite wall, and it was closed. That meant that the two had locked in some of the gang, since the gang wouldn't have bothered to close it behind them. But how many of them were in it? And where were Phwombly and Doc Ravage?

It didn't need any Sherlock Holmes to figure that out. They'd gone up the stairs to the second floor and on up to the roof.

Using his good leg and the banister, cursing modern technology and two stubborn old men, Silver hauled himself up the steps. He had to crawl over several bags of money and their former bearers, snoring away, their jaws a little out of line. Doc Ravage's still mighty fist had undoubtedly been responsible for that.

Then he was sweating to get up the almost vertical ladder. Through the open trap above him he could see the blimp and the car at the end of the cable. The car was two-thirds of the way up, about twenty feet above the roof. It held the Mad Fokker, who was grinning over the side of the car and thumbing his nose.

Silver got to the top of the ladder and stuck his head out. The object of derision was, as he'd expected, Phwombly and Ravage. They were weaponless, and so helpless to do anything now. But they had forced the gang to abandon much of the loot. Bags of money lay in a pile directly behind them.

The Mad Fokker would not have been so happy if he had known what was happening above him. A pair of bolt cutters was extended through the opening for the car, and their jaws were closed on the cable. Above them was a white beard like Santa Claus', a grin like the Devil's, and a sea officer's cap. Surely, that was Blimp Kernel himself, Silver thought.

Since Phwombly and Ravage were directly under the car, they could not see Kernel.

Phwombly screeched, "8-•!"

The face of the man in the car sagged, and his mouth gaped. It took him some seconds to recover, and during that time the car had gone a few feet higher.

"How did you know I am 8-•?" he screamed down.

"Only I know!" Phwombly screamed back.

That wasn't exactly true, since he had told Silver, but this was no time for nitpicking.

"8-•! Don't you know who your leader is, who's hiding behind that fake face and the beard? It's your old enemy, your archfoe, Herr Doktor Krogers himself! He's been using you, 8-•, and laughing at you all the time! I've been trying to figure out for some time who Kernel could be, and finally I hit on the truth! Do you know anybody else who could fit the bill? Tell me, 8-•, haven't you thought from time to time there was something familiar about him? Did you ever detect a slight German accent in his speech?"

"No! No! No!" 8-• shrilled. He reared up in the car and looked upward. And then he screamed.

A thin voice fell down to the men on the roof. "That's right, *verdammenswert Schweinhund*! I'm the man you've been seeking for sixty-two years. At first, I was going to kill you. And then I thought, what a joke if I use the man who foiled me over and over again, the man who was really responsible for my beloved country's losing the war! And worse of all, making an idiot of me, Herr Doktor Krogers, the greatest brain in the world, in the universe, even!"

The old man in the car screamed again, grabbed the cable, and began pulling himself up it toward Krogers, ten feet above him. He had to be in his late eighties, and yet he went up the thin cable like a baboon. That his rear was bare made the simile even more appropriate.

"Vengeance is mine!" he cried once, but thereafter he quit. No doubt, he was out of wind, because a few feet from reaching the opening, he stopped. His gaspings for breath were so loud that Silver could hear them.

"*Leben Sie wohl, Schwaschsinniger*! Have a nice trip!"

Doc Ravage bent over and seized a bag, probably containing

silver dollars, by the neck. Agony passed over his face, quickly replaced by his normal stoical expression. But he remained bent over, and it was evident that he'd "caught" his back. He was unable to straighten up again.

Silver, understanding what he had meant to do with the coins, pulled himself out onto the roof. At the same time, he shouted to Phwombly and Ravage to get out from under the car.

"Kernels' cutting the cable!"

Ravage, stooped over, scrambled over the pile. Phwombly dived over the bags, hit his shoulder hard against the roof, and lay there groaning.

Kernel saw the whole thing. He laughed and then shouted down at them. "Look at this *dummkopf*, you *dummkopfs*. You sweat while he sweats. Ho! Ho! Revenge at last!"

Silver, sitting down, pulled his pants off. Then he twisted his false leg a quarter turn, feeling no pain in the connections to his nerves. The minute connections had come away easily.

He struggled to his foot, hoping that Kernel, or Krogers, would be so curious about what he was doing that he'd delay the cutting. 8-•, hanging on the cable, was looking down at him, and though Silver was angered by what he'd done, he also felt a twinge of pity. After all, the old guy was insane.

"So what gives?" Kernel screeched down at him. "You are going to do a one-legged dance? Are you an Indian medicine man, you're going to make it rain yet? Only on one side of the sky, ho, ho!"

Balancing on the one leg, Silver swung the false leg back and then hurled it up and outward.

Krogers cried out, and his face disappeared. He'd probably run back to the end of the gondola in a purely irrational reflex, since there was nothing he could do to prevent the leg from hitting the propeller.

Turning over and over, the limb went into the whirring blades. There was a clang, and the leg flew back to one side, still turning, and landed on the corner of the roof.

The propeller faltered for a minute, then resumed its original rate of rotation. If any of the blades had been damaged, they gave no evidence of it.

Silver grimaced with chagrin. He had hoped that the irradiated plastic of the leg, hard as steel, but much lighter, would snap off a blade or at least bend one considerably.

The grimace turned into a grin. Though the casting of the leg had failed in one way, it had succeeded in another. While

Krogers had been at the stern of the gondola, 8-• had made a final effort. He had pulled himself to the opening and was reaching in. Krogers' scream of fury came all the way down to the man on the roof. A second later, he had seized the bolt cutters and torn them from 8-•, who had to release them to keep from falling.

Krogers, leaning over, placed the jaws of the cutters again on the cable. His face became red with the effort, but the jaws closed. The cable parted, and the car fell toward the roof. But 8-• had grabbed Krogers' leg and pulled himself up just enough to grab Krogers' long white beard. The two fell, screaming, while the blimp, released of the weight of the car and two bodies, soared upward.

The car struck the roof with a loud crash and went on through it. The building, weakened by the blast, fell in. Silver could do nothing except fall with the roof. Then something struck him, and he was unconscious.

In the ambulance on the way to the Bisbee hospital, Greatheart awoke. He murmured to the attendant, "Was anyone left alive in the bank?"

"Just you," the attendant said.

"Then I guess they're all in Valhalla," Greatheart whispered, and he passed out again.

"Hey, Jack," the attendant said to the driver. "Where's Valhalla?"

"There ain't no such place in Arizona," was the answer.

WHAT LIES IN THE FUTURE FOR GREATHEART SILVER? WILL HE ONCE AGAIN WALK THE BRIDGE OF A ZEPPELIN? WILL HE TALK TO HIS RAVENS? WHAT HAPPENS WHEN OLD BENDT MICAWBER FINDS OUT THAT HIS BEAUTIFUL DAUGHTER AND GREATHEART ARE IN LOVE? WILL GREATHEART EXPERIENCE MANY STRANGE ADVENTURES IN STRANGE PARTS OF THE WORLD? READ THE CONTINUING EXPLOITS OF GREATHEART SILVER!

Afterword

I've been asked to explain why and how I conceived the character of Greatheart Silver.

Hell, I don't know.

If any explanation is possible, it may be found in the verb "conceived" above. A writer of fiction is a big mother continuously balled by the universe. The spermatozoa are inputs, what the writer sees, hears, smells, touches. Inputs, or take-ins, or data sperm, range from light from a star a billion years dead to a toilet that won't work. Most of the sperm die before they reach the ovum, the writer's unconscious mind. Those that survive seldom unite with the ovum at once. They go into suspended animation for forty or maybe sixty years. And when fertilization occurs, it's done not by one tiny wriggling data-input but by a thousand. It's a form of superfetation, multiple and simultaneous impregnation of that great egg we call the unconscious.

There's no uniformity in the shape or size of the eggs. One writer's looks like a plumber's helper; another, like a Moebius Strip. Mine looks like a streetcorner pissoire designed by Michelangelo. Or maybe it's the other way around. I never asked it.

Nor does any writer get the same inputs, the same data-sperm, as any other writer. The person sitting on the bus next to me isn't in quite the same environment. He or she is encased in a unique mini-environment. Nor is he or she the same receptor as I am. What one takes in, another bounces.

Another analogy: An idea is the output of a protein and protean circuit that, like a mushroom, has been growing in the dark for years. One day, the final spurt to growth penetrates the darkness, all circuit paths are completed, what had seemed unconnected is revealed as connected, and, click, the light!

Byron Preiss called me on the telephone (an invention I detest; it has its uses but the abuses far outnumber them). He asked me to write a story for *Weird Heroes*, I suppose because I've written much about the pulp heroes of the thirties and forties. And so there went a character (me) in search of a hero. The hero (read: he or she or it) must derive from the old pulp protagonist but be a product of modern times. So, a final confrontation between the great pulp-villains and the pulp-heroes, most of whom will be in their eighties and nineties. Kill them off in a grand finale with tears and laughter.

This is why Silver is, in this initial tale, not as rounded or as much an active participant as he should be. I have to usher the old ones into the terminal wings before I can really bring my hero onto the uncluttered stage.

When I kill them off, I am in a sense killing myself so I can be reborn. My hang-up on the old pulp heroes (and the greats of the late nineteenth and early twentieth centuries) are hang-ups from my childhood. I love them, but my ardor may be keeping me from going on to more "mature" writing. So, writing about them is for me a form of therapy. But I'm paid for the therapy. It's as if a doctor came to me and asked me to let him pay me to cure me of cancer.

(That's an idea for a story, by the way. Doctors moonlight, sweep streets or sell lottery tickets, so they can afford to pay their patients for permission to treat them.)

But art is long, and so is therapy, and there are no rain checks.

Meanwhile, back at the heroizing . . . . When I was a child I read *Treasure Island* and *The Pilgrim's Progress* (both splendidly illustrated) many times. Long John Silver and Mr. Greatheart (with Tarzan, Odysseus, Sherlock Holmes, Og, the Oz Gang, Captain Gulliver, the Ancient Mariner, et. al.) were my favorite heroes. I was also impressed by the two ravens, Huginn (Thought) and Muginn (Memory), who rode the great god Odin's shoulders. In recent years I've become a zeppelin buff, though this goes back to the many pop-lit books about dirigibles and their dauntless captains which I devoured when a child. (Roy Rockwood, and Victor Appleton where are you now?) As a forty-year-oldster, I lived in the Phoenix, Arizona area, in the Valley of the Son of Abominations, and I've been to the village on which Shootout is modeled, Tombstone. And I've wakened in the dead of night and seen "ghosts" parading before my bed, things that shed their own light, gave their unspoken warnings, and faded back into the night. Of course, the "ghosts" were exteriorizations projected by my mind, but they looked real enough.

And then there is Mr. Micawber. The one in this story is a descendant of Dickens' character. He's an example of my hobby of integrating classical and pop-lit characters into one family, into one genealogical history that their originators did not dream of. However, my Mr. Micawber is a bad apple in the family barrel. He has more affinities to Heep and Murdstone than to his bombastic but compassionate ancestor. But then there's his daughter, who is lovely and loving and who falls in love with Silver.

If I try to analyze what I've done (and I'm against the try), I might say that the name and the character of Silver were picked through the unconscious' symbolic process. Silver is not all good, like so many of the pulp-lit heroes or all bad, like so many of pulp-lit's villains. He is, being human, both. And so his name represents his physical makeup, the pirate at one pole and the stout-hearted, pure-minded ogre-slayer at the other. But mostly he's gray shot with bright colors, like dusk and sunset. And remember that Long John Silver had his redeeming traits and Mr. Greatheart must have been rather insufferable at times.

As for our hero's amputated leg, that seems to have been suggested by the similar condition of his ancestor of the Spanish Main. But it might also stand for the universal crippling effect (more or less) that all societies (past and present) have or have had on mankind. Maybe. I don't want to go into that.

Though it's not apparent from my tale, there is a linkage between Harlan's Ellison's *The New York Review of Bird* and *Showdown at Shootout*. Cordwainer Bird is Harlan's TV nom de plume, the byline he uses when his scripts have been butchered by directors and producers. If the production is good, he uses his own name. If it's bad, he uses Cordwainer Bird. You've probably seen it on the tube from time to time.

Now, back up a little. In early 1974 I started to write a series of fictional-author stories. That is, stories by writers who are characters in fiction. My own name (except in one case) is not mentioned. Each story is prefaced by a short biographical account of the author, and the fictional author's name is the byline. David Copperfield is one example of this. Martin Eden, the protagonist of Jack London's semiautobiographical novel, *Martin Eden*, is another. H. P. Lovecraft's Robert Blake (based on Robert Bloch) is another, and Bloch's own character, Edgar Henquist Gordon, is a fourth. The list of fictional authors is long, and many names will spring to the mind of the reader: John H. Watson, M.D., Kilgore Trout, Gerald Musgrave, Bunny Manders, Eugene Gant, Nick Adams, Anna Karenina, Gustave von Aschenbach, Don Quixote, Jubal Harshaw, Archie Goodwin, Enoch Soames (a poet), Ernest Pontifex, and so on. I don't plan to do all of these, and indeed someone has already written a novel by Kilgore Trout. (But I was responsible for the suggestion that it be done.)

The name of Cordwainer Bird has intrigued me for a long time. I could not, however, write a story by Bird because he was only a TV byline, not a person in a story. But there's more than one way of kissing a duck, so I decided to put Bird as a character into a story, then I could write a story *by* him. I phoned Harlan, and he gladly gave me a free hand. But, before I could get around to writing a story that would have Bird in it, I found out that Harlan had promised to write a tale for this collection. So I used the detestable instrument again, and Harlan told me that Bird would be the hero of the story herein. We discussed his physical and psychical character and chronologies because we didn't want any discrepancy between his Bird and mine. As a result of this ornithologicocolloquy, Harlan's Bird has his adventures before 1978. My Bird will have his experiences after this date. Harlan's bucks the super-villains of the New York literary establishment. Mine will then fall in with and be the Boswell/Watson/Damon or Pythias of my character, Ralph von Wau Wau.

Von Wau Wau is a German shepherd or police dog whose I.Q. has been made equal to Sherlock Holmes' through the genius of a French scientist. Von Wau Wau gets tired of working for the Hamburg police, resigns, and goes into business for himself as a private eye. Eventually, he moves to Los Angeles where he shares an apartment, and adventures, and occasionally his portable fire plug, with Bird.

In addition, Bird is now included in the genealogy of the Wold Newton family described in my *Tarzan Alive* and *Doc Savage: His Apocalyptic Life*. After proper (and some improper) thought, and much research, I discovered that Bird is indeed a member of that family which includes so many classical and pop-lit heroes and villains of the past and present. Bird is the shortest person in that family of giants, but in spirit, attainments, and direction and intensity of purpose, he walks tall. And so you who will refer to the revised edition of the Doc Savage biography (Bantam Books) will find that Bird's uncles are those archenemies of evil of yore, the Shadow, G-8, and the Spider, and that Bird is a direct descendant of the Scarlet Pimpernel.

See what you started, Byron, when you called me via that two-headed instrument, the telephone? Things thought unconnected suddenly became linked.

And that is what "creativity" is all about.